AN EXCEPTIONAL HOUND

Book II of the Ryland Creek Saga

JOSEPH GARY CRANCE

ISBN: 978-1-4834-8725-0 (sc)
ISBN: 978-1-4834-8726-7 (hc)
ISBN: 978-1-4834-8724-3 (e)
ISBN: 978-1-7947-6791-1 (cb)

Library of Congress Control Number: 2018907214

Because of the dynamic nature of the Internet, any web addresses or
links contained in this book may have changed since publication and
may no longer be valid. The views expressed in this work are solely
those of the author and do not necessarily reflect the views of the
publisher, and the publisher hereby disclaims any responsibility for them.

Lulu Publication Services rev date: 1/27/2022

www.rylandcreektwo.com

Dedication

*This book is dedicated to my wife
Brendalyn, my first editor,
who has waited patiently so many a dark night for me,
her coon hunter, and his hounds
to return from the forests once more.*

Acknowledgments

I must thank some very special people who have constantly supported my writing endeavors: Carey May Stephens, Cheryl Ward, Tracey Yorio, Judy Janowski (author, *Life Is a Garden Party*), Gloria Williams, Chanon Landenberg, Dutch Van Alstin (author, Life Behind Bars series), and Leonard and Colleen Mourhess.

I would be remiss to not mention the Corning (New York) Area Writers Group for their constant encouragement and feedback. I'd like to specially notice Melora Johnson (author, *Earthbound*), Tarren Young (writer), Christy Nicholas (author, the Druid's Brooch series), Mattea Orr (contributing author, *Transcendent*), Dave Muffley (poet, *Admonitions of Ares*), Chris Esperanza (aspiring author), Levi C. Bradigan (writer), Ron Palmer, Michelle Pointis Burns (author, *Say Cheese and Murder*), M.A. Hoyler (contributing author, *It Calls From The Sky*), A.V. Rogers (author, *Dollhouse*), and Morgan J. Bolt (author, *The Favored*).

A warm, familial call out to my cousin, Wayne Foit, who provided me information and sources to speak to on Native American customs.

My deep gratitude to Lisa Telehany Dewitt, whose own tale of perseverance is nothing short of inspiring.

To Elizabeth Laubach, my high school freshman English teacher, who planted the seed in me to become a writer someday—thank you!

A call out to my copy editor, Joyce Mochrie for her superb professional review of this manuscript. Visit her website at www.onelastlookcopyedits.com.

A special thanks to my mother, Jeanne Crance, and daughter, Samantha Crance—my constant cheerleaders. To my father, Gary Crance, who started teaching me about coonhounds and coon hunting from the time I could walk—and continues to this day.

And to the woodland hollows of Upstate New York: There is a magic in these places, if you know where to look.

Contents

CHAPTER 1
And So It Begins

October 1987

Jason Canton peered down the metal sights of his .22-caliber rifle's blue-black barrel. Resting on a decaying log, the youth's gun had its nylon sling pushed to one side to help steady his aim. The twelve-year-old with long, dirty-blond hair could easily spy the large ebony hound nearly a hundred yards away.

Upwind, the canine had not yet detected any human scent. With his nose down, the hound followed some captivating smell along a small runoff creek next to a massive sugar maple. The deep woodland's fall colors were spectacularly bright with oranges and yellows this early afternoon in Upstate New York. The vivid contrast of coonhound and foliage in the mostly oak forest made the unsuspecting dog an easy target.

"Oh, man!" the redheaded Bobby encouraged over Jason's left shoulder. "You can plug that old hound right here and now, and no one would be the wiser!"

"We shouldn't be shooting someone's dog in the middle of the woods, Bobby!" Jason replied in a harsh whisper.

"C'mon! Just this once!" Bobby egged on.

"Well, all right," Jason said reluctantly. The youngster closed one eye and took careful aim. As he'd been taught, the preteen controlled his breathing and slowly squeezed the trigger. The small caliber rifle cracked, and the bullet impacted the maple tree's trunk, missing the hound by a mere inch.

The coonhound's body jerked reflexively, and the hound quickly disappeared behind the safety of the gray-barked maple. The

1

canine slowly peeked around one side of the tree, searching desperately for his assailant, and let out a resounding, "Harrumph!"

"Ah, man, you missed!" Bobby the tempter carped. "But he's sticking his head out again—you've got another chance at him!"

Smoothly working the gun's bolt action, Jason loaded a new shell into the chamber as the spent brass from the first attempt ejected to land on the colorful leaves covering the forest floor.

The large hound tested the air, trying to ascertain the whereabouts of his attackers. Unfortunately, the wind still worked against the canine. The hound then seemed to look directly at Jason, as if the dog suddenly knew precisely where the boys were. The ebony cur stepped boldly from behind the maple into the open, giving the youngster an easy target.

"Oh man! Do it! Do it! Do it!" Bobby spoke in rapid-fire whispers. "He's almost daring you to take the shot!"

Again, Jason aimed down the weapon's open sights. He placed the front bead on the dog's chest. It truly was a sure shot. For what he thought would be the last time, the boy slowly squeezed the trigger.

An oak staff came down violently with a loud ringing thud on the rifle's barrel, and the weapon discharged harmlessly into the ground a few feet away. Shock covered Jason's face as he stared into the angry eyes of a young man wearing a gray fedora, greenish coat, and faded blue jeans, all of which blended naturally into the surroundings.

"That's my dog!" the tall stranger seethed, and then slid his walking staff up the gun's barrel to catch Jason in the chest. The powerful blow sent the would-be killer of hounds to the ground on his back, knocking the air from the youngster's lungs. The rifle fell with a clatter several feet away as the young man—perhaps in his twenties—put his boot on the kid's chest, pinning Jason to the leafy ground.

With a craven scream at the surprising appearance of the adult, Bobby turned at a full sprint to leave Jason to his demise. Craning his neck, the trapped youth watched as his accomplice quickly disappeared into the forest. When Jason looked back, he found the ebony hound's muzzle only inches from his face.

The large dog let out a low growl.

"Easy, Seth," the man spoke gently, calming his agitated companion. "It's okay now."

"Harrumph!" Seth snorted but never took his eyes off the boy.

"How d'you find us out here, mister?" Jason blurted.

"The two of you make more noise than any four people I know." He turned his attention back to the frightened boy.

"You and that hound leave a fair amount of sign yourself," came a deep voice from behind.

The man who held Jason to the ground closed his eyes momentarily, but instead of alarm, a smile slowly crossed his face. His focus still on Jason, with just a slight turn of his head, he replied, "Didn't know you were in town. It's been a long time, Uncle Arthur." Reaching down, he took a firm hold of Jason's jean shirt and hoicked the boy to a full standing position with little apparent effort.

Shaking, Jason glanced over at the newest arrival. About twenty yards away, an even taller man stood, clad in a long, dusty-brown drover. This stranger was older—forties maybe—and wore no hat with his mostly salt with some pepper locks hanging far below his broad shoulders.

The man called Uncle Arthur looked admirably at the solid-black dog. "I thought I'd come see this Seth whom I've heard so much about. But tell me, Nephew, who's the young'un what would shoot such a magnificent coonhound?"

"This is Seth," the nephew confirmed with a smile. But then the younger man turned his ire back to Jason. "And that's a good question. What's your name?"

"I'm Jason Canton," the frightened boy blurted.

"Will and Beth's son?"

"Yes, sir! I'm sorry, mister!" Jason trembled.

"What of the other kid—the one who turned tail and left you all alone?" the younger man continued.

"That was my friend, Bobby Bensen," the preteen quickly confessed.

"Not much of a friend," Arthur interjected, as he produced a large red apple from his coat and took a loud bite.

"W-w-who are you?" Jason sputtered, looking at the man who still held his shirt.

"I'm Nathan Ernst, and you're on *my* land."

"That makes you an attempted felon and a trespasser to boot, young'un," Arthur noted in a matter-of-fact tone, taking another mouthful of apple.

"You're Nathan Ernst?" Jason's eyes went wide, recognizing the family name so well known in their small hometown of Painted Post.

"That would be me," Nathan said. "Let's get you home to your parents. They need to know what you tried to do here today."

"Please no, Mr. Ernst! My pa will whoop my butt for sure if you tell him!" Jason pleaded.

"That's between you and your pa," Nathan noted as he retrieved the boy's rifle, removed the ammunition clip, and ejected the used shell. He looked up just in time to watch Arthur suddenly produce a braided bullwhip from beneath his drover coat with his free hand. The whip's leather cracked loud as it quickly reached out, resulting in a screeching yelp came to Nathan's left.

Also hearing the pained yell, Jason looked about to see the whip's end wrapped several times around Bobby's forearm. The harsh sting of the bullwhip's tassels caused the red-haired preteen to drop a rock he'd been holding.

"A scoundrel as well as a coward!" Arthur proclaimed, giving his whip a vicious tug that brought Bobby closer by a few feet. With a subtle movement of the man's wrist, the bullwhip's end unfurled and released the errant boy. Bobby turned to run, and Arthur immediately lashed out with the whip one last time as the braided coil's biting end crossed the fleeing youngster's buttocks.

"Ow hooo-hoooo!" Bobby screamed with a quick hop as he felt the leather viper's bite. At a full sprint, the boy screeched in agony until he was long out of sight.

Arthur shouted after the escaping redhead, "Go ahead and run, you little, no good, sonofa—"

"Uncle!" Nathan interrupted, looking back at Jason. "The youngster here is on the cusp of beginning a bad habit of shooting someone's hound. Not much sense in teachin' him to cuss as well."

With a begrudged look, Arthur slowly rolled the whip into a coil, and hung it on a strap inside his coat. As if nothing unusual had transpired, the whipmaster took one last bite of his apple and threw the core into the forest.

"You were a little harsh on Bobby, don't you think, uncle?" Nathan asked.

"You and his parents can thank me later. All I did was show that young villain the dire consequences of his inappropriate behavior." Arthur gave a short nod.

Stifling a laugh, Nathan then peered at Seth, who snorted in agreement. "I'll get Jason here home and meet you at the farm. The front door to the house isn't locked, and you can help yourself to some coffee. If you plan to stay, I've a guest bedroom you're more than welcome to use. See you in a couple of hours."

"Might' hospitable of you, Nephew, and I kindly accept your invitation." Arthur started to turn but added with a wink, "And it was nice meetin' you, young Jason." Taking a few steps that yielded no sound, the tall man moved into the thick forest brush and disappeared.

"We'll cut over the hill to your parents' farm," Nathan informed Jason. "I'll carry your rifle." He quickly threaded his shoulder through the weapon's sling, so it hung diagonally across his back.

"Okay, if you say so, Mr. Ernst. But are you sure you want to take me home? I know these woods well, and I can make it back by myself. I promise to tell my pa what I tried to do here today."

"Well then, I imagine you wouldn't mind me listenin' to your rendition of the story." Nathan smirked. "Let's go," he said more sternly, using his oak staff to indicate the direction they should walk.

The boy's shoulders fell, knowing full well the punishment that awaited him once back home.

"C'mon, Seth," Nathan called, and the hound obediently heeled close to his master's side.

The trek through the bright autumn forest brought little solace to the youth as he silently practiced his alibi. Every step, the boy knew, brought him closer to his strict father.

After nearly an hour of hiking, they came to the edge of a long cornfield that had been recently cut. The bent-over stalks rattled noisily in the light wind. Several hundred yards away stood a grayish farmhouse and a large, white barn with the Tioga River in the background reflecting the afternoon sun.

"That's my home down below." Jason motioned. "I can make it the rest of the way, Mr. Ernst. Sure wouldn't want to put you through any more trouble."

"I need to talk with your parents, but nice try, young'un." Nathan grinned. "I give you points for persistence."

"You can't blame a fella for tryin'," Jason moaned.

"Whoa!" Nathan said suddenly, scanning the ground.

Jason stopped when the adult kneeled.

Using the oak staff to help balance his weight, Nathan examined a small patch of soft mud with a single, huge imprint.

Seth sniffed the area with interest.

The boy could see Nathan intently studying the spoor. "What left that track, Mr. Ernst?"

"Bear," Nathan responded, "and a big one at that—probably a mature boar. Hopefully, it's just passing through." He used his fingers to press against the still-pliable mud. "This track is fresh. We might have only missed this bear by an hour or so."

"What happens if it ain't just passin' through?" Jason asked, honestly curious.

"Wouldn't be good for the folks around here," Nathan replied. "This town has seen its fair share of bears over the years. Those that stayed often became a nuisance and had to be dealt with."

Standing, Nathan motioned with his head to continue to Jason's home. But after taking just a few steps, Seth turned quickly, looking at the far corner of the field. While the humans could see nothing unusual amidst the dense and colorful brush, the hound let out a low growl.

"What's gotten into him, Mr. Ernst?"

"Not sure. Seth smells something he doesn't like."

"Do you think it could be that bear?" Jason persisted.

"Hard sayin', but doubtful. Most bears would break out at a dead run at the sight and sound of humans." Nathan scanned the forest, hoping to get a glimpse of what had caught his dog's attention. "C'mon, Seth, let's go," he said after discerning nothing unusual.

The faithful hound seemed reluctant to take his eyes off the faraway spot. After a few moments, Seth obeyed, but positioned himself between the forest and his master.

The walk down the cut cornfield demanded little effort. Within ten minutes, Nathan and Jason stood on the Cantons' front porch as Seth dutifully stayed a few feet behind.

Nathan knocked on the door, and Jason's mother soon answered.

7

"Well hello, Nathan," Beth Canton, a pretty brunette, greeted warmly. "It's been a long time! How have you been?"

"I've been fine, thank you, Beth." Nathan replied, tipping his hat politely. "But it's your son who needs to tell you about today's events."

"What on earth did you do, Jason?" Beth's smile turned to a sudden frown.

"Who's at the door?" A deep voice came from somewhere inside the house.

"It's Nathan Ernst with our son, honey," Beth shouted over her shoulder. She waited patiently, hearing her husband's approaching footsteps.

"Well, if it isn't Nathan Ernst!" William "Will" Canton greeted as his large frame filled the doorway. "How've you been? Still chasing raccoon through these hills, I suspect." Will was a tall, heavyset man with a thick beard. With his red plaid shirt and jeans, the big man looked every part the professional logger that he was.

"I'm fine, Will," Nathan replied, unslinging Jason's rifle, accepting the other man's proffered hand, and giving the man the weapon. "Appreciate you not cuttin' down those den trees over near Hunters Creek."

"Those oaks are much more valuable as homes for wildlife than for timber, being hollow and all." Will smiled, looking at the ebony cur standing near Nathan. "There's talk all over town about your hounds, but what brings you here with our son in tow?"

The coon hunter's look hardened. "I'll let young Jason explain."

Shamefaced, the youth looked down and hesitated.

"Jason, dear, what happened?" Beth prompted.

"I took a shot at Mr. Ernst's hound in the woods," Jason replied and quickly added, "But I missed and didn't hurt him, Pa!"

"You did *what*?" Will's countenance went instantly from congenial to sheer anger as he set the rifle just inside the doorway. "Which of your hounds did my boy shoot at, Nathan?"

8

"That would be Seth." Nathan motioned at his dog, who now sat on his haunches, watching. The coon hunter then took a step back, showing little sympathy for what undoubtedly would follow.

"I'm sorry, Pa!" Jason pleaded when his father reached out, grabbed his arm, and yanked him closer.

"Not sorry enough, young man. Not yet anyway!" Will bellowed. He loosened his belt buckle, pulled his belt free from the pant loops, and folded it over. "You mean to tell me that you almost killed one of the greatest coonhounds Painted Post has ever known? And you're the one always telling me that you want to be a coon hunter someday!"

At the revelation of the youngster's desire, Nathan's look softened considerably.

"I'll handle this," Will said, dragging his son inside and slamming the door, leaving Beth with Nathan on the porch.

"I'm so sorry." Beth shook her head. "Jason is usually a good boy, although his grades in school have gone down lately. I just don't know how to talk to him anymore. Children don't come with an instruction manual."

"Reckon not," Nathan acknowledged, overhearing Jason's punishment commence inside. "Your son had an accomplice—a Bobby Bensen. That young'un ran off into the woods and is as much to blame as Jason."

"I know Bobby's parents. I'll give them a call and tell them what happened." Beth winced, hearing her only child cry out.

With a nod, Nathan looked beyond the worried mother as young Jason howled in pain once more while his father continued to mete out the punishment.

"I best go now," she said. "It was good seeing you again."

"Likewise," Nathan responded with a parting tip of his fedora.

Beth turned the knob, stepped inside, and shut the door promptly.

As his master descended the porch steps, Seth let out a short bark. "Harrumph!"

"You're right." The coon hunter stopped and sighed, slowly turning to take a long look back at the closed door.

———•———

About ten minutes later, a swollen-eyed Jason came outside and ever so gingerly sat on the front porch's uppermost step. With his hands folded before him, the boy rested his head on his forearms and began to sob uncontrollably. His father's discipline had been just. Jason had known it had been wrong to shoot at the hound and only had himself to blame for the deserved repercussions.

Suddenly, a wet nose touched his cheek, and the youngster startled to find the black hound's snout immediately before him. Seth wagged his tail as Jason stroked the dog's head. The twelve-year-old looked up to see Nathan Ernst waiting silently, leaning on his walking staff.

"So you want to be a coon hunter?" Nathan asked gruffly.

"Y-y-yes, sir, I do!" Jason replied.

"Be at my house tomorrow night around sunset. Your parents know where I live," Nathan said. "Wear some good boots and a warm coat. Painted Post won't care how cold you get out in the woods. I'll have a headlamp that you can use."

The youngster only stared with his mouth agape.

As Nathan turned and began to walk away, he called over his shoulder, "Seth! C'mon, boy!"

Seth started to follow but stopped for a moment to give the kid a sloppy lick of his tongue. The incredibly fast hound then spun about and soon rejoined his master.

"Thank you, Mr. Ernst!" Jason shouted after the departing figures.

With his pace slowing only a little, Nathan turned his head slightly over his shoulder and nodded.

The mammoth black bear had watched the man and boy from the distant corner of the field. The forest had obscured their sight, and the humans had been oblivious to its presence.

However, the vigilant hound had known exactly where the bear had lain in wait.

Had the beast attacked as it had wanted to, the dog would have given far too much warning, ruining the element of surprise. The brute seethed with a harsh grunt at the thought of the hound's interference.

There was something unusual about that black canine, the bruin sensed.

It then had watched, frustrated, pawing at the ground, as the trio made their way to the safety of the farm below. There would be other opportunities, it knew.

But now, a gnawing hunger drove the huge omnivore's needs.

It had a meal to kill.

CHAPTER 2

A Hint of Trouble

Sharon sat on a large rock beside the flowing water of Ryland Creek. It was summer—it was always summer in the dream—and she wore a long, white dress that remained immaculate despite the woodland surroundings.

The pretty brunette put her small, bare feet into the water and walked to Nathan with her ever-impish grin, her dress billowing about as she neared him.

"He needs you." Sharon's brown eyes searched Nathan's soul like she always could in life.

"Who needs me?" He cocked an eyebrow.

"The young boy—the one you met in the forest yesterday," she explained, her voice kind.

Her voice had always been kind.

"Jason Canton?" He sighed, on the verge of protesting. "The young'un has good parents. He doesn't need me."

"Yes, he has a wonderful mother and father," Sharon said, putting the back of her hand gently against his cheek. "But he requires you in his life nonetheless."

"I don't understand."

"Nor can you—at least not at this place in your life." Her grin grew, leaning in to kiss him. "But trust me, my love, he needs you."

Somewhere deeper in the forest, a robin sang.

Nathan jerked upright in his bed, gasping. Sharon's final words echoed in his slowly waking mind.

He needs you.

A welcoming aroma wafted through the house, and the lifelong bachelor tried to make sense of it. The coon hunter gradually calmed, recognizing the delicious smell of frying bacon. Nathan realized that Uncle Arthur must have risen early to start breakfast.

The young man rose quickly, throwing on a pair of jeans, warm socks, and a red, thick cotton shirt. Coming down the stairs, he walked into the kitchen.

Even with his back turned to Nathan as the woodsman buttered some toast, Arthur greeted in a loud voice, "Good mornin', Nephew! Considering you're a farmer by trade, the day's now nearly half over with you gettin' your beauty sleep and all."

Partially laughing, partially grunting, Nathan glanced at the clock on the wall, which read a little after 8:00 a.m. Another aroma, that of percolated coffee, bade him to pour a cup of the steaming drink, and he sat at the table.

"How many eggs do you want, and how do you like 'em?" Arthur turned around with a wild gleam in his eyes and a silver spatula in one hand.

"Two over easy, would be fine, Uncle Art."

No sooner had Nathan responded when the front porch door swung wide open, and a giant's frame filled the doorway. The man cradled something small in his left arm as he walked into the kitchen.

"Nate, whose truck is that on your lawn?" Mead Ernst asked as he neared his brother.

"Nephew Mead?" Although tall himself, Arthur had to adjust his eyes upward and grinned, recognizing the visitor who entered the kitchen. "My, how you've grown! Last I saw you—you were but chest high. Now look at you!"

"Uncle Arthur McCutcheon," Mead said warmly, stepping forward to shake his uncle's hand. "It's been a while. Pa used to tell tales about you all the time."

Spying the bundle in his nephew's arms, Arthur smiled and spoke softer. "What kind of stories did your father, Jacob, tell about

13

me? And have you had your morning meal yet?" He then turned his attention to cracking some eggs in a bowl.

"We're good. My wife, Sarah, whipped up a big breakfast this morning," Mead replied. "As far as stories about you go, Pa told us that you were so quiet in the woods, you once stole a chicken roasting over a campfire from some Indians over near Salamanca without them ever seein' you!"

"That's not entirely true." The elder man held a nostalgic look.

"Wasn't stealin'?" Mead asked.

"Wasn't chicken." Arthur turned around to smirk before returning to his task.

"Pa said that's why the Seneca gave you the name 'The Forest Ghost.' Is that also true?"

"My Seneca-dubbed appellation more accurately translates as 'The Ghost That Belongs to the Forest,'" Arthur's smile widened. "But you're close enough."

"Do you believe in ghosts, Uncle?" Mead pried further.

"I most certainly do! Heaven knows the woods of Ryland Creek has its fair share of ghosts." Arthur's tone was serious. On a merrier note, he quickly asked, "What else did your pa have to say about me?"

"Pa said you could track a bobcat on a rocky stream bottom," Mead replied, mentioning the notoriously furtive wild feline that haunted the forests of Painted Post.

"Hard clay, maybe, but not over hard rock for an extended period," Arthur said.

Nathan spoke up. "Uncle Art found Seth and me in the woods yesterday easily enough."

"Did Jacob say anything more about me?" the woodsman asked.

"He also said you were half crazy." Mead grinned.

14

"Ah, that's where your good father, my best friend, was quite mistaken," Arthur intoned with mocked disappointment and then laughed. "I don't do nothin' halfway!"

The tiny package in Mead's arms stirred. The beautiful, blonde-haired little girl dressed in a hooded pink coat, shiny red boots, and jeans opened her bright-blue eyes. Realizing where she was, the child immediately scanned the room. "Unc'a Nat'n!" she squealed with delight.

"How's my Lill?" Nathan reached for her.

"This is my oldest, Sharon, but we call her Lill. She's three years old and going on thirty." Mead looked at Arthur. "She was sayin' 'Uncle Nathan' before she said 'daddy,' much to my chagrin." He deposited Lill into his brother's welcoming arms.

"There's no accountin' for taste, brother." Nathan grinned and kissed the little girl on the forehead.

"Lill," Mead said, "this would be your Great-Uncle Arthur."

"It's nice meetin' you, young lady." Arthur bowed deeply.

"Nice meet you, too," Lill returned happily as she nestled into Nathan's arms.

The silver-maned woodsman smiled at the precious child, now comfortably resting. "She's beautiful and looks like your ma, my sister, Rose." Arthur turned around to continue cooking breakfast.

Mead gave a tight-lipped nod upon hearing mention of his mother, who had died during his childbirth. "I stopped by Brian Wilkins' farm on the way here." He sat at the table near his brother.

"The sheep farmer?" Nathan's brow furrowed. "What took you over that way?" He returned his attention to Lill and smiled at her.

"Brian called early this morning and asked me to stop over. Seems he had a big bear visit his farm last night."

"Take a sheep, did it?" Arthur kept his focus on the eggs, now crackling in the hot, cast-iron skillet.

"Not *a* sheep, Uncle Art. It took four of Brian's flock," Mead replied.

15

"A bear killed four sheep in a single attack?" Arthur turned to look at his nephews.

"Yep," Mead said.

"One very hungry, very large bear!" Arthur whistled through his teeth.

"Oh, it was big all right. Nearly ate all of one sheep, but it left the other three it slaughtered alone. Just killed 'em and let 'em lay out in the open field."

"Sheep scatter immediately when they're scared," Arthur noted pensively. "That bear must've been lightnin' fast."

"Why would it kill four and only eat the one?" Nathan asked.

"It's not that a big bear couldn't eat more than one sheep at a single sittin'." Arthur scooped the cooked eggs out of the frying pan, onto a platter, and then set the hot food on the table. "But what makes this incident quite strange is that this bruin didn't carry away the sheep that it didn't eat, nor attempt to cover the carcasses with some dirt."

"It doesn't make sense." Mead shook his head. "A weasel will break into a henhouse and go into a blood frenzy, killin' more chickens than any lone weasel could ever eat. But I've never heard of a bear doin' the same."

"Does sound a bit problematic," Arthur noted. "Very unusual, this bear's behavior. My Native American friends would say there's something wrong—even evil—with its spirit."

"Bad bear! Very bad bear!" Lill declared.

Nathan chuckled. "Yes, it's a very bad bear."

Grabbing two more plates heaped with bacon and toast, Arthur placed them near the eggs as he sat his large frame in a chair.

"This whole thing sounds looney," Mead said, helping himself to some bacon.

The Forest Ghost laughed hard. "Ha! Just so happens that crazy is my area of expertise!"

"I came across a big bear's track on the Canton farm yesterday," Nathan added. "That would be about four miles from Wilkins' sheep."

Chomping on a piece of toast, Arthur said, "That distance between those two farms is well within a bear's normal home range."

"You mentioned seein' a track." Mead continued. "I studied that bear's prints. It has a large, diagonal scar on its left rear foot. You can see it as plain as day."

"Guess we should call it Scar Paw then, huh?" Arthur slapped the table, laughing.

"Works for me!" Mead replied.

Likewise, Nathan grinned. "I only saw the front paw print on the Canton farm. Although it was a large track, we can't be sure it's the same bear."

"What were you doin' over by the Cantons, anyway?" Mead asked.

"Young Jason Canton and a friend of his named Bobby Bensen took a potshot at Seth in the woods. I escorted Jason home to explain to his parents what he attempted," Nathan replied.

"Seth! My Seth!" Lill exclaimed happily upon hearing her beloved hound's name.

"Yes, your Seth!" Nathan smiled at her.

"What of the other kid . . . this Bobby?" Mead asked.

"Last that we saw of that rascal," Arthur quipped, "young Master Bensen was headed eastwardly with a howl incentivized by the crack of my whip!"

"It may have been a while since you've been in town, Uncle Art," Mead replied, "but J.P. Smith tells of your prowess with a bullwhip."

"My, oh my—J.P. Smith!" Arthur exclaimed, eyes widening at the mention of Painted Post's favorite storyteller. "Does that old bugger still own the general store downtown and tell wild tales at the counter?"

"Yes and yes," Mead replied. "J.P. told a story where you used your whip to take a deerfly off a horse's ear while that horse was pullin' a wagon, and the horse never broke stride!"

"I believe my good and learned friend Mr. Smith exaggerates on occasion. It was a horsefly, not a deerfly." Arthur's serious tone broached no argument from his nephews.

"Well, I'm betting those two boys stay away from now on." Mead chuckled.

Turning his attention from Lill to his brother, Nathan added, "I'm taking Jason coon huntin' tonight. If he shows up, that is."

"Seems a mighty strange reward for someone who almost killed your prized hound," Mead said, cocking an eyebrow.

"It may do the young man some good," Nathan replied, recalling Sharon's revelation in the dream.

"Maybe," Mead said. "How are your hounds doing?"

"I think Remmie will have pups in two to three weeks." Nathan took a mouthful of eggs and handed Lill a piece of bacon.

"Who's the sire?" Mead asked.

"Seth," Nathan responded.

"My Seth!" Lill exclaimed once more, lifting her half-eaten piece of bacon like a baton.

"Your Seth!" Nathan playfully mimicked. "Would you like to go see the hounds?"

"Yes!" she shouted with her entire body.

"Well, there you have it." Arthur smiled at his grandniece. "Let's have a gander at these fine coonhounds after we finish breakfast."

As Arthur and Nathan quickly downed the rest of the sumptuous meal and their steaming mugs of coffee, Mead continued to tell his uncle about his growing family.

"You have a son as well?" Arthur asked at one point.

18

"Yes, his name is John. He's only a little over a year old now, but he's been very sickly of late. Sarah won't leave the house much with John being ill."

"I suspect he has the Ernst constitution," the Forest Ghost spoke confidently, "and young John will turn out just fine."

Once finished with the meal, the men stood. Nathan gently placed Lill on the floor and took her hand. The family walked outside, and the porch's wooden floor groaned slightly under their weight. They paused in the fresh, fall air of Ryland Creek.

The farm was well kept. Nathan Ernst would not have it any other way. The barn had a fresh coat of red paint. A small tractor partially protruded from one of the barn's doorways. To one side of the barn were the kennels that housed the coonhounds.

The hills' gentle grade rose to form the small basin that surrounded the farm. A half-cut cornfield held the remaining brown stalks supporting ears of corn that hung at various angles. On the far side of the field, the forest gently wrapped its arms around the farmstead.

Taking in the familiar landscape, Arthur gave an audible sigh. The Forest Ghost then pointed out to his kin the different trees by their bright fall foliage. The duller oranges and dark reds of the oaks were interspersed with the bright yellows of the sugar maples and the equally vibrant umber of the hickories. Not to be outdone, the red maples showed off their namesake crimson leaves, while a smattering of hemlocks and towering white pines maintained their persistent green.

As they descended the front porch steps, a loud braying came from within the tall, red barn near the house.

"Is that ol' Butch I just heard?" Arthur asked.

Mead and Nathan shared a confused look.

"It sure is," Nathan replied, "but I don't recall you and that stubborn mule knowin' each other."

"Stubborn and our family go hand in hand most days, Nephew," Arthur said, grinning.

Nathan only nodded.

"Pa and Butch didn't get along too well, as you may recall," Mead noted with a chuckle.

"It wasn't entirely Butch's fault!" Arthur replied. "In fact, I was there that wintry day when the two of them had their falling out."

Now the brothers shared an amused look.

"It was a specific incident that caused the rift between those two?" Nathan's curiosity took hold.

"Sure was," Arthur said, nodding.

"Well, I'd like to hear about that!" Mead smirked.

"That would be a story for another time," Arthur said, returning a grin of his own. "But for now, we have a young lady who wants to see her hounds."

"Seth! My Seth!" Lill shouted, again looking up at her uncle.

"Yes, he's your Seth, for sure," Nathan said. "Let's go see your dog."

Walking to the kennels, all listened as Nathan called out each hound's name: Remmie, who was a black and tan, Bill and Sally, who were walker hounds, and finally, the regal ebony cur who was Seth.

Looking at Remmie's pregnant state, Arthur noted, "I'm saying she'll have pups closer to two versus three weeks."

"Seth!" Lill shouted with glee, approaching the hound's cage.

Wagging his tail, Seth rushed to the wire mesh and stood on his hind legs, causing the entire kennel to shake beneath the powerful hound's bulk.

And Seth roared!

The toddler showed no fear and only giggled in delight.

"Pet him, please?" Lill pleaded.

"Sure, honey." Nathan worked the latch to open the pen door. "But you have to be care . . ." Before he could complete the warning, though, the little girl rushed headlong toward the large dog.

"Lill!" Mead cried out, knowing that while Seth might not intentionally hurt the child, it would not take much for the well-muscled hound to knock his small daughter to the ground.

Instead of pouncing joyously on top of the child, the King of Hounds lay on his stomach, proffering his head to the tiny hands that gently stroked his ears.

Nathan kneeled close to his niece and the ebony cur.

Arthur began, utterly amazed. "Well, I'll be dipped in pig s—"

"Uncle Art!" Nathan interrupted, looking from the woodsman back to Lill. "Remember the young'un's tender ears."

"Right you are, Nephew," the woodsman conceded.

"We best head home before Sarah gives me the what for." Mead smiled. "Lill, honey, say goodbye to Uncles Nathan and Arthur—and Seth, too. Mommy is waiting."

The little girl looked up at her gargantuan father with a smile. With a slight lean over the hound, Lill kissed Seth's furry head. "Goo' boy," she whispered. Then, righting her tiny frame and with her arms outstretched, Lill hugged Nathan's neck. "Take care of my Seth, Unc'a Nat'n!" the tot happily commanded.

"I will, little lady," Nathan replied.

"Seth! My Seth!" Lill tee-heed and ran to her father, who lifted her skyward.

"Stayin' long, Uncle?" Mead asked, beginning to walk toward his truck.

"For a bit, I think. It's been some time since I've had the chance to grace this town with my presence."

"Bye-bye, Great-Unc'a Art'ur!" Lill interjected with a tiny wave.

Arthur beamed. "Well, just one more person in this town who thinks I'm great. Goodbye, young lady." The tall man bowed again, but deeper this time.

"I'm sure Father Simmons remembers you well." Mead returned a wicked grin, referring to a local Catholic priest. "He's retired now, but I'm certain he still hears confessions."

The broad smile quickly disappeared from Arthur's face.

CHAPTER 3
A Clear Understanding

The sun had sunk low in the western sky when the truck pulled down the driveway and came to a stop on the Ernst farm. Nathan and Arthur stood on the porch, watching as young Jason and his mother exited the vehicle.

"Evening," she greeted warmly.

"Evenin', Beth," Nathan replied. Turning to his left, he added, "This is my—"

"Uncle Arthur McCutcheon." Beth climbed the steps and offered her hand to the handsome, silver-maned man. "I've heard so much about you."

"Does everyone call you 'uncle'?" Nathan cocked an eyebrow slightly, looking at the woodsman.

"I get around," Arthur acknowledged with a slight turn of his head and then looked back to Beth to accept the lady's hand. "And it's nice to meet you as well, Mrs. Canton."

"Please, call me Beth."

Bowing at first, Arthur stood tall again and then turned his attention to the youngster. "So you think you're up for chasin' ringtails?"

"Ready as ever!" Jason shouted.

Descending the porch steps to be close to the preteen, Nathan said, "Let's establish some clear rules about what it takes to go coon hunting with me and my hounds. I'm sayin' this in front of your ma so there's no misunderstandin' of any sort."

"Yes, sir." The boy gulped.

"You're to study hard in school. My pa wouldn't let either me or my brother go huntin' unless we maintained at least a B average in every class. The same rule applies to you. Is that clear?"

Jason nodded. "The only grade I don't have a B or better in right now is math."

"You'll need to work on that."

"I'll get my grades up, Mr. Ernst."

"And no bellyachin' once we're in the woods. The fall and winter nights around here can get so cold it'll cause your teeth to clatter. Complainin' about it won't make it one degree warmer. Understood?"

"I won't complain, sir," the lad replied.

"Good to hear." Nathan nodded.

"Well, I will leave you men to your hunting." Beth smiled politely, smiling appreciatively at Nathan and Arthur. "I know better than to ask when you're going to get home tonight. So, Jason dear, we'll keep the front porch light on with the door unlocked." As she leaned over to embrace her son, Jason kept his arms straight down with his gaze fixed on the two men.

"You can hug your mother, young'un," Arthur said. "That ain't against the rules of coon huntin'."

Jason smiled and, if somewhat perfunctorily, returned his mother's embrace.

"You're growing up so fast," Beth whispered in her son's ear and not without her eyes watering slightly. Straightening, she looked at the men. "Thanks again, Nathan, and it was so very nice to meet you in person, Uncle Arthur." With a hurried walk, she entered her vehicle, and the hunters watched her drive away.

Returning his attention to the youngster, Arthur said, "If you learn from an Ernst, you stand a decent chance of becomin' a good coon hunter. And remember the rule about not complainin'! If'n I hear you utter a single, whiny word, I'll scalp you, kick the leaves over you, and leave you there in the woods." He grinned wickedly and then added nonchalantly, "I'll load Seth and Sally in the truck." The whipmaster walked by and proceeded toward the kennels.

When confident Arthur was out of earshot, Jason looked at Nathan. "Did he really mean that, Mr. Ernst?"

"About loading the dogs? I believe so." Nathan turned toward the house, motioning for the boy to follow.

"No, no! I meant about him scalpin' me and leaving me in the woods!" Jason said as they ascended the porch steps.

Stopping at the doorway, looking back to cast his eyes at his uncle's departing figure, Nathan shrugged. "Hard sayin'."

Jason gulped again.

"Come on, then." Nathan turned the knob and held the front porch door open. "Let's get your gear so you're ready. The ringtails should run tonight." He led the youth inside the house and handed him a hard plastic helmet with a wide leather belt that supported a heavy red battery. The coon hunter then showed the youngster how to connect the headlight assembly, adjusted the helmet's harness to Jason's noggin, and explained how to operate the lamp.

"Got it?" Nathan asked when he'd finished.

"Easy enough," Jason replied. "Can I shoot the raccoon tonight, Mr. Ernst?"

"Don't you think we ought to tree one first?" Nathan smirked.

"Yes, sir. I'm not a good shot just yet, but I'm still learning how, and—"

"A fact I'm quite certain Seth is eternally grateful for." Arthur stood in the doorway, seeming to have materialized out of nowhere, and the boy startled.

Jason's face then reddened as his chin dropped. "I'm real sorry about trying to hurt Seth, Mr. Ernst."

"That's in the past, young'un. Let it go." Nathan's reassuring tone caused the youngster's smile to return.

"The dogs and gun are loaded in the truck," Arthur said. "We're ready."

When the youth looked up again, the woodsman had vanished. "How does he do that?" Jason wondered aloud.

"Do what?" Nathan asked.

"Disappear like that without a sound!"

"They don't call him The Forest Ghost for nothin'. But the reason you didn't hear him is because you're caught up in the future and not the present. Be mindful of where you are."

"Well, what should I call him? The Forest Ghost or Uncle Arthur?"

"I s'pose 'Uncle Arthur' like the rest of us." Nathan laughed. "Let's get to the truck."

Without further ado, the boy ran out of the house with a speed fueled by youthful enthusiasm, leaving the coon hunter shaking his head and following in Jason's wake.

Stepping outside onto the porch, Nathan pulled the door closed. He found his uncle and Jason already waiting in the front seat of his club cab pickup. When Nathan entered from the driver's side, the two large men sandwiched the small boy between them.

"Where are we going hunting tonight, Mr. Ernst?" Jason asked.

"Wildcat Hollow." Nathan shifted the truck's transmission and drove down the driveway and onto Ryland Creek Road.

The youngster's eyebrows raised. "I've never heard of that place! How'd it get that name?"

"You mean to tell me, young Jason," Arthur shook his head in make disbelief, "that all the while growin' up in Painted Post, you haven't heard the story of the Beast of Wildcat Hollow?"

"No, sir!"

Flabbergasted, the woodsman continued, "My, oh my! There are some pretty serious gaps in your upbringin', young'un, but let me school you on this one."

Nathan only cast his uncle a sidelong glance.

"Perhaps you have heard rumor the Eastern Cougar has long since been hunted out of existence in these parts," Arthur began.

"Some say the last lion was killed in the 1920s in the Nittany Mountains of Pennsylvania where—"

"My pa says some people claim to have seen mountain lions in the woods around here," Jason interjected. "But he also says those folks are just seein' things—like a bobcat or something. I know I've never seen a cougar before." He folded his arms across his chest.

"Do you believe in things sight unseen?" The woodsman's eyes squinted discerningly.

"Well, I believe in God, and I can't see Him. So yeah, I guess I believe in *some* stuff that I've never seen."

"Can't think of a better example of faith." The silver-maned man nodded. "So let me tell you the story about this terrifyin' beastie that legend says lives where we're goin' tonight.

"Seems back in the 1960s, a Mr. Wilbur Millwright, known to be a fairly decent coon hunter, decided to run his hounds up on Wildcat Hollow one night. He had a young son, Dave, whom he took along with him on that hunt."

"That would be 40-odd years after that last lion you mentioned died in Pennsylvania," Jason said. "And over 20-some years ago from now."

"Well, I suppose there's hope for you gettin' your math grade up after all!" Arthur grinned. "Where was I?"

"Wilbur and his son, Dave, were about to go hunting up Wildcat Hollow," the preteen dutifully responded.

"Right, right." Arthur nodded. "Bein' a lifelong resident of our little hometown, Wilbur had also heard the stories of some mysterious, fierce, cat-like creature sometimes seen in that old forest, but he didn't pay it any mind. Just like your pa, ol' Wilbur suspected people were seein' somethin'—but certainly not a mountain lion.

"So Wilbur, Dave, and their hound called Midnight drove to Wildcat Hollow. They hadn't gone more than a mile up the holler when the men heard Midnight let out a booger bark from inside his dog box."

The neophyte interrupted again. "What's a 'booger' bark? Does that mean there was some snot running out of the dog's nose?"

Nathan couldn't help but laugh. "No, young'un, that means the dog smelled or saw something that had him scared. Pretty unusual for a coonhound to make that bark."

"Right you are, Nephew!" Arthur exclaimed. "Of course, bein' a decent coon hunter, the hair on the back of ol' Wilbur's neck stood up. Somethin' told him somethin' wasn't right, but he was determined to hunt in that hollow and nowhere else that night."

"Wait, wait!" Jason gave a skeptical look. "If Wilbur suspected something was wrong and all, why not just go hunting somewhere else?"

"Pride, son, plain old stubborn pride." Arthur shook his head. "You see, Wilbur had up and told a lot of his coon-chasing friends he was headed to Wildcat Hollow. In fact, he even laughed at them when they tried to warn him against huntin' in that forest. Sadly, pride has been the downfall of many a man."

"Couldn't Wilbur have just gone somewhere else and told everyone that he hunted the hollow?" Jason countered.

"Well, that would be lyin' now, wouldn't it? Wilbur might have been a prideful man, but he was no liar! Not that some coon hunters aren't prone to stretch the truth occasionally about their dogs, but sayin' you hunted somewhere when you didn't is a bit blatant. Where was I?"

Smirking, Nathan turned the truck onto a lesser-traveled but still paved road. "Wilbur's hair was standing on end."

"Oh, right! Well, accordin' to Dave—who at the time was only about your age, young Jason—it seems Midnight wouldn't leave their side for most of the night. They hunted for hours and walked for miles all over that mountain, but their hound stayed close to them and refused to hunt.

"When they had almost returned to where they'd started, with Wilbur quite down in the mouth, Midnight finally struck a coon's track and ran deep back into the hollow.

"But poor Dave was worn out at this point and asked his pa if he could go to the truck and sleep. It had been a tough hunt without result. Not wantin' to break the boy's spirit and never have his son coon huntin' with him in the future, Wilbur let Dave head back to the truck alone.

"Well, Dave made it to their truck and fell fast asleep." Arthur paused, seeming to steel himself for what was to follow. "Most folks figured Wilbur must have gone through those brambles that night after his hound Midnight had treed that raccoon."

"What do you mean they 'figured' Wilbur went through thorn bushes?" Jason's head perked up. "Why not just ask him?"

Throwing his hand in the air, Arthur replied, "That's because no one ever saw Wilbur alive again! When he awoke the next morning, Dave discovered Midnight crouched in terror just outside the truck. But Wilbur was nowhere to be found.

"For weeks, New York State Troopers and Forest Rangers searched Wildcat Hollow, but they couldn't find Wilbur. They even tried to use search dogs to find the missin' hunter, but like Midnight, those dogs didn't seem to want to leave the searchers."

"So, they never found Wilbur?" Jason asked, his voice only a weak whisper.

"*They* never found him. About a month after Wilbur's disappearance, a deer hunter, who also decided to hunt that wicked hollow, just happened to take a gander up into a large white pine. There he saw Wilbur's cold, dead eyes staring back from about forty feet up that tree. That hunter is said to have nightmares to this day and never hunted in Wildcat Hollow again!"

"But how'd Wilbur's body get so way up in that tree?" Jason's eyes widened.

"It remains a mystery to this day." Arthur shrugged his broad shoulders. "Some say ol' Wilbur must've tried to climb that pine after the coon that Midnight treed, and the exertion caused that old man to have a heart attack. It could be his stubborn pride got the best of him right up until the end.

"The odd thing is that Wilbur's body was horribly scarred and scratched as I mentioned. Some contend those cuts and bruises were due to climbin' the tree, or maybe from goin' through some brambles. But others say the ill-fated coon hunter received those marks from the claws of the Beast of Wildcat Hollow!"

Jason's face blanched for several moments, but then he managed to say, "And *that's* where we're hunting tonight?"

"Coon are where you find 'em, young'un," Nathan replied, slowing the vehicle down to make a turn onto a dirt road. He then pointed to a corroded, white metal road sign, which was slightly askew on a likewise rusty pole, that read in black letters, "Wildcat Hollow."

"But what happens if we come across that mountain lion tonight?" the youngster asked.

"How fast can you run?" Arthur inquired.

Now, young Jason smirked. "Pretty durn fast when I'm scared!"

Nathan and Arthur burst out laughing, which eventually caused Jason to chuckle as well.

As the trio drove into that darkened ravine, many times the narrow sides of the hollow came together to squeeze their way ahead. Large hemlocks draped their piney branches over the road, making the night even darker.

After traveling more than a mile, Nathan finally pulled the truck over to park on a small grassy patch. The hunters exited the vehicle, and Arthur then released his hounds from their dog boxes. Tails wagging in excitement, Seth and Sally promptly ran into the forest, disappearing into the night down a narrow path.

The hunting party donned their helmets, with Nathan slinging the scoped .22 caliber rifle over his shoulder to hang diagonally across his back. Within a minute, the men and boy followed the same trail the hounds had taken. They hadn't gone far when Seth's barreled voice echoed throughout the woods. Sally soon followed her mentor's lead and let out a long bawl.

"Seth and Sally have . . ." Nathan began.

But Jason was too excited and blurted out, "They've opened on a coon!"

The glow of the headlamps revealed a shared surprised look between the adults.

"And just how d'you know that, young'un?" Arthur asked.

"Oh, I went coon hunting once with my cousin Terry Wilkerson. We didn't get anything that night. After that hunt, Pa said I couldn't go with Cousin Terry any longer. Pa told me later that Terry often abuses his dogs."

"Your pa would be right about that." There was no shortage of contempt in Nathan's voice.

"Well," Arthur rocked his tall frame back and forth on his heels, "you don't get to choose your relatives." Seeing a somewhat amused look from his own kin, the whipmaster quickly added, "Present company excluded, of course, good nephew."

Jason leaned in close to Nathan and confided, "Wilkerson is only like my third cousin, Mr. Ernst—a *very* distant third cousin—by marriage, not blood."

For several long minutes, the hounds tracked the wily raccoon across the hollow's bottom, crossing several creeks, but Seth and Sally finally settled into a short, chopping bark.

"They're treed!" Arthur exclaimed, delighted the dogs had found their prey.

"Oh boy!" Jason shouted. Taking off at a quick run, the youngster didn't make it more than a few feet before his foot caught a tree root and went tumbling hard onto the forest floor.

The two men soon caught up with the fallen youth.

Hurt, but knowing not to complain, Jason brushed the leaves and mud off his clothes as the adults stood over him.

"Young'un," Nathan said, grasping Jason's shoulder, "that raccoon is up a tree and ain't goin' anywhere. Listen and learn—I don't run to or from anything, is that clear?"

"Yes, sir, I'll be sure to walk from now on. No running to or from anything," Jason repeated. He could see Nathan smile before his new mentor turned and headed toward the beckoning coonhounds.

"We might just make a coon hunter of you, yet," Arthur said with a nod of admiration.

After several minutes, the hunters joined their loud barking hounds beneath a tall, leafless red maple. Although the raccoon perched in the highest branches of the ancient tree, Jason spotted the furbearer almost immediately.

"I see him, Mr. Ernst!" Jason pointed at the ringtail with glee. "Right there!"

"Well done, young'un," Nathan said, unslinging the rifle from his back. "Pet the dogs up and tell them they did good."

More than happy to comply, Jason shouted, "Good girl, Sally! Good boy, Seth!" He carefully approached the treeing hounds and stroked their backs.

"Come over here now, young'un." Arthur motioned to Jason. "We don't want you gettin' hit on the head by a fallin' ringtail. I wouldn't know what to tell your mother if'n that happened."

Producing a loaded ammunition clip from his pocket, Nathan smoothly inserted it into the bottom of the .22 rifle. Aiming through the scope and clicking off the safety, the coon hunter squeezed off one shot. His aim true, the raccoon, dead instantly, plummeted to the ground.

Commanding the hounds back, Arthur lifted the sizeable boar coon into the air. "One very large and prime hide! This old fellow should bring a pretty penny from those no good, cheatin' fur buyers—may they all rot in h—"

"Uncle Art!" Nathan's castigating tone cut the older man off.

Silently nodding his admission of a near slip of the tongue, Arthur walked over and handed the ringtail to his nephew.

Pulling a short, braided silver chain from his hunting coat, Nathan used the chain to hang the lifeless animal on a nearby sapling. He then produced his razor-sharp knife from another pocket. Unfolding the blade, the hunter quickly put the knife's edge up to one of the inverted carcass's hind legs. He then hesitated, turning to look at Jason. "You ever see a raccoon skinned before?"

"No, sir," Jason replied.

"Have you ever seen *anything* skinned?" Arthur asked the youth.

"No, Uncle Art, I can't say that I have."

"Well then, are you squeamish around the sight of blood?" the woodsman continued, shaking his head.

"No, sir!" Jason shouted, but then added, "Leastways, I don't think so."

"Hmmm," was all Nathan said, and then put his knife to the task. The sharp instrument easily sliced through fur and sinew. With Sally watching and sitting nearby, the skilled hunter began to pull the hide off the dead ringtail.

"Mr. Ernst, I don't feel so good," Jason said, barely above a whisper. The preteen then fainted and fell toward the soft leaves.

Both men turned to see Seth holding Jason's coat collar in his maw, keeping the boy's head several inches above the ground.

"Reckon that answers whether or not he's squeamish around blood," Arthur noted sarcastically. "And your Seth is quick! That hound likely rescued the young'un from a might' serious headache."

"That's not the first time Seth's come to the rescue," Nathan replied. "He saved my hide on the small bridge over Ryland Creek not that long ago."

Seth snorted, even with a mouthful of boy.

Before the woodsman could ask about the specifics of Seth's heroism, the disoriented youth, still supported by the ebony cur, came to and shook his head. "What happened?"

"You passed out, young'un," Arthur replied with a smirk.

Jason moaned. "Oh man! I did?"

Continuing to process the pelt without looking at the youngster, Nathan said, "You were holding your breath while watchin' me skin the coon. Always remember to keep breathing. And you can thank Seth for catchin' you before your noggin hit the dirt."

With a slight nod from his master, the obedient hound opened his powerful jaws to have the boy drop the last few inches to the ground.

Earning a mouthful of leaves as he landed, Jason let out a muffled, "Oooomph!" Spitting out the fall foliage, embarrassed but still grateful, he rose to his knees and leaned over to hug the hound's neck. "Much appreciated, Seth."

The ebony cur wagged his tail as the boy stood.

"That hound is truly somethin' else," Arthur declared, smiling broadly.

A few hours later, Jason's first coon hunt with Nathan and Uncle Arthur would end with three more large raccoon taken that evening.

When they had returned to the truck, Sally lifted her head in the air, catching something carried on the wind. The ordinarily fearless hound suddenly darted beneath the vehicle, her tail tucked between her legs.

Also catching the scent in that soft breeze that had so unnerved his hunting mate, the King of Hounds stepped between the hunters and the night. The ebony cur searched the darkness, and his powerful body tensed.

And then, Seth roared! A warning to a threat unseen.

"What's gotten into him, Mr. Ernst?" Jason asked.

"Hard sayin'." Nathan shrugged. "I've never seen Seth do that before."

"You don't suppose he smells that old mountain lion, do you?" Jason's jaw dropped open. Again.

Arthur's stare seemed to pierce night's veil. "Whatever has Seth's attention, it can't be good."

The men then loaded the dogs into the truck. As they departed Wildcat Hollow, the vehicle's lights faded away.

The nighttime reclaimed the woods, and a loud, feral scream broke the silence.

Scar Paw had heard the hounds trailing and treeing throughout the mountains and had closed the distance from afar to confront the hunters and the dogs. The bear had been less than a hundred yards when the black cur's unmistakable challenge resounded in the cool autumn night's air.

This coonhound, the beast's nascent nemesis, showed an uncanny ability to detect its presence and had thwarted the bruin's attack once again.

The beast then heard the truck doors slam, the sound of the engine start, and a maddening silence as the men and their hounds drove away.

An old, moss-covered oak stump, just a foot before the bruin, had stood there for decades and would likely have lasted many years hence had it not been for the bear's seething rage. In a single, powerful swipe of the brute's front paw, the stump splintered into dust.

With its uncanny senses, the black bear looked up a nearby white pine tree into the starlit eyes of an Eastern cougar.

The giant cat didn't pounce on Scar Paw. The lion remained still, thankful for the safety of its high perch. For despite the dark night, the stealthy cougar could readily discern that it was no match for the massive bear.

Further, the wild feline knew nothing in the forests of Painted Post—not even its razor-sharp claws—could confront the darkness radiating from the unnatural thing below.

CHAPTER 4

Lost and Found

A rthur wore an amused look, watching Jason bite heartily into a second double cheeseburger. "Where in the world do you put all that food, young'un?"

With his mouth half full of the juicy burger, the youngster took a long sip of his chocolate milkshake from a straw and shrugged. "I don't know. I just eat it."

"And how!" Nathan was forced to agree.

It was the first Friday night in November, and Jason's second time to head out coon hunting with Nathan and Uncle Arthur. The sun hadn't quite set when Jason arrived at the Ernst farm, so the preteen readily accepted Nathan's suggestion to get something to eat at a local favorite restaurant, Shirley's Diner, before they went to the woods. The meal was a reward of sorts, too, as the student reported he had scored a perfect one hundred on his latest math test.

Not so surreptitiously, Jason slipped a long french fry to Seth, sitting patiently on his haunches next to the boy. The hound readily accepted the tidbit.

This evening, the eatery was experiencing a substantial patronage as the hunters sat in a booth away from the main entrance. Martin "Marty" Rigby, the handsome black man who owned the establishment, was busy greeting customers and assisting the waitstaff to get the many orders served.

One customer, Thomas "Tommy" Phelps, a known drunkard and already half inebriated, pointed to the ebony cur, shouting to anyone who would listen, "Hey, I thought dogs weren't allowed in here!"

Not having any of it, Marty waved his finger at the man. "For Seth, I'll make an exception. Besides, Tommy, I let you in here, didn't I?" The dinner crowd listening exploded with laughter. "And I know Seth is housebroke, which is more than I can say for you!" The patrons hit an even higher pitch, silencing the sot.

However, another patron, sitting by himself and spying the hunters, silently scowled.

Arthur took a spoon, dipped it into a large bowl of beef soup, and slurped loudly.

"Better make sure you keep your white hair out of your soup, Uncle Arthur." Jason smirked.

"It's silver, not white." The woodsman kept his focus on the sumptuous broth, plowing his spoon into the bowl again.

"What's the big deal—silver or white?" Jason took another large bite from his rapidly disappearing cheeseburger.

When Arthur seemed just about to school the youngster, Nathan interjected. "Legend in these parts has it that if'n your hair turns white, you'll die in the forest."

"Really?" Jason replied and then added hastily, "Then I'm certain it's silver and not white, Uncle Art."

"Much obliged, young'un." Arthur laughed before sipping his next spoonful.

"Well, bless me if it isn't Artie McCutcheon!" an excited, feminine voice shouted from across the diner.

Both Nathan and Jason watched curiously as the woodsman's back arched ramrod straight upon hearing his name called out. Closing his eyes, Arthur spoke in a whisper, just loud enough so his hunting partners could hear. "Don't make any sudden moves, and maybe she'll leave."

Stella Wharton's black high heels clicked loudly on the tiled floor. The wealthy widow wore a red dress and pink pearls in stark contrast to the sea of other diner patrons clad in blue denims and brown canvas coats. When she'd neared, Stella slipped her arms over Arthur's broad shoulders and spoke in a sultry voice into his ear. "It's been a very, very long time since I saw you last, Artie."

"Artie? Artie!" Jason put one hand over his mouth to stifle a laugh.

With a slight shake of his head, the woodsman gave the youth a tacit don't-encourage-her-young'un glare.

"And still no wedding ring on your finger yet?" the huntress of men noted.

The utensil dropped out of Arthur's hand and clanged noisily on the floor. "Oh, we were just about to go coon hunting."

Even Seth let out a loud snort.

Glancing at Nathan, Stella said, "I'm glad you're keeping your father's tradition alive by raising hounds. I do miss him so. Jacob was a very good man."

"Thank you, Ms. Wharton." Nathan nodded slowly.

"And are you still taking those long walks in the woods, Artie?" Stella returned her attention to the whipmaster. "Are you sleeping in the forest beneath a blanket of stars . . . all alone?"

With some measure of composure, Arthur turned to smile at the woman. "I do, and I'm doin' quite well. Thank you for asking. Did I mention we're going coon huntin' tonight?"

Cocking her head slightly with a knowing smirk, Stella sighed. "I see you haven't changed one little bit, Arthur McCutcheon, and I approve. If you ever need anything, Artie, and I mean, *anything*," Stella's lewd look was unmistakable, "you know where to find me."

Sharing another muffled laugh, Nathan and Jason watched the ordinarily outspoken woodsman remain dumbfounded.

As Arthur's strong frame shuddered slightly, Stella sashayed to the counter, took her meal to go with a thank you for her business from Marty, and departed through the front door. When he was sure it was safe, Arthur reached down to retrieve his utensil from the floor. "A woman like that would drive me crazy!"

"I reckon that would be something of a short trip, huh, Uncle *Artie*?" Jason quipped with a half smirk and handed the big man a clean spoon.

Hesitating for a moment before accepting the silverware, Arthur then laughed. "Ha! But tell me, Master Canton, is there a young lady in your life?"

"Well, there is Tara, I suppose." Jason turned to Nathan. "I have to use the restroom."

Looking at the boy's empty plate, the coon hunter nodded. "I'm not surprised."

Excusing himself, Jason walked to the back of the diner. The men's and ladies' restrooms were down a long, narrow hall. On the walls were color as well as black-and-white aerial photographs of the beautiful Painted Post region in all its seasons.

Turning the lavatory's doorknob, Jason disappeared within.

The humorless patron followed the boy's movement, stood, and likewise meandered toward the narrow hallway.

Seth growled as the small man walked across the diner.

Nathan tried to ease his faithful dog. "I see him, boy."

Because he liked to read the graffiti on the restroom walls, Jason took a little while longer than he'd expected. Washing his hands, he then rushed out of the bathroom, into the waiting grasp of his cousin, Terry Wilkerson.

"What have we here?" Terry grabbed the boy's shoulder and pushed him against the opposite wall.

Jason wasn't amused. "Let me go, Terry!"

"Not so fast." The rat-faced man sneered. "I heard rumor you went coon huntin' with Nathan Ernst, and here I catch you at Shirley's eatin' with him and his hound."

"My pa doesn't want me hunting with you anymore. Besides, Mr. Ernst is twice the coon hunter you are!" Jason looked defiantly at his *third* cousin—by marriage.

40

"You don't know about the Ernsts, and Nathan Ernst in particular, do you, boy? If you knew what he supposedly did out there on Ryland Creek, you'd run away real fast like." Terry squeezed Jason's shoulder with excruciating pressure.

"Stop it! You're hurting me! I'll tell my pa!"

"Your pa ain't goin' to do a thing to me," Terry smiled confidently. "I'm your ma's cousin. And further. . ."

The force that threw Terry to the other wall was such that it knocked the air from his lungs, and one of the pictures slipped off one nail to hang at an angle.

"I'm not your kin." Nathan's eyes burned as his fists twisted Terry's shirt to hold the man in place.

"I'm . . . I'm sorry, Nathan!" Terry stammered.

Appearing just behind his nephew, Arthur looked very displeased at the small man pinioned against the wall. "Oh, you certainly are one sorry sonofa—"

"Uncle," Nathan interrupted with a motion of his head to Jason but did not take his eyes off the bully of a cousin.

"Right, right," Arthur conceded once more. "No cussin'."

With words more promise than threat, Nathan said, "Never let me catch you hurting Jason again. Because if you harm him, if you even look at him in a cross manner, I *will* find you."

"I won't ever touch the boy!" Terry blurted out, patting the air in surrender.

Keeping the villain trapped against the wall, Nathan spoke in a softer voice to the still-shaken youngster. "Are you okay?"

"Yes, sir, Mr. Ernst, I'm all right now." Jason smiled appreciatively.

With a hard stare, the coon hunter released Terry. "Leave and be sure to pay your tab on the way *out*."

Freed, Terry scrambled away from the hallway. His exit was hurried even more so, for when he passed the ebony cur, Seth growled ominously.

With a satisfied grin, Jason watched his third-by-marriage cousin hastily retreat. The youngster said nothing but went to the off-kilter picture of Painted Post and righted it to hang perfectly once again. Walking back, he put a hand on Nathan's forearm and smiled. "Thank you, Mr. Ernst."

Nathan only nodded.

Upon finishing their meal, the coon hunter paid the entire bill to Marty at the cash register.

The sizeable tip brought a broad smile to Marty's face, who quickly added with a knowing grin, "Thanks for cleaning up the rest area, if you know what I mean." He then winked at the large dog by Nathan's side. "It's always good to see you, Seth."

The hound wagged his tail and whined happily.

Stepping outside into the parking lot, still crowded with cars, the hunting party walked to Nathan's truck.

"There'll be a big storm tonight." Arthur looked skyward as a cool breeze blew. "And it'll come in fast and hard. Not as bad as the storms from Lake Erie, but bad enough."

"How do you know that?" Jason gazed up at the now-starry sky with a puzzled look.

"The trees told me, young'un," the woodsman replied.

"Enough time for us to get a quick hunt in, do you suppose?" Nathan deferred to his uncle.

"Just, if'n we make it to the woods soon." Arthur dropped the truck's tailgate and opened the dog box. Seth easily jumped up and proceeded through the open door.

In less than half an hour, the hunters stood in the darkened forest on a broad path, one of many interconnecting trails in this state game preserve. Arthur's prescient forecast held true as thick cloud cover had already rolled in, hiding the stars, and the wind had started to pick up.

"Will the coon be out and about tonight, Mr. Ernst?" Despite his warm coat, Jason shivered beneath his bright headlamp as the temperature dropped rapidly.

"They'll run until the storm's fury hits," Nathan replied. "The raccoon will want to get a drink and some food so they can den up for the rest of the night."

On cue, Seth's voice boomed somewhere far beyond their light's reach.

"Ha, ha!" Arthur cackled. "There's at least one ringtail that ventured out!"

The first snowflake of winter floated down past Jason's nose. "Oh man, it's going to snow!"

His open trail bark continued as Seth worked out the woods bandit's curvy trek. The wily creature must have sensed the coming storm and had been frantically searching for a bite to eat to fill its stomach. While the ringtail's hunt for a meal had made the erratic track difficult to sort out at times, the ebony cur was too skilled to be thrown off the scent.

Within ten minutes, Seth finally settled into his tree bark. Meanwhile, the snow fell noticeably harder, and a white blanket covered the ground.

"Wow, Uncle Arthur." Jason's breath rose as a misty cloud in his headlamp. "You certainly were right about the storm coming in!" The young boy shivered with the temperature continuing to plummet nearly as fast as the snow fell, and the windchill made it feel even colder.

Following the trail, the hunters started walking toward the beckoning coonhound. They were thankful to find Seth treed less than fifty feet off the manmade path.

The hound continued to bark rapidly as his master arrived. This chase, the raccoon had scaled a large hemlock, the conifer's flat needles providing a protective wall against both the storm's wrath and the hunters' detection.

"How are we ever going to see that ol' coon up this tree?" Jason moaned.

"Have patience, young'un." Nathan looked calmly at the youth through the thick, falling snowflakes. "When you shine the branches with your headlight, look for the coon's eyes to come back as one or two amber dots. Likely, the ringtail will be near the very top."

The hunters spread evenly out about the hemlock, using their lights to methodically scan the large pine tree.

"Hey!" Jason called out, hopping up and down. "I see him! I can see the coon, Mr. Ernst!"

"Well done, young man!" Arthur shouted over the growing wind.

Nathan laughed at the youngster's joy. "Stay there, Jason. I'll be right over with the gun." As the hunter passed beneath the tree, he patted the cur's head. "Good job, Seth." The hound momentarily stopped barking to place his large front paws on his master's chest and lick his face. The King of Hounds then resumed treeing.

Once Nathan had joined Jason, the coon hunter readily spied the reflection of the raccoon's eyes peering through the piney boughs, verifying the boy's claim.

"That's not much of a target!" Jason said.

Again, The Forest Ghost silently materialized next to the youngster, startling the lad. "Sometimes, in coon huntin' as in life, that's all the opportunity you'll ever get." The big man then winked beneath his plastic helmet. "But take the shot anyway."

"Yes, sir," Jason replied.

Loading the clip into the gun, Nathan then took careful aim. The heavy snowfall forced him to peer through the rifle's scope longer than usual, but when the shot finally rang out, the raccoon crashed through the pine's branches to land dead at Seth's feet.

"Another large ringtail!" Arthur exclaimed, walking over to retrieve their bounty. "A sow this time, but a prime hide nonetheless!"

"Are you cold?" Nathan said, noticing Jason shuddering.

"Yes, sir," the youth admitted, but quickly added, "but I'm not complaining!"

"No sense in you waitin' while I skin this raccoon. Do you remember where the trail is? You can head back to the truck while I take care of this hide. Uncle Art will stay and help me lead Seth out of here. We'll call it a night on account of this storm."

"Thanks, Mr. Ernst. It is getting a little cold out here."

"There's a fork in the trail just before you get to my truck. Be sure to take the right branch. If you go left, the trail eventually circles back to where we're parked, but you'll end up hiking an extra two miles if you do."

"Okay, sir." Jason nodded. "I'll see you in a bit."

"Let me know when you're on the path." Nathan used his light's beam to direct the youngster. "It's only just over there."

Walking in the indicated direction, Jason soon found himself on the trailway that had brought them to Seth. However, the frozen precipitation had come down so heavily that it had erased any sign of their passing only fifteen minutes before.

"I'm on the trail, Mr. Ernst!" The cold was seeping into the youth, and his thoughts were of the stinging snow. "I'm supposed to take the left fork to get to the truck, right?"

In a loud voice, Arthur responded from the darkness, "Right!"

"Got it!" Jason shouted back.

Setting off at a good pace, which also helped warm him some, the neophyte went down the path. In less than ten minutes, Jason finally came to the split in the trail. The youngster then took the left fork—just as Uncle Arthur had said—and headed into the thickening blizzard.

———◆———

The frigid cold stymied Nathan's effort to skin the raccoon, but nearly ten minutes later, he successfully completed the task.

45

Slinging the .22 rifle over his shoulder, the hunter snapped a leash on Seth's collar and handed the lead to his uncle. "Let's call it a night."

"A successful night!" Arthur clarified with a broad smile.

On the trail, they could still make out Jason's tracks, if with some difficulty due to the mounting storm. The men and leashed hound moved slower than the anxious boy, but when they came to the trail's fork, Arthur put his hand up to stop his nephew.

Studying the rapidly fading prints in the snow, Arthur said, "Our young'un took the wrong trail."

Nathan replayed Jason's last words in his mind. "He must have misunderstood you! He thought you were agreeing with him takin' the left trail. With this snowstorm, it'll take him a long time gettin' back to the truck—too long. We can't take the chance he might get lost."

"Agreed," Arthur replied. "Let's head after him. If we keep a good pace, we should catch up with him soon enough."

They started out but hadn't gone a hundred yards down the trail when another massive set of tracks appeared next to Jason's smaller footprints.

Easily heard above the mounting winds, Seth growled ominously

"What in the world?" The coon hunter bent over to study the tracks.

The whipmaster's light beam focused on one large print with a diagonal line running through it. Arthur's pronouncement sounded like an epitaph.

"It's Scar Paw!"

"No, it can't be!" Nathan shook his head in disbelief. "How could that bear be out here—and just now?"

"Can't know for sure, Nephew." Arthur had to shout over the howling wind. "It ain't right. Most bears would've denned up in a storm such as this. But one thing is for certain—it's huntin' the boy!"

"We can't get to Jason before that damned bear does." Nathan reached over and unsnapped the hound's leash. "But Seth can."

The exceptional hound dipped his nose to smell the track and read the scents in the blowing wind. Like Arthur, the dog clearly understood the strange bruin's motives.

"Find Jason," Nathan said, looking at his steadfast canine companion and motioning with his head down the trail. "Find the boy, Seth."

With one last look at his master, the large coonhound sprinted into the night, and in seconds, absorbed by the darkness.

———•———

"I must've taken the wrong trail," Jason muttered. After thirty minutes of walking, his pace had slowed by half. The cold sapped his will, and his ungloved fingers were numb. Further, the storm viciously whipped ice crystals into his face, causing his eyes to tear.

The trail circles back to the truck, he remembered Mr. Ernst saying. With a deep breath, and the cold air stinging his nose, Jason felt certain he'd already gone at least a mile. That meant the truck and the other hunters should only be minutes away.

Against the raging storm, the youngster continued on. The crusty snow caked his headlamp lens, substantially reducing the bulb's ability to pierce the night. But the path was wide and now very white, making it easy to follow. After a few more steps into the biting wind, Jason determined he could walk backward to protect his face and still negotiate the trail.

As Jason turned, his light's compromised illumination revealed a huge, dark form through the swirling whiteness less than forty yards away. Whatever it was, the shape lumbered at him, and the youngster knew it was no longer the cold causing his teeth to clatter.

To his right, only a few yards off the trail, Jason spied a massive red oak. Sprinting as fast as his frozen limbs would allow, the boy ran to the far, storm-exposed side of the enormous tree. Despite the stinging ice and freezing windchill, the boy's numbed fingers found his headlight's switch and turned the dulled beam off. He remained quiet, stifling a sob.

Even above the wind's howl, Jason heard it distinctively—the unmistakable sound of footsteps crunching in the new snow just on the far side of the tree. In the corner of his eye, a massive, dark head slowly emerged from around the tree's trunk.

Shutting his eyes, Jason drew his body into a tight crouch.

It was close now. So near, the boy could hear it step closer, crunching the snow beneath its weight. Its warm breath washed over his neck, providing a stark contrast to the bitter winter storm. His breath likewise froze, feeling no comfort in the unknown.

Then, there was a warm tongue on his hand, forcing the boy to open his eyes and find the familiar crown of a king.

"Seth!" Jason immediately wrapped his numbed arms around the large coonhound's neck. As he released his hold, it wasn't just the wind that produced the tears. "I'm so happy I didn't shoot you the day we first met."

Stepping back, Seth cocked his head. "Harrumph!"

But then the dog's superior senses caught something in the air, and the hound suddenly reared on his hind legs to better course the scent. Seth leaped into the swirling mass of snow and disappeared once more.

The silence seemed to last forever.

And then, Seth roared!

Through squinted eyelids, Jason leaned around the tree's trunk to determine if he could locate the hound, and from behind, a giant paw grabbed his coat. He screamed.

"You scare sorta easy, boy." Nathan's voice came as a warm tonic. Scrambling to stand, Jason then hugged the man.

48

Carrying his bullwhip in one hand, Arthur appeared with Seth by his side. Seeing the lad safe produced a quick smile from the woodsman, but he spoke directly to Nathan. "It's gone."

"What's gone?" Jason looked at both men.

With a shake of his head, a tacit understanding for his uncle to not broach the subject, Nathan said to Jason, "Nothing. All's well. Let's go back to the truck and get you warmed up."

Wiping the snow from his headlamp lens and allowing the light to challenge the storm's growing might, Jason said, "Hey, Uncle Art! Your hair is all white now!"

Looking down at the long, frozen locks on his chest, Arthur grinned. "Yes, it is, young'un, but only for a little while."

CHAPTER 5
Dual Mysteries

The two-toned song of a red-winged blackbird sounded somewhere in the forest.

Sharon sat on the mossy rock, barefoot, the spray from the waterfalls wetting her long, brunette hair.

She was always barefoot in the dream.

Their faces were but inches apart, as Sharon bowed her head slightly. "Speak with him," she repeated, her voice urgent. "Listen to Gray Eyes."

Nathan's face scrunched up a bit. "The Seneca chief near Salamanca? The one who raised Uncle Arthur as a teenager? He can tell me about this bear?"

"Yes. He will explain the beast and its kind. You'll need his knowledge to defeat the thing you call Scar Paw. You've never faced a creature like this before."

"Sharon, it's only a bear. A big, mean one, I'll grant you." Nathan shook his head. "But it's just a nuisance animal that'll have to be put down."

"No, my beloved," she spoke patiently. "This creature is so much more than anything nature intended."

"Then what exactly is it?" Even in the dreamscape, his skepticism remained.

Putting her hand up to his cheek, caressing it softly, a hint of sadness clouding her eyes, Sharon spoke one final time this night.

"Destiny."

———◆———

Tara cocked her head puppylike. "You're weird."

With her short, brown hair and matching eyes, the preteen leveled her impish smile as Jason concluded his story about chasing raccoon in the snowstorm several nights ago.

Sitting in the kid-filled, noisy middle school cafeteria, Jason made a loud crunching noise as he bit into his taco. "Yeah, you're probably right." He did not pretend to understand girls, but didn't let that consternation bother him, either.

She persisted. "Why do you hunt them? What did those raccoon ever do to you?"

"Do to me?" Jason spoke with a mouthful of lettuce and meat. "They didn't do anything more to me than the cow in this taco. Did the cow in your taco do something to you?"

She momentarily stared at the taco in her hand, conceded Jason's point with a brief nod, and took a noisy bite. "But what do you do with the raccoon after you kill them?"

"Mr. Ernst says he'll let me come watch when he sells the hides to a fur buyer. His uncle, Uncle Arthur, said fur buyers and used car salesmen are cut out of the same cloth."

"What does that mean?"

"I dunno," Jason replied. "Come to think of it, Uncle Arthur says a lot of things that I don't understand."

"You're so weird." She laughed, taunting him.

"Yep, uh-huh." Jason slurped his chocolate milk through a straw. He had to admit that he liked it when she laughed.

"Weren't you scared, though, getting caught in that snowstorm all by yourself?" Tara's tone morphed into maternal concern.

"A little, I suppose, but I knew Mr. Ernst, Uncle Arthur, and Seth wouldn't let me down." Jason had never put his sentiment into words but knew the truth of it.

"Who's Seth again?"

"The best coonhound ever!" He chomped into his taco again, with some of its lettuce falling to his plate.

"How do you know he's the best?"

"Well, I dunno that for sure," Jason admitted, "but Mr. Ernst says he's the best coon dog they've ever owned."

"And Seth did save you from that storm."

"Yeah—that, too." He laughed. "You kinda sound like my mom!" When her expression changed suddenly, he asked, "Is everything okay?"

"My mother divorced my father last year. I don't see her very much anymore because she moved to another state."

"Really sorry to hear that."

"It's all right." She braved a smile. "Now, it's just Dad, my little sister, Becky, and me, but we'll get through it. At least, that's what Dad always says."

Jason gave the girl a kind, shy nod.

"Mind if I join you?" Bobby Bensen stepped behind Tara, holding his tray in both hands. Before they could respond, he sat next to her and set the tray down hard on the table's gray top, trying to look "cool" but desperately falling short of the mark. Putting his arm around the girl's shoulders, he asked, "How are you doing today, Tara?"

"I was just leaving." The young girl made no attempt to hide her disgust at Bobby's overt affection and immediately stood, leaving more than half her food uneaten. Looking directly at Jason, she grinned. "See you in gym class this afternoon. I hear we're playing dodgeball today, and I'll take you out!"

"Yeah, right." Jason returned the smirk.

Tara's eyes narrowed. "And one of these days, Jason Canton, I'm going to beat you arm wrestling, too."

"Uh-huh." Jason squinted his eyes, mimicking hers.

"Will you take care of my tray?" she asked, never looking at Bobby.

"Sure, no problem," Jason replied as she turned to go.

Without so much as a hint of a goodbye from the girl, Bobby watched her depart. "She really likes me," he confided. "She's just playin' hard to get."

Jason rolled his eyes. "If you say so."

"Yessiree," Bobby continued. "I hear you're coon hunting with Nathan Ernst. Is that true?"

"Yep, and with Uncle Arthur, too." Jason used a spoon to attack the succotash piled in a corner slot on his tray. "You met him—the guy with the whip."

"He's still around?" Bobby's eyebrows raised, a slight trepidation creeping into his voice.

"Sure is!" With a smirk, he quickly added, "How's your butt?"

"It hurts when I sit on it sometimes." Bobby reflexively rubbed his keister.

"We got what we deserved after what we tried to do." Jason finally cornered the last kernel of corn and a lima bean and put them in his mouth.

"Do you think I could go coon hunting with you and Mr. Ernst someday?"

"Don't see why not. But you should ask him yourself."

"I'm not so sure. . . ." Bobby looked down with a shake of his head.

"Can never hurt to ask." Jason stood, grabbing his and Tara's trays from the table.

"Yeah, you're right. Maybe I'll have my pa call and see if Mr. Ernst has room for one more to go hunting."

Later that day during gym class, Tara took both Bobby and Jason out over several games of dodgeball. She scored against Bobby repeatedly.

———— • ————

The drive to Salamanca, New York, was over 120 miles.

Earlier, Arthur had insisted Nathan join him. "It's important we talk with my adopted father, Gray Eyes. He's an elder sachem of the Seneca tribe and something of a shaman. He'll know how to handle this Scar Paw bear."

Sitting at the breakfast table with a cup of coffee, Nathan had agreed to make the trip, making no mention of his dream with Sharon. Her warning and his uncle's sudden desire to speak with the chief were too much of a coincidence.

"We'll take my truck since I know the way." Arthur said, donning his long, brown drover.

"Mind if Seth rides along?"

"Not at all!" The woodsman smiled. "And he can ride in the front seat with us."

They drove for over two hours on New York's rural Southern Tier thruway. There was only a hint of snow on the ground. The snowstorm's fury that had passed by Salamanca on the way to Painted Post just a few days ago had mostly melted away.

Sitting patiently next to his beloved master, Seth studied the many wooded hills as they drove.

It was close to noon when they finally spied their exit. Nathan noticed a sign for a restaurant that read, "The Sunset Inn" and suggested they stop at the diner to have lunch.

"No, no, nephew," Arthur explained. "Gray Eyes would take great offense if we don't eat with him."

Once off the thruway, Arthur drove his truck down some secluded back roads. There were many small houses along the way, but then he finally took a dirt road that didn't look like much more than an overgrown path.

No stranger to the woods, Nathan viewed the giant trees they passed. "Lot of raccoon in these hills, Uncle Arthur?"

"More than you can shake a dried-up pine stick at!"

Seth whined happily and wagged his tail.

54

Driving on that pathway for nearly a mile, Arthur pulled up to a large, chinkless, full-log cabin surrounded by tall, white pines and smoke pouring from its chimney. A sizeable, field dressed, eight-point buck hung from a wooden pole structure beside the home.

Not far away was a smaller log house that Nathan noticed his uncle studying with a reminiscent smile. The coon hunter then exited the vehicle with Seth, who naturally fell into step by Nathan's side.

When the younger man proceeded to the cabin's front door, Arthur caught his kin's shoulder. "Hold on, Nephew. Be sure when you address Gray Eyes, refer to him as 'sachem' and not 'chief.'"

"I thought you said he was a chief." Nathan's eyebrows raised.

"Gray Eyes *is* a chief."

"Then why can't I say so?"

"You can call him by his proper title once he knows you know what it truly means." Arthur smiled kindly, although Nathan still held a confused look. "You'll understand, in time." He then shouted, "Father! It's me, Arthur McCutcheon! We need your counsel."

The cabin's front door creaked open, and the barrel of a heavy caliber rifle appeared first. Slowly, a red face, creased with many lines and topped with long, silver hair pulled back in a ponytail, peered out.

"Who's 'we,' Ghost?" John "Gray Eyes" Cornplanter turned to focus directly on the younger man.

Arthur nodded. "Let me introduce you to my nephew, Nathan Ernst, and his hound, Seth."

The sachem stepped onto the porch to reveal his tall, lean frame, holding the rifle before him. "Seth, you say? Would this be the coonhound of such renown from the Land of the Three Rivers—what the white man calls Painted Post?"

"One and the same!" Arthur grinned, giving a curt, deferential bow.

Smiling broadly, Gray Eyes set his rifle just inside the doorway. "Who am I to deny my lodge to such a magnificent animal? Come, my friends!" He slipped from sight, leaving the entrance wide open.

"Good thinkin', nephew, bringing Seth along!" Arthur slapped Nathan hard on the back but couldn't resist adding, "It would seem your hound is more famous than you."

As his uncle walked into the home, Nathan shrugged. "Seems so." With a quick look at Seth, he grinned, "Don't let it go to your head."

With a quick snort, The King of Hounds dutifully followed his master inside.

Inside the cabin's darkened interior, the tanned hides of many different animals hung from the walls. Besides the few windows, the flames from the burning firewood within a flat-black iron woodstove with a glass front were the only sources of light. A large kettle rested atop the stove, which Nathan assumed to be the source of the delicious aroma wafting throughout the cabin.

"Did you eat?" The sachem directed his guests to a long wooden table with pine benches on either side.

"Course not! How could we pass up your wonderful cookin'?" Arthur quickly sat near one end of the table and motioned for Nathan to sit across from him.

"Excellent." Gray Eyes beamed. "This is one of my better beaver recipes, and I'm sure you'll like it."

"What part of the beaver is your stew made from?" Arthur cocked an eye in pretend apprehension.

"Depends on what part you happen to get," Gray Eyes replied.

Surprisingly lithe, the older man went to some cupboards and removed dishes and silverware. Going to the kettle, he ladled the meal of meat, potatoes, and white, wild carrots onto two plates. Setting the steaming food before his guests, the gracious host then retrieved a bowl from another cupboard and a nearby uncut loaf of bread. Gray Eyes filled the bowl with stew and placed it before Seth and then put the bread on the table.

"Just one more thing!" The chief went to an old, whitish refrigerator on the far side of the room and removed something. Returning, he handed two cups to Nathan and Arthur and produced an unlabeled, green glass bottle. "The blackberries were very juicy this year."

With a broad smile, Arthur hoisted his cup. "Is this juice fermented?"

"Not yet, damn the luck." Gray Eyes chuckled, filled both cups with juice, and sat at the table's end between his guests. "It's been too long, my dear son, Ghost. What brings you home?"

"We've come seeking your advice, Father. We have a bear problem, a big bear problem." Arthur tore a hunk from the loaf of bread and dipped it into the stew.

The older man's eyes smiled as he waved one hand in the air. "Shoot it—end of problem."

"It's a little more problematic, my father." The Forest Ghost spooned a mouthful of meat and potatoes, the pace of which showed his sincere appreciation for the chief's culinary prowess. "This creature has killed livestock—more than it could eat at one time—and didn't drag off the carcasses nor bury them."

Shaking his head, Gray Eyes said, "Not unusual for an animal to kill more than it could eat in a single attack. This bear of yours could have simply been scared off before it could carry its kill away and bury it."

Likewise enjoying the stew, Nathan spoke up. "This bear also tracked a young boy who was coon hunting with us—in the middle of a snowstorm. I think the only reason this thing didn't get the young'un is because it sensed Seth."

The hound stopped eating just long enough to look up and give a snort at the mention of his name.

With that news, Gray Eyes' face grew pensive. "It hunted a human, this bear did?"

"Yes, Father." Arthur separated another hunk of bread from the loaf and used it to sop up the remaining gravy on his plate. "The tracks in the snow told the story."

Taking a deep breath, the chief leaned back in his seat. When he finally responded, Gray Eyes spoke slowly. "Your tracking ability is second to none, Ghost, so I know the truth of what you say. You truly have a problem, my friends. For it is a *Nyah-gwaheh*, a Great Bear, that now haunts the lands of the Painted Post—and that is never a good thing.

"One of these spirit animals has not been seen by my people for a very long time. When I was young, my grandfather told me of such a creature that inhabited the hills of Salamanca when he was only a boy. In those dark days, the children would go into the forests to hunt and play, but they did not return at nightfall.

"Hunters would search the woods for the missing children but only find much blood and a gigantic bear's tracks. These warriors would follow its trail, but the bear would stay just ahead of them, taunting them with a sound much like a man's laugh, and vanish when the hunters were certain they had the beast cornered."

While their host paused, Nathan spoke up. "Sachem, why did you call this thing a 'spirit animal'?"

Smiling gently, Gray Eyes replied, "Because this creature is not completely of this world, Seth's Master. Being from the Land of the Three Rivers, you should know better than most there are spirits in the forest."

Recalling many ghost stories about his hometown, Nathan nodded. "But what can kill it then?"

"A bullet from .30-30 rifle should do nicely." The old Seneca laughed heartily but then continued seriously, "Legend has it that a Nyah-gwaheh can only be killed by stabbing it through its paws."

Arthur and Nathan shared a surprised look.

"This thing, this spirit bear," Arthur began, "has an unusual mark on one of its rear feet—a diagonal scar across its pad. We call it 'Scar Paw' because of its distinctive track."

"Then someone has tried to kill this Great Bear before." The old chief took a keen interest, leaning forward. "And that is a very big problem, my friends."

With a large measure of respect in his voice, Nathan dared ask, "Why is it such a big problem, Sachem?"

Oddly, Gray Eyes first studied the empty air beside Nathan. He smiled and then turned his attention back to the younger man after several long moments. "Because, Seth's Master, someone has already tried to kill this thing you call Scar Paw and failed. This creature's spirit must be unusually strong, even for a Great Bear."

The coon hunter shook his head. "But if it can be killed like any old bear, what makes it so unusual?"

Arthur grimaced, knowing his young nephew had made an honest mistake—but a misstep, nonetheless.

"You white men," Gray Eyes chuckled, his voice still kind. "Just because something can be killed with a mortal weapon does not mean it is simple to kill. You must know this truth, Seth's Master—this creature will hunt you with as much skill and cunning as you hunt it."

"I see." Nathan nodded slowly.

"But you have an advantage," Gray Eyes continued, motioning with his chin at the black hound.

"Seth?" Arthur's eyebrows raised slightly. "He's a great coonhound but not a bear dog, Father. How can he help us with Scar Paw?"

The old chief studied the magnificent cur for some time before speaking again. "Seth is much more than just a coonhound, my son."

Then, as if the topic of Scar Paw had never been broached, Gray Eyes spoke with Arthur for over an hour of the great many hunts they had enjoyed together in years past.

59

Nathan and Seth sat patiently, listening to the other men laugh and reminisce.

Finally, Arthur slapped the table. "It's time for us to go, my father. We thank you for the knowledge of the *Nyah-gwaheh*. We shall be cautious in the forests if'n we should ever run across this beast again."

"Rest assured, Ghost, the Great Bear will find you. Be ready when it does." The Seneca smiled sadly.

"Ready?" Nathan asked. "As in armed with a .30-30?"

"No, Seth's Master." Gray Eyes shook his head, leaning over the table and lightly tapping Nathan's chest with one finger. "You must have only courage in your heart when you face it. This thing you call Scar Paw will be able to sense your fear, which will only embolden its attack."

"I don't run." Nathan's visage hardened—his words slow but steady. "And I won't show any fear."

Studying his new friend with a slow nod, the sachem said nothing more.

Accompanying his guests to their truck, Gray Eyes produced a piece of dried meat from his shirt pocket and gave it to Seth, who readily devoured it. He then gently patted the hound's head and spoke in his native tongue.

Seth looked at the wise man and wagged his tail.

As they loaded into Arthur's vehicle and drove away, Nathan could see Gray Eyes waving until a turn in the road obscured the older man from sight. "Uncle Arthur, you speak some of the Iroquoian languages. What did Gray Eyes say to Seth?"

Arthur nodded knowingly. "My father said, 'Exceptional One, you must follow your destiny to whatever end.'"

When Gray Eyes reentered his cabin, he saw the pretty ghost who had arrived with his guests.

Forever barefoot, she walked across the floor and planted a gentle kiss on his cheek, which felt like a warm summer breeze. "Thank you, Chief."

The old man smiled. "I did what I could for them, Sharon of Ryland Creek."

Her aura brightened the dark room. "They are better prepared now to face this thing, thanks to your great wisdom."

"I fought with Nathan's grandfather, Paul, in Europe during the second World War," Gray Eyes said. "If the nephew of The Ghost That Belongs to The Forest has half his grandfather's courage, then he is a very brave man. If a Great Bear now haunts the Lands of the Painted Post, then he will need every ounce of that courage in his heart."

"Nathan is very brave," Sharon said. "He won't run from a fight." Her ethereal form slowly faded from sight.

"And Nathan has the hound Seth watching over him as well," the chief replied, offering some final solace in the near emptiness of his home. "Only if they face this terror together, can they defeat the beast called Scar Paw."

CHAPTER 6

The Winged Raccoon
of Channery Creek

J.P. Smith, Painted Post's resident storyteller, had his usual gaggle of youngsters surrounding the checkout counter of his namesake general store.

"And that's how Dead Man's Curve got its name!" the heavyset purveyor concluded to the cooing and applause of the youngsters.

Behind the crowd, Nathan and Arthur had waited patiently to purchase a few items.

As the children dispersed, it didn't take J.P. long to spy the tall, silver-maned man. "Well, if it isn't Arthur McCutcheon!" he greeted warmly. "Stella Wharton mentioned you were in town. I figured it was just a matter of time before Painted Post's native son made his way through my doors."

"It has been a long time, J.P. and always good to be home." Arthur returned the smile. "And you haven't aged a day since we last met!"

"Oh, I assure you I have!" The store owner put one hand on his lower back and grimaced. "My daily aches and pains remind me of just how old I truly am."

"We should all age so gracefully." Nathan placed the few items on the counter.

"Stella tells me you're still unmarried, young Master McCutcheon." J.P. began ringing up the purchase on the loud, mechanical brass cash register. "She has her sights on you like a fisher cat on a cottontail!"

"I can run much faster than a rabbit when frightened." Arthur chuckled, if a bit nervous. "And Stella scares the livin' daylights out of me!"

Grinning at the woodsman who would not be caught, the yarn spinner then looked at Nathan. "How's your coon hunting going with that magnificent hound, Seth?"

"It's goin' well," Nathan responded.

"Hi, Mr. Ernst!" a familiar voice called out from behind.

"Hello, Jason, how are you doing?" Nathan smiled without first looking back. As the coon hunter turned, though, he saw Jason accompanied by another.

"I'm doing swell! Mom went to the post office for some stamps, so we thought we'd get some candy bars." Jason then turned to his companion. "Mr. Ernst, this is Bobby Bensen."

"I remember." Nathan smiled, more curious than surprised.

"As do I." Arthur's tone was considerably harsher, which caused Bobby to swallow hard under the whipmaster's stare.

"Got something you wanna ask Mr. Ernst?" Jason elbowed his friend in the side.

Bobby spoke so rapidly the sentence came out as a single word. "Sir-I-was-wondering-if-you-wouldn't-mind-me-go-coon-huntin'-with-you?" He then held his breath, waiting for a response.

"Sure, as long as your parents agree." Nathan nodded, amused.

"Oh, thank you so much, Mr. Ernst!" Bobby exhaled loudly.

"Put their candy on my tab," Nathan said to J.P., causing both boys to smile as they placed two large chocolate bars on the countertop.

"You could not be learnin' to chase ringtails from a better coon hunter, Masters Canton and Bensen." J.P. beamed. "And you'll also get the chance to hunt with Seth!"

Another then spoke sarcastically. "If you're such a great hunter, Ernst, and Seth is supposed to be the best coonhound ever, then why don't you hunt Channery Creek?"

63

All eyes turned to focus on Terry Wilkerson, who had joined the checkout line.

"Garbage pickup runnin' late today?" Arthur cast a sidelong glance at J.P., who only smirked.

Dripping with contempt, Wilkerson continued, "You don't have the guts to hunt that cliff and go after the winged coon that haunts that place!"

When Jason turned to stare at him with a curious look, Nathan answered the boy's unasked question. "There's been a ringtail on Channery Creek that no one has been able to tree."

"A raccoon," J.P. warned, "that's also been thought to have led many hounds to their deaths over the years. In fact, Lloyd Hanson lost his best hound, Champ, up there just last week. Ol' Lloyd found his poor dog dead at the bottom of Channery Creek's cliff." Turning to Jason and Bobby, he added, "Some believe that ringtail even has wings and grabs pursuing hounds in its claws to pull them over the cliff's edge!"

"You wouldn't dare take Seth there, Ernst," Terry egged.

"We will hunt Channery Creek." Nathan stepped forward so forcibly the other man cowered. "And we will get that coon."

"Nephew," Arthur cautioned with a shake of his head. "I grew up in Painted Post. That's a treacherous place."

"We'll do it!" Nathan handed over the money for his purchase, picking up the items J.P. had bagged. With a smile, he slid the chocolate bars across the countertop to Jason and Bobby.

"Yeah, let's see if you really hunt there or not, and if you get that coon." Terry placed his item on the counter, smiling at his goading the other man into the dangerous pursuit. Paying his bill, he then said to Jason, "And you still don't have a clue about who you're huntin' with, do you, boy?"

Staring straight at his third cousin, by marriage, Jason replied, "I know this much—Mr. Ernst is a far better coon hunter than you'll ever be!"

64

The *real* coon hunter looked at Terry with a slight grin.

"We'll just see who's better!" Terry scowled and proceeded to the exit. But as he tried to leave, the small man bounced off a mountain blocking his way and stumbled to the floor.

"Goin' somewhere?" Mead grinned.

"Dang Ernsts!" Terry nearly shouted. When Mead's eyes narrowed, Terry gingerly stood, scampered around the giant, and hastily departed.

"Unc'a Nat'n!" A child in a hooded, bright-pink coat rushed from behind Mead straight at his brother.

"Lill!" Nathan said, bending on one knee to hug her.

"So, what was all that hubbub with Wilkerson?" Mead stepped closer.

"Your brother," Arthur interceded, "has just committed to huntin' that troublesome ringtail on Channery Creek."

"Nate," the big man shook his head, "you know Pa wouldn't hunt that place for fear of gettin' a hound killed."

"Mead's right!" J.P. interjected. "Your father, Jacob, knew better than to hunt that hill."

"Said I would, and so I will." Nathan scooped Lill into his arms and stood.

"Principle or pride, nephew?" Arthur cocked an eyebrow. "The latter has been the downfall of many a man."

"Uncle Art is right, brother." Mead nodded. "Don't let that snake Wilkerson trick you into doin' something foolish. There's no sense getting yourself or Seth hurt."

"Unc'a Nat'n hurt? Seth hurt?" The almost-four-year-old child could read the concern on her father's face. "No! Bad! Very bad!"

"I won't let anything happen to Seth or myself, little lady," Nathan replied.

"Promise?" Lill's eyes went wide, leaning closer.

"I promise—no harm will come to either Seth or me."

"Seth! My Seth!" she shouted, raising her small hands above her head.

"Well, Nathan," J.P. shook his head, "all I can say is you are your father's son. In all my years, I've never seen an Ernst back down from a fight."

"And you two." Nathan swung around to look at the young boys. "Neither of you are to get outside of my light on this hunt, understood? Are you ready to go tomorrow night?"

"Yes, sir!" they shouted in unison.

"Thanksgiving vacation is coming up, Mr. Ernst," Jason said. "We have all next week off from school!"

"As for you, young'un." Arthur pointed at Bobby. "Take heart that we won't lose you in the woods. I've never done the math proper, but I estimate seventy-five percent of the time, I've come out of the forest with the same number of folks that I went in with."

"*Only* seventy-five percent of the time?" Bobby gulped.

"Yep, or at least close thereabouts, and that's a pretty good percentage for anyone!" Arthur turned his attention to Jason. "As for you—you're responsible for makin' sure neophyte here is dressed proper for the hunt."

"Yes, sir!" Jason's chest puffed with pride and gave Bobby a hard slap on the back. "C'mon, nerdo-oh-fight, I'll explain what you need to wear."

"What's a nerdo-oh-fight?" Bobby's face scrunched up.

"Dunno." Jason laughed. "But it must be you!"

The excited boys, candy bars in hand, thanked Nathan again and ran out of the store.

"Are you sure you want to hunt Channery Creek, brother?" Mead dared to broach the subject one last time. "No sensible person would fault you if you reconsidered."

With a steeled look, Nathan spoke evenly, "Someone's gotta get that coon. And if'n there were ever a hound capable of takin' that particular 'winged' ringtail, it would be Seth."

66

The next night, Beth Canton dropped Bobby and Jason off at the Ernst farm just as the sun dipped behind the western hills. For a moment, she spoke privately with Nathan, who promised to keep close watch of both boys. Her concerns assuaged, Beth hugged both children and drove home.

Walking up to them, Arthur greeted the youngsters. "Jason, we've set aside an extra light for Bobby in the cellar—you know where it is. Get his helmet adjusted, and we'll head on to Channery Creek."

"Where'd Mr. Ernst go?" Jason looked about.

"He's talkin' with Seth." The woodsman motioned to the kennels.

The boys spied Nathan kneeling as coon hunter and coonhound stared at one another.

"Are we hunting with just Seth tonight?" Jason asked.

"Nope," Arthur replied. "We're huntin' with Sally, too."

"Oh boy!" Jason shouted, grabbing the other boy's forearm. "C'mon, Bobby! Let's get your helmet."

As the boys ran into the house, Arthur shook his head and grinned at the youths' seemingly endless energy.

Ten minutes later, the young hunters stepped onto the front porch, proudly wearing their headlamps. They saw Arthur and Nathan patiently leaning against the truck, with Seth and Sally already loaded into the dog boxes.

"Load up into the truck, young'uns." Nathan motioned to the sky. "It's a moonless night, and the coon should be runnin'."

"Don't raccoon need the moonlight so they can see, Mr. Ernst?" Bobby's face puckered.

"Most wild game likes to move on dark nights," Nathan replied. "Only people need a light to guide them through the darkness."

Opening the rear door of Nathan's club cab, Arthur motioned for the youngsters to sit in the back seat. Bobby jumped in first, and as Jason neared, the silver-maned man said, "You're sittin' in the back since one of us needs to lose some weight!"

"Well, it can't be me 'cause I don't have any to lose!" The wiry-thin Jason gently tapped the older man's stomach. "But you, on the other hand. . . ."

Arthur smirked. "Get in the truck, boy."

The drive to Channery Creek was short, with Nathan taking an unnamed dirt road that climbed the steep hillside. After he'd parked in a small field, he said to the boys, "There are cliffs due east of us by about a mile. Always stay behind Uncle Arthur and me—especially if we get near those cliffs. There are some places here where the drop-off is twenty feet or more straight down. A fall like that would kill a person. Got it?"

"Yes, sir!" Both preteens replied, nodding vigorously.

"I'll carry the gun tonight," Arthur said, putting his hand on his nephew's shoulder. "You pay attention to the hounds and the young'uns."

With a nod, Nathan proceeded to the back of the truck. As he unlatched the tailgate and opened the dog boxes, Sally sprinted away and disappeared beyond the hunters' bright headlamps. Seth stepped regally out of his box and onto the tailgate to look his master in the eye.

"You know what to do." Nathan stroked the large dog's head. "Go get this coon, boy."

Licking the man's face, the ebony cur then jumped to the ground and followed Sally's path into the darkness.

———— • ————

Sitting in the upper boughs of a huge, leafless red oak, the old ringtail watched the truck's headlights making the way up the steep hill. Long experience had taught it that the only men who invaded its home at night were those after raccoon. Just a few nights ago, another hound had learned the fateful mistake of hunting on this mountain.

The wily woods bandit climbed down the tree. But unlike others of its ilk, the coon moved toward the truck's sound so any coonhound would be sure to catch its scent.

Tonight, the world of men would again learn the bitter lesson of invading this creature's domain.

———◦———

It wasn't three minutes later when Seth's voice boomed in the night.

"Seth has opened!" Jason shouted eagerly.

Bobby gave a short hop, hearing the hound's incredibly loud bawl for the first time.

"That was a quick strike," Nathan said, his tone curious but likewise happy. When Sally's voice then joined Seth's, with both coonhounds racing across the hillside, he added, "That must be a hot track for sure."

Much more reserved, Arthur turned to his nephew. "A little *too* quick for my likin'."

"Understood." Nathan looked at Jason and Bobby. "Boys, fall in line behind me and Uncle Art."

And the hunters began following the hounds' singing.

Headed due east.

———◦———

Despite its intent to be found, the old coon was still surprised by how quickly the hound with the deep voice had caught its scent. The other dog chimed in soon afterward.

No matter. It was confident in its scheme to bring both canines to their deserved fate.

69

The raccoon then ran apace, realizing the coonhounds were only about a hundred yards behind. In under five minutes, it came up short of Channery Creek's steep cliff's edge by less than twenty yards, climbing a massive, shagbark hickory, but stopping about four feet above the ground.

Any other ringtail would have gone aloft, high into the tree's upper boughs, safely away from its pursuers. But this raccoon was different, for it perched where the hounds would easily see it.

Just as it hoped.

———————◦———————

"That coon is runnin' fast and headed straight for the cliffs." Nathan's former confidence now filled with apprehension.

"Nothin' we can do now but follow the dogs, Nephew." Arthur's grim tone didn't ease the tension in the air.

Nathan turned to the children. "Stay close to me. Let's see where this hunt leads."

———————◦———————

Still racing hard on the raccoon's scent, Seth looked ahead. Even in the darkness, the hound could readily make out the large ringtail on the hickory's trunk. Then, to the hound's surprise, the ringtail came down the tree and began running again. Now, only about fifty yards behind the coon, Seth instinctively slowed his pace.

But the less-experienced Sally surged past her hunting mate, determined to catch the prey on the ground and finish this chase. With single-minded grit, she charged forward.

The ringtail made its way to an old log that had long ago fallen at the precipice's edge, with its other end resting firmly against an oak that grew from the cliff's face. Quickly crossing the natural bridge into the tree, it again perched upon an eye-level branch where the pursuing hounds would easily see it. The coon glanced down the

30-foot chasm, with a solid ten feet separating it and the edge of the drop-off.

The female coonhound came barreling toward it with the large male close behind. Unmoving, the ringtail waited for the coondogs to plunge over the cliff to their deaths, like so many other hounds had before. Without exception. The canines' doom was inevitable.

Her sharp vision easily made out the coon resting on the low-level branch. Sally made a final leap into the air . . . . And then there was no earth below her. She howled in terror, confused as her rear feet slid over the cliff's edge.

But she did not fall.

Dangling over the abyss, Sally hung there suspended—caught by the nape of the neck in Seth's powerful jaws. The ebony cur slowly stepped back until his hunting companion had her feet on solid ground once more and then gently released her.

The King of Hounds, as black as the night itself, stared victoriously at the Winged Coon of Channery Creek, the age-old nemesis of many a hunter and coonhound.

And then, Seth roared!

———— ◆ ————

The hunting party halted as Seth's booming voice echoed throughout the hills. Then, both coonhounds began barking rapidly.

"Yes! They did it!" Jason shouted.

"Whoo-hoo!" Bobby joined in but then added, "Did what?"

"The dogs have found the racoon, young'un," Nathan replied. "They seem to be treed, but it sounds more like they're bayin'."

Jason cocked his head. "Baying? Treeing? What's the difference, Mr. Ernst?"

"Seems like they're barking as if they can see that ringtail," Nathan explained.

"I further estimate those hounds are very nigh the cliffs," Arthur said, listening intently.

"Agreed," Nathan said. "Let's take it easy from here on out. There's no need to hurry—that coon isn't going anywhere."

At a pace that seemed painfully slow to the boys, the hunters made their way to the calling coonhounds. When they arrived where Seth and Sally were treed, the men readily spotted the raccoon. For not only was the ringtail almost eye level and strangely not at the very top of the tree, it snarled viciously from across the gap.

The preteens began hollering alongside the hounds.

Furthermore, The Ghost That Belongs to the Forest, seeing the old log connecting the cliff's edge and the tree, read the story precisely. "What in the h—"

"Uncle Art!" Nathan laughed. "Remember no cussin', especially since we have *two* young'uns with us now."

"Right, right," Arthur replied. "Old habits and all."

In that moment of distraction, Bobby took a step forward. "The raccoon is right there!"

"Bobby!" Jason shouted. "You're too close to the edge!"

The rocky ledge began to crumble where Bobby had stepped. The boy's arms windmilled in the air as he slipped inexorably over the cliff. "Whoa, whoa, whoa!"

Time seemed to stop, and even the raccoon ceased its taunting growls as it watched the small human start to slip over the precipice.

Bobby screamed, beginning to fall headfirst. His headlamp came off and disappeared into the chasm.

The leather whip coiled several times around Bobby's chest, and a violent tug pulled the neophyte backward to land hard on his back and the safety of solid ground. A steady hand then grabbed the gasping kid's coat. Despite the blinding light, the frightened youngster could still make out long, silver hair protruding beneath the helmet directly above him.

"What're you tryin' to do, boy?" Arthur chuckled. "Ruin the percentage of people that I come out o' the woods with?"

"Thank you, Uncle Arthur!" Bobby sat up and quickly hugged the man's leg. "I'm sure glad you always carry that whip!"

As the hunters took a collective sigh, Jason quipped, "You weren't too happy Uncle Arthur carried a whip a few weeks ago!"

"Do you remember what I told you about staying behind me?" Nathan spoke sternly.

"Yes, sir. I'm sorry," Bobby replied, red-faced.

With a nod, Nathan sighed and said no more.

"But how will we take that ol' raccoon with it hanging over the cliff like that?" Jason scratched the side of his face.

The .22 rifle cracked in the night, and the bullet caught the old ringtail between the eyes. The Winged Raccoon of Channery Creek died instantly, plummeting into the gorge like so many hounds that had once chased it.

"I'll make my way down the cliff to retrieve the coon and Bobby's light." Arthur lowered the gun, speaking nonchalantly. "I will meet you at the corner of Channery Creek and the River Road."

———— ◆ ————

Nearly an hour later, the hunters arrived at the Ernst farm on Ryland Creek, returning Seth and Sally to their kennels and rewarding the hounds with a hardy scoop of feed.

But it was Bobby who caught the strange sounds emanating from Remmie's pen adjacent to Seth. "What's making that noise?"

Opening the kennel door, the hunters used their headlamps to peer inside the coop of the black and tan mother and beheld six tiny, squirming balls of fur.

"Puppies! Remmie had her pups!" Jason shouted gleefully.

"This has been an amazin' night, Nephew." Arthur smiled. "We took a notorious raccoon, and now we celebrate the birth of a new litter of coonhounds."

"You're a father, Seth!" Nathan looked up to see his exceptional hound, who had also heard the soft yelps, standing just on the other side of the shared wire wall.

The ebony cur took in the scent of his progeny and snorted.

Bobby's eyes went wide. "Are all nights like this when you go coon hunting?"

———— • ————

Killing the bull could be difficult, Scar Paw knew but likewise relished the challenge.

The old bull outweighed the bear by more than twice. The nearly one ton of muscle and sinew charged the intruder with an incredible burst of speed across the pasture.

But Scar Paw was faster.

The Great Bear wheeled impossibly quick and clamped its jaws around the bull's windpipe. As blood pulsed between its teeth, the bruin sensed the other animal's intense fear, which only caused Scar Paw to tighten its jaws more viciously. A mighty shake of the bruin's head forced its victim to the ground. With its sharp claws, Scar Paw eviscerated the dying animal, hastening the bull's short-but-excruciating end.

Nearby, a young calf stood frozen at the sudden onslaught of the huge beast that had killed its sire with relative ease.

Slowly turning about, the Great Bear sensed the calf's delicious fear. The terror then charged the innocent, and beneath a silver blanket of stars, a pasture on Ryland Creek became bright crimson.

With a sound akin to human laughter, the Killer of Bulls and Calves breathed hard.

"Huh, huh, huh."

CHAPTER 7
The Naming

"You can't be serious?" Nathan shook his head. "Her, too? What am I doing? Starting an orphanage?"

Sharon smiled sweetly, the pooled water below the falls reflecting her kind image.

She always smiled in the dream.

Softly laughing, she responded, "They already have parents, silly."

"Exactly," Nathan replied, throwing both hands in the air, "so they don't need me."

"My love, I assure you, these children need you."

"Are their parents bad at being parents or something?" Nathan suggested.

"No, it's not that at all."

"Then I don't understand."

Sharon's lips morphed into a knowing smile, and her brown eyes narrowed ever so slightly. "Exactly."

In the coniferous branches directly overhead, a Barred Owl hooted its soft melody.

In the dawn's soft light, Arthur stood, gently stroking the mule's gray-brown head. "How are you doin' today, old fella?"

His muzzle sticking outside the barn stall, Butch brayed contently.

They weren't alone.

"Well, let's hear this story." Mead laughed with Nathan by his side.

"What story in particular?" Arthur turned to look at his nephews.

"You know," Mead said. "The one about how Butch and Pa had their fallin' out a long time ago."

Nathan smirked. "As far as I can recall, those two were always at odds. It's hard to believe Pa and Butch ever liked one another."

With a soft, conceding chuckle, Arthur said, "That's what you remember because Jacob and Butch here parted ways years before either of you were born." At the mention of the name "Jacob," Butch bucked his head several times. "Easy now, fella," the woodsman spoke softly, continuing to stroke the long-ear's face, and the equine calmed once more.

"This ought to be good." Mead laughed.

With a sentimental smile, The Forest Ghost peered back through time. "When we were just boys, your pa and I would chase ringtails with your grampa Paul, who himself was a hunter of much renown in these parts. In fact, coon huntin' was how your father and I became best friends, which eventually led to us being kin, I suppose. Over the years, I'd tag along many a night coon huntin'— those were some memorable times, for certain.

"Anyway," Arthur continued, "your grandfather would ride Butch through the woods at night whenever he went chasin' ringtails alone. I don't need to tell you havin' a surefooted mule to take you through these rugged hills would make an otherwise miserable climb considerably easier."

Mead nodded. "I can recall Pa takin' Butch on some coon hunts now and again."

"Yes," Arthur chuckled, "but at that point in their relationship, those later hunts were more or less a temporary ceasefire between those two."

Both Nathan and Mead laughed, knowing every word their uncle spoke was true.

"There was a time they were inseparable," Arthur hastened to add. "Jacob often rode Butch for miles and miles in the woods—trips that would solidify your father's knowledge and understandin' of this land."

"What's the difference between knowledge and understanding, Uncle Arthur?" Mead asked.

Arthur cocked his head. "Knowledge is what you see, young'un. Understandin' is what you feel. Now, where was I?"

"The falling out," Nathan prompted.

"Yes, yes," Arthur continued. "Well, one day in February, I went with your father as we rode Butch to the Tioga River. I don't think I could've been much more 'n fifteen years old then, and it was brutally frigid that day. We had no business being out of doors, but Jacob had it in his head we were goin' for a ride, so we did.

"When we made it to the river, I dismounted from Butch to look at some coon tracks in the snow. Painted Post had experienced a harsh winter that year, and your pa figured the ice must have been so thick, he could take ol' Butch straight across the Tioga. I advised against the notion and stayed on the riverbank, but Jacob was adamant he was goin' to do it.

"I think they only made it about fifty yards when your pa, atop Butch, broke through the ice. It was deep water there, and at first, both boy and mule disappeared beneath the ice. Jacob later told me that he got caught in the river's current. But Butch grabbed your father's coat in his teeth and pulled him above the ice.

"I sat there and watched as that tough mule used his front legs to break through the ice, with Jacob holding on to Butch's neck for dear life, all the way back to shore."

Nathan looked bemused. "Well, after that episode, you'd think those two would have been best friends forever."

"You'd reckon such if the story ended there." Arthur shook his head, laughing as vivid memories flooded back. "Once Butch was on solid ground again and certain Jacob was okay, that old mule knocked your pa back into that cold river! Then Butch grabbed Jacob's coat and dunked him in that freezin' water several more times for good measure!"

Mead guffawed. "That must've been one miserable ride home!"

"No, no!" Arthur bent over, laughing harder. "There was no ride back because Butch ran off and left us there. Your father was half frozen to death by the time we got back to the farm. And to add insult to injury, your grandpa Paul, who'd already put Butch up in the barn and dried him off, was waitin' there for us."

"What did Grampa Ernst say?" Nathan had joined in the laughter with his kin.

"He said, 'When I'd seen Butch make it home alone without you two, I knew the old saying was true—a fool follows stubborn's path.' Jacob never lived that story down."

With his body seemingly shivering at the memory, Butch brayed stiffly and walked to the back of his stall.

Mead turned to his brother. "Congratulations on taking that coon on Channery Creek last night, Nate. That was quite the feat—one I'm sure Pa would've been proud of."

"It was all Seth and Sally. I was just along for the walk," Nathan replied.

Looking at his watch, Arthur said, "We best get movin' if'n we're not to be late for the diner."

"Uncle Art and I are treatin' Jason and Bobby to breakfast this morning—a reward of sorts for last night," Nathan explained, seeing his brother's consternation.

"You have quite the huntin' party with you now, brother." Mead grinned.

"I suspect we're to have another join us," Nathan said. When Arthur and Mead looked at him for an explanation, he simply added, "Let's get a move on, Uncle Art. We're going to be late. Mead—please tell Lill I love her."

Today, Shirley's diner was full of noisy patrons this bright midmorning, with talk of upcoming Thanksgiving festivities filling the air.

Staring at the tall stack of pancakes with a side of bacon on Jason's plate, Arthur said to the youth, "There's no way possible on God's green Earth you can eat all that, young'un!"

"You just watch me!" Jason accepted the challenge with a smirk. "Wanna bet me a dollar I can't eat it all?"

"I wouldn't take that bet, Uncle Art," Nathan said, grinning. With a quick look at the other lad, he asked, "Do you have enough to eat, Bobby?"

While he'd only ordered two of the plate-sized blueberry pancakes, Bobby hadn't hesitated to begin eating once the food was brought to the table. "I'm fine, Mr. Ernst, thank you!" he replied with his mouth already half full.

Holding the order pad in her hand, the pretty waitress, Danielle "Dannie" Gorton, looked Nathan over several times before she asked, "Will there be anything else? *Anything?*"

"No, thanks. I think we're good for now," Nathan replied.

"Well, you let me know if there's *anything* you need, okay?" She gave the eligible bachelor a quick pout before tearing the top piece of paper from her order tab to set it on the table.

"Will do. Thanks again, Dannie." Nathan nodded politely.

She then sashayed away from the hunters to serve another table.

Watching the exchange between his nephew and the young lady, Arthur smiled but said nothing as he started to eat his breakfast of eggs, sausage, and hash browns.

One elderly patron spotted the feasting hunting party and came over to greet them.

"Rumor has already spread about how you and Seth took that devil coon on Channery Creek." Lloyd Hanson put his hand on Nathan's shoulder. "Is that true?"

Taking the mug of coffee away from his lips, Nathan said, "Yes, sir, we finally got that ol' critter, and it was this crew right here what did it." He motioned to Arthur and the boys, who continued to attack their breakfasts. He then added more slowly, "J.P. Smith told us you lost a hound up Channery Creek only last week."

Despite his many years of experience—knowing well the perils that could happen on any given night as all coon hunters did—Lloyd's eyes moistened. "Yeah, lost Champ there. The dog still had a lot of huntin' seasons left in him. I miss him sorely."

"Yes, Champ was a great coonhound." Nathan nodded in respect. He looked at his coffee for a moment and then back at the other houndsman. "I know how I'd feel if'n I lost Seth. Tell you what. I was goin' to tan that hide and keep it, but perhaps you'd like to have it?"

"No, no!" Lloyd brought his hands up. "That belongs to you. I couldn't impose."

"I insist," Nathan said. "You can have that fur in memory of the great hound that Champ was."

"Well, thank you, young man. I'm much obliged." Lloyd turned away momentarily, wiping something from his eye, and quickly changed the subject. "You hear about what became of Bill Welty's prized bull, Rebel, last night?"

"Haven't heard anything about such." Taking another quick sip of his coffee, Nathan asked, "What happened?"

Whistling low through his teeth, Lloyd replied, "Well, Billy went up to his pasture this morning and found old Rebel and a calf torn to pieces!"

That news caught Arthur's attention, and the woodsman put a forkful of hash browns midway to his mouth back on his plate. "Torn to pieces, you say? A full-grown bull?"

"Not just any bull, Uncle," Nathan replied, eyes wide. "Rebel was known to be big and aggressive."

"Yes, he was huge, and a fine stud for the Weltys for many years," Lloyd replied. "From what Billy could tell, it was an enormous bear that did the killin'."

"I suspect it wasn't any old bear." Arthur's voice was grim.

With two pancakes down, and starting the last, Jason looked intently at the whipmaster. "Do you think it was Scar Paw, Uncle Art?"

"Who's Scar Paw?" Lloyd asked.

"A bear with a distinctive track we've run across in the forest," Arthur explained. He then said to Jason, "I don't know for sure, young'un, but I suspect so. It would take a huge bear to attempt such an attack. Scar Paw fits the bill in that respect."

"Well, I'd best be movin' along. Always good seeing you again." Lloyd smiled at the hunters and sauntered back to his table.

Looking at his hunting crew, Nathan downed the rest of his coffee. "Seems our bear has graduated from sheep to bulls."

"Agreed." Arthur watched as Jason, true to his promise, added a little more maple syrup and took the final bite of his pancake while the preteen eyed his order of bacon on another plate. "Anymore, I'm thinkin' it'll take a miracle to find and kill that beast."

"Did someone say 'miracle'?" A tall, gray-haired man in a cleric's collar walked up to the table.

"Father Simmons!" The woodsman smiled. "It's been a while since we last met."

"It has been *too* long, Arthur," the retired priest replied. "And I'd wager the altar wouldn't burst into flames if you showed up at Mass this evening."

Wringing his hands, Arthur noted, "That's not a sure bet, Father."

"And who are these two young men you have with you?" the priest asked.

"This would be Jason Canton and Bobby Bensen, Father," Nathan responded. "We're teachin' them how to chase raccoon."

Smiling at the youths, Father Simmons said, "I'm certain you boys have been told this already, but you're learning from the best when you hunt with Nathan Ernst and Arthur McCutcheon."

Suddenly overcome with decorum, their mouths still stuffed with food, the boys only nodded.

Nathan chuckled but added more seriously, "Father, is it possible an animal could be, or perhaps become, evil?"

The cleric looked pensive for a few moments before speaking. "The great philosopher Saint Thomas Aquinas reasoned animals have souls. He considered these souls different from humanity's, being innocent of right or wrong."

"So, the answer is 'no'—an animal couldn't be evil?" Nathan replied.

"Normally, one would think so. But if something has a soul, it stands to reason that soul could become corrupted in some manner akin to a person."

"Normally," Arthur said, letting the thought hang in the air.

"Yes," the priest agreed. "If one supposes a normalcy to anything, then you must also allow there could be some semblance of abnormality, no matter how improbable." He caught a tacit, shared look between Arthur and Nathan. "Is there some animal you have in mind?"

"Honestly, I'm not sure what to think." Nathan ended with a shrug.

"I find when praying about such things, the answers normally become known in time, particularly when I pray *in church*." Simmons cleared his throat, smiling at the silver-maned woodsman.

"Loud and clear, Father!" Arthur laughed. "Loud and clear!"

"Have a blessed day," Simmons said as he waved goodbye and stepped away.

With the priest out of earshot, Bobby let out a loud burp as he finished another bite of his breakfast.

A young girl with short brown hair walked up to the table, directing her attention to only one of the boys. "Hi, Jason! Did you go hunting last night?"

"Yes, we did!" Jason beamed. Remembering his manners, he added, "Mr. Ernst and Uncle Arthur, this is—"

"Tara," Nathan said. The hunter's insight caused the youngsters to share a surprised look.

"Yeah, but how d'you know her name, Mr. Ernst?" Jason spoke first with his face scrunched.

"You mentioned Tara before. I'm Nathan Ernst," the coon hunter introduced himself.

"Oh, I did?" Jason shrugged. "I guess I must have."

"Good meetin' you, Tara," the woodsman chimed in. "You can call me Uncle Arthur."

"It's nice to meet you, too, sir." The pretty girl nodded politely. "Jason tells me all about you."

"Oh, he does, does he?" The Forest Ghost looked at the blond youth with a piece of bacon in his hand.

"We had a great time chasing raccoon last night!" Jason said, avoiding Arthur's gaze.

"I was there, too!" Bobby shouted, clearly vying for the girl's attention.

Rolling her eyes at the redhead, Tara stepped closer to Jason. "Tell me about it."

While the other hunters finished their meals, Jason relayed the story of the hunt on Channery Creek, chasing the troublesome ringtail. Tara listened to his every word, utterly rapt. When he recounted where Bobby had almost fallen over the cliff, she only glanced at the other boy and quickly shook her head. Then Jason ended the tale on a high note.

"Puppies? You have puppies?" Tara's eyes reflected the happiness of children everywhere at that news.

"Yes," Nathan replied. "And we'll need some help naming them."

"The namin' is a critical thing in a dog's life and always a particular challenge." Arthur interceded with some exaggerated nodding. "Somethin' young'uns excel at."

"Can I help name them, Mr. Ernst?" Tara asked, holding her breath.

"Of course," Nathan replied. "We'll name them several days from now if you'd like to join us."

"Oh, thank you, I would! I'll tell my parents!" she all but shouted. "It was good seeing you again, Jason."

Upon hearing his name, the boy beamed.

Not to be outdone, Bobby added quickly, "It's nice to see you, too, Tara!"

"Yeah." Her enthusiasm drained as she turned to leave. "You, too, Bobby."

No sooner had she departed when another familiar face arrived.

"Well, hello, young Nathan." J.P. Smith sauntered to the table.

"We seem to be quite popular this mornin'," Arthur said, grinning at his nephew and the boys.

Nodding at the woodsman, J.P. said, "Tongues are waggin' this morning about your success on Channery Creek! You must tell me the tale sometime, so I may add it to my repertoire!"

"News certainly travels fast in Painted Post," Nathan said. "I promise to tell you about the hunt someday."

At first smiling broadly, J.P.'s countenance turned more serious, looking directly at Nathan. "I have something to give you. Would you mind accompanying me to my car?"

The sudden request caught Nathan off guard, and he reached for his wallet. "Sure, no problem. I just have to pay the tab."

"I've got it." Arthur snatched the bill that Danielle had left. His eyes went wide in mock disbelief when he studied the tally on the order pad. "Although, I may have to take out a bank loan to feed these young'uns!"

Jason and Bobby smirked.

"Ready?" J.P. asked.

"Sure, let's go." Nathan stood and followed the taleteller out of the diner.

When they had made their way to his vehicle, J.P. inserted his key to open the trunk. He then pulled out two identical cardboard boxes. Handing one to the younger man, he motioned with his chin. "Go ahead and take a look."

"What's this for?" Puzzled, Nathan opened the box to reveal an unused, well-oiled, .30-30 lever action rifle.

"Something I think you'll need in the near future. This other box contains another just like it."

"These are too large of a caliber for a coon." Nathan closed the box as J.P. stacked the other rifle on top.

"They're not for raccoon, my dear boy." J.P. seemed to look past Nathan's shoulder. "Rumor abounds that our little town has a big bear problem, and I'm thinking these could come in handy."

"Well, thank you." Nathan hesitated, not knowing quite what to say. "I'll surely pay you for these."

"No, sir. They are a gift." When the younger man made a befuddled look, J.P. quickly added, "Please, just take them—no arguments." He then placed two cartons of .30-30 shells atop the other boxes. "I must be on my way. I'll see you when you're in town next." He then turned about and entered his car, leaving Nathan holding the weapons.

The puzzled coon hunter looked at the mysterious gifts and could only shrug as J.P. drove out of the parking lot.

But then again, it was Painted Post after all.

Several days later, with Ryland Creek sporting a white, crusty snow covering, six tiny balls of dark fur had opened their eyes for the first time to see the world.

Sitting on his haunches, Seth watched through the wire mesh of his cage as the young people—Jason, Bobby, and Tara—neared.

Catching sight of the ebony cur, Tara walked closer. "So, you must be Seth, whom I've heard so much about." She put her fingers on the cold wire mesh.

Standing on all fours, The King of Hounds approached her and then jumped up to place one large paw against her hand on the mesh. He brought his muzzle nearer to her, taking in the scent of their newest guest.

"It's nice to meet you, too." She smiled.

Whining happily, Seth wagged his tail and dropped to the ground, returning to sit and watch the spectacle.

"C'mon, Tara." Jason opened the door to the adjacent pen. "Let's see the pups!"

The children walked into the puppies' kennel and removed the lid of the coop to reveal the small squirming bodies close to their mother, Remmie. There were three males and three females waiting to be named.

Hearing footsteps, the kids looked up to find Nathan and Uncle Arthur walking toward them.

"Go ahead," Nathan said when he was close. "Don't be afraid to pick them up. Remmie won't bite."

As each youth selected a pup, the little ones squealing when taken from the warmth of their mother, Remmie watched anxiously. A soothing word from Nathan eased the good mother's angst.

Tara held the first squirming female, nearly completely black like her sire, Seth, except for the smallest markings of brown under her eyes. "Let's call this one Night!"

"That would be perfect," Nathan replied.

Holding the largest male high, Bobby offered a suggestion. "Can we name him Prince?"

"Seein' how his father is the king around these parts, I reckon that'll work just fine." Arthur cackled.

In turn, Jason held up the biggest female. "Well then, we'll call this one Queenie."

This time, Nathan only nodded.

Per luck of the draw, Tara lifted the remaining female. "Oh, she's so cute!" The young girl noticed small patches of white on each of the pup's feet. "Can we call her Snow?"

"That's quite appropriate, considerin' all the frozen stuff we get in this town," Nathan replied.

The boys picked up the last two unnamed puppies.

Although the smallest of the litter, the pup in Jason's hands let out a loud bellow. "Whoa! You're certainly a feisty one! Can we call him Tye?"

"My pa would have approved of such a name," the coon hunter replied with a reminiscent smile. "It's easy to say."

Smiling from ear to ear, Bobby held the last male, who had the classic markings of a black and tan, much like his mother. Like Tye, this pup showed a great deal of spunk. "How about we call this one Buck, Mr. Ernst?"

"That sounds perfect." Nathan smiled.

Walking to the mesh that separated the adjacent kennels, Jason and Bobby brought the newly dubbed Tye and Buck close to Seth.

The King of Hounds took in a deep breath of his sons and then looked back at the boys with a slight dip of his head.

Still cradling the squirming Snow, Tara asked, "Mr. Ernst, would you mind if I went coon hunting with you, Uncle Arthur, Jason, and," she paused, swallowed hard, but finally managed, "Bobby?"

As if expecting the request, Nathan replied, "Yes, with your parents' permission, of course."

The young girl beamed as she looked from the pup in her arms to Jason.

"Nephew," Arthur said, grinning, "you're goin' to need a bus whenever you go huntin'."

CHAPTER 8
Yesterday's Promise, Tomorrow's Hope

Circling high above, a red-tailed hawk cried out a mournful, almost lonely, screech.

There was always a bird in the dream.

"She's pretty. Very pretty, actually." Sharon dipped her foot into Ryland Creek and caused the pool's placid surface to gently ripple and obscure her reflection.

Sitting close beside her, Nathan watched the water's gentle undulations. "Who's pretty?"

"The waitress at Shirley's." Sharon turned to look at him.

"You mean Dannie Gorton?"

"Yes."

"I suppose so, but why do you mention it?"

"Aren't you lonely?" she asked, her brown eyes searching.

"Well, I have my dogs, and—"

"I know you have your hounds, but that's not the same thing, is it? My beloved, you have to live your life."

"It's enough. It's all I need." Nathan looked away.

"Is it?" She reached over, cupped his chin, and gently turned his head to face her again. "Is it really enough?"

"I still have you."

"But only in a dream!" She laughed softly, but with sincere appreciation.

"Besides," he said, grinning, "Dannie falls far short of the mark."

"What mark?" Sharon cocked her head, her eyes squinting with a curious intensity.

As the ripples in the water subsided, their images reappeared in the still pool.

Nathan used his fingers to wrap her long bangs behind her ears, to see her face clearly. He smiled and said, "You."

Arcing gracefully through the blue sky, the hawk screeched again.

Not so mournfully, this time.

———— • ————

Beth Canton looked up from the book she'd been reading as her only child gently tugged her arm to garner her attention. Sitting comfortably on their large sofa, she glanced out the frosted window at the small, heated woodshop where her husband, Will, was working on his latest project. It was the day before Thanksgiving, and while her thoughts would soon be of cooking with her extended family, she turned back to Jason, instinctively knowing from her son's face that something was amiss.

"Yes?"

"Mom, I'm not sure where to begin, but there's something I've been wanting to ask you." Jason was dressed in his flannel shirt and jeans, looking much like his father, and causing her to think again how quickly her "little" boy was growing up.

"What is it, honey?" She set her book aside.

"I really enjoy coon hunting with Mr. Ernst and Uncle Arthur. They've taught me a lot more than Cousin Terry ever could!"

The good mother laughed, hearing Jason's unmistakable contempt. "I understand you don't see eye to eye with Terry—and that's all right. But as long as Nathan Ernst will take you hunting, it's okay by your father and me."

"But there's more." Jason paused. "I've run into Cousin Terry a few times lately, and he keeps saying there is something about Mr.

Ernst that I don't know about. He said if I knew, then I wouldn't go hunting with Mr. Ernst anymore. I figured Terry was just mouthing off like he usually does, but is there anything to what he says?"

Glancing again at the woodshop, Beth wished Will was nearby to help tell the tragic story of the Ernst family. She patted the seat beside her, and Jason quickly sat close. Gently placing an arm around his flannel-covered shoulders, she said, "It happened a few years ago, so you might not remember."

"Not remember what, Mom?"

"Nathan was set to marry Sharon Helm. They were several years behind your father and me in high school, but everyone knew those two were the perfect couple—soulmates if there were ever such a thing."

"So why aren't they married now?" Jason cocked his head like a puppy. "Did they break up or something?"

"No, honey, Sharon died in a car accident on Ryland Creek. It was so sad, and many believed Nathan would never recover. I guess, considering he doesn't even give a glance at all the eligible women his age in this town, perhaps he never truly did."

"That's very sad, for sure, Mom." Jason's face grew pensive, nodding. "But why would that good-for-nothing Terry say anything about it in the first place?"

"Jason," she gently reproached, "Terry is still our cousin."

The boy smirked. "Third cousin—and only by marriage, Mom!"

She laughed. "Yes, you're right—there's more, if only rumor. Some say Sharon's car accident wasn't accidental at all. The story goes some nasty man from Chicago with a vendetta against the Ernsts had damaged her car's brakes, causing her to crash on the bridge on Ryland Creek."

Jason absorbed his mother's words but still held a confused look.

91

She answered her son's unspoken questions. "That man from Chicago would later die on that very same bridge. The newspapers reported he accidentally fell over the railings and died from the fall."

"So, what's that got to do with Mr. Ernst?"

"Nathan was there when it happened. Some say that stranger confessed to causing Sharon's death and then tried to kill Nathan. Supposedly, he even shot Nathan in the shoulder, but that villain lost his balance and fell to his death just after firing his gun."

"Then it still wouldn't be Mr. Ernst's fault either way, huh?" Jason's voice seemed to protest a not-present third cousin.

"No, it would be self-defense." Will Canton appeared in the doorway, apparently listening in. "As for your cousin, Terry—"

"Only by marriage, Pa!" Jason interrupted vigorously.

Smirking, Will continued, "Terry would have you believe otherwise. I'll talk to him about that next time I see him. Rest assured, son, if we thought anything bad about Nathan Ernst, we wouldn't allow you to hunt with him."

"Terry will tell you that he's kin, Pa, and you won't do anything about it." Jason smiled at his large father.

"Yeah, we're kin." The giant winked at his son. "But that's on your mother's side."

Beth grinned with a disapproving shake of her head.

"Is it okay if I go hunting tonight with Mr. Ernst, Pa? Bobby and Tara are going, too."

Will was about to speak, but the mother in the room interrupted. "Tara, hmm?" She eyed her "not-so-little-anymore" boy.

"Yeah, Mom." Jason blushed.

"I suppose that would be perfect." Beth hugged her son.

Watching his nephew search for something in the basement, Arthur asked, "With all these young'uns comin' along for the hunt tonight, aren't you getting a bit short on headlights?"

"We've always had some spare lights. But you're right—we need more." Nathan feverishly removed some clutter from a bench holding hunting gear. Then he finally spied what he'd been seeking—hefting an old headlight and its heavy battery. "There you are!"

"Is that what I think it is?" Arthur studied the older-style light.

"Yeah," Nathan confirmed, his eyes still fixed on the dusty light. "This belonged to Pa. He wore it the night he died. No one has worn it since."

Remaining quiet for a moment, Arthur then replied respectfully, "There's nobody more fittin' to wear that than you, Nephew."

Nathan gave his uncle a slow, appreciative nod. Buckling the wide leather belt with its heavy battery around his waist, and then adjusting the helmet's headband, he gently eased the assembly onto his head. Reaching down, he flicked the light's switch. The beam, if somewhat dull, shone on the basement wall. "I can't believe there's still a charge on this thing!"

"That's 'cause your father's light isn't extinguished," Arthur spoke reverently.

"What's that supposed to mean?" Nathan cast his uncle a curious look.

The woodsman gently sighed. "You have become a great coon hunter, like your father before you, but you've got a lot to learn about life, and Ryland Creek, in particular, Nephew." With that, the silver-maned man left the room, leaving his perplexed kin alone.

Nathan could only shrug at yet another mystery.

Well, it was Painted Post, after all.

———— • ————

Dusk's temperature hovered around freezing when the children began arriving at the Ernst farm to go hunting that night. As usual, Bobby came with Jason and Beth. Tara rode with her father, Michael.

93

"I appreciate you taking my little girl hunting with you." Michael offered his hand as he walked up to Nathan.

"Good to see you again, Mike." The coon hunter grasped the other man's hand. "And it's our pleasure to have Tara join us tonight. I'll make sure the boys don't pick on her."

"Don't think she'll need much in the way of protection." A grin grew on Michael's face.

The men then heard Tara's voice, loud and firm.

"Touch me again, Bobby Bensen, and I *will* break your arm."

Nathan and Mike watched as a red-faced Bobby quickly removed his arm from around the young girl's shoulders.

"I see what you mean." Nathan grinned, turning back to the beaming father. "We'll drop Tara off at your house when we're through huntin'."

"Thanks again. I have to pick up my other daughter from daycare now." Michael walked over and told his oldest child goodbye, entered his vehicle, and drove away.

The trio of youngsters rushed up to Nathan.

"Which dogs are we taking?" Jason asked.

"We'll hunt with Seth and Bill tonight," Nathan replied. "Help Tara get set up with the gear."

"Where's Uncle Arthur?" Bobby asked.

Nathan pointed to the front porch, where the woodsman stared trancelike at the surrounding hills.

"What's he doing?" Jason queried.

"Talkin' with the forest." Nathan's gaze also swept the leafless, darkening woods.

"Does it ever talk back?" Bobby laughed.

Staring at the youngster for a curious moment, Nathan said, "All the time." When the children's expressions begged for an explanation, he just smiled. "Someday, you'll understand."

"If you say so, Mr. Ernst," Jason shrugged. Then, turning to the other kids, he waved them forward. "C'mon! Let's get our lights!"

The trio of preteens ran into the house past Arthur, who remained unmoving.

With a light laugh, Nathan shook his head as he watched them scamper inside.

Ten minutes later, the children emerged from the house, proudly wearing their helmets, to find Nathan and Arthur near the dog pens.

"Jason!" Nathan shouted, standing by one of the kennels. "When I turn Bill loose, he'll run to you and jump into his dog box. Just open the door and then close it behind him."

"Yes, sir!" Jason ran to the tailgate and reached over to unlatch the first box's door. "I'm ready, Mr. Ernst!"

"Okay, here he comes!" As soon as Nathan unfastened the kennel's gate, the well-trained walker hound rushed to the truck, jumped onto the tailgate, and quickly entered the dog box.

Jason locked the door latch, with Bobby and Tara cheering on.

"Good job!" Nathan shouted and stepped over to the next pen. "Now here comes Seth."

Once free, the ebony cur raced for the truck. Suddenly, Seth stopped. Spying Tara, the large hound went over to her, jumped up to place his paws on her shoulders, and licked her face, causing her to giggle.

"Seth!" Nathan shouted as he walked nearer. "Quit showin' off and get in the truck!"

The hound looked at his master, back at the girl, and gave a quick snort. Dropping to the ground, the King of Hounds jumped onto the tailgate and into the box, with Jason securing the box's latch.

"C'mon, young'uns," Arthur opened the club cab door, "the night's half over, and we've got some ringtails to chase!"

The children quickly climbed into the truck's back seat. Tara made sure Jason sat in the middle.

"Is that a new light, Mr. Ernst?" Jason asked, eyeing the different headgear when Nathan sat behind the steering wheel.

"It belonged to a far greater hunter than I'll ever be." Nathan paused while Arthur silently watched. But before Jason could ask more, Nathan started the truck, shifted the transmission, and drove down Ryland Creek Road.

"Where are we going tonight?" Jason leaned forward to poke his head between the two adults.

"We're headed to the Black Swamp," Nathan responded.

A simultaneous, communal "huh?" brought the other children forward cheek-to-cheek, sandwiching Jason's face.

"The Black Swamp?" Bobby asked. "I've never heard of anything around here called the Black Swamp before."

With a grin, Nathan looked at his uncle, who immediately picked up his nephew's cue.

Shaking his head in mock sadness, Arthur asked, "How is it you young'uns, livin' in such a magical town as Painted Post, ain't never heard of the Black Swamp?"

The whipmaster's query only garnered a collective shrug from his adolescent audience.

"Well, first off, a swamp—just about any swamp—is always a good place to hunt raccoon. Wetlands provide a variety of meals—frogs, fish, grubs, and the like—that the woods bandits love to fill their stomachs with."

"Grubs? Ick. That's gross!" Bobby grimaced but then swatted the air dismissively with one hand. "Oh, so it's just any ol' swamp then. There are lots of swamps around here, Uncle Arthur."

"That's certainly true," the woodsman conceded. "But did I say the Black Swamp was any ol' swamp, young'un? There's many a story surroundin' that particular marsh, and how it came by its name."

"Is it because that swamp's water is black, Uncle Arthur?" Tara leaned closer, her chin almost over the man's shoulder.

"As a matter of fact, young lady," Arthur smiled, "the water is the deepest black! However, it's *why* that water is as dark as a moonless midnight is how this swamp got its name!"

Now a veteran of Arthur's fantastic tales, Jason smile broadly. "Oh, this ought to be good!"

"The words 'good' and 'Black Swamp' have no cause to be used in the same breath, youngster!" The whipmaster's eyes narrowed in dramatic flare, with his overture causing the preteens to gasp. They nodded for the whipmaster to continue. "A long time ago, an evil warlock entered the Land of the Three Rivers—"

"Wait!" Bobby interrupted. "What's a warlock?"

"A male witch." Tara shook her head. "Don't you know anything?"

"You're quite correct, young lady!" Arthur exclaimed. "But don't be too hard on Bobby—he's simply learnin' something new as we all should. Now, where was I?"

"At the beginning!" Jason sounded exasperated. "The wizard had just arrived in Painted Post."

"Of course, of course," Arthur nodded. "Let truth be told, this sorcerer wasn't the first to come to our beautiful lands. There was at least one other, but this evil man was determined to leave his mark on our valley 'cause he was disgusted with its goodness.

"So, this sinister being found an area on top of a high hill with mighty oaks. For months, the warlock said spell after spell, and slowly, the trees died as a result of his black magic, leaving only hideous, lifeless trunks behind. Then he cast another incantation such that water bubbled up from the heart of Painted Post herself.

"But then somethin' happened he had not expected—the land fought back!

"The water that rose at his summoning was pure. Soon, all manner of wildlife began to thrive in abundance around the spell-made swamp. This turn of events drove the wizard insane with rage—his evil plan was being thwarted right before his very eyes!"

"Hold on!" Jason shook his head. "If the water was so pure, how'd it become black?"

"I'm gettin' there, son." Arthur gesticulated. "Never rush a storyteller."

Jason returned a begrudged smirk.

Winking, Arthur continued. "The wizard thought long and hard about how to solve his dilemma. And then it came to him. He needed the fresh blood of young'uns to make his hideous designs work! For what could be more evil than that?

"Thus, he set the wind in motion to swirl through the dead oaks' branches and holey trunks to create a song that could be heard far and wide. Slowly, over time, the youth of Painted Post would hear the music and walk into the swamp, trying to discover its source." Partially turning about, Arthur saw each of the youngsters with mouths agape. "But as soon as they were deep in the swamp, a thick fog would form, and the children couldn't find their way out. One by one, each unfortunate young'un who entered the swamp perished, and their decayin' bodies eventually turned the water pitch black!"

"B-b-but what happened to that wizard? Is he still there?" Bobby finally managed to ask.

"An excellent question, young Master Bensen! For you see, wickedness might exist for a short time in the Land of the Three Rivers, but it cannot last for long.

"The forests cried out for help, and a powerful shaman dedicated to goodness responded. When the righteous man arrived—himself a wizard—he confronted the evil sorcerer. Soon they began a terrible fight!

"Legend has it that a ferocious storm centered above the Black Swamp. Thunder and lightning came, the likes of which no one had ever seen before or since as the two magicians fought one another.

"The battle lasted for three days without cease! Eventually, the good man got the upper hand, and he turned the evil wizard into a huge, lifeless oak, akin to what the evil one had perpetrated upon the forests here. Some say that you can still find that ol' dead tree in the middle o' the swamp."

"And *that's* where we're gonna hunt tonight?" Bobby moaned.

Grinning, Jason couldn't let the opportunity pass. "Coon are where you find 'em, nerd-o-fight!" Looking into the rearview mirror, the boy saw Nathan's eyes smiling at him.

"But, Uncle Arthur," Tara said, "you mentioned another evil wizard that was here before the Black Swamp was made. What about him?"

"Ah, yes!" The whipmaster grew a mischievous smile. "The tale of the Gandalark—a hideous beastie, that one." He paused and shuddered. "But that would be a story for another time."

"Oh man!" the kids moaned in unison.

A short while later, Nathan stopped the truck beneath a huge weeping willow. The hunting party exited the vehicle's cab, and Arthur released Seth and Bill from the dog boxes. Knowing their roles well, the hounds sprinted into the darkness in search of raccoon.

"Wow, this place really stinks!" Tara pinched her nose upon taking in the dank odor.

"Must be all those dead bodies!" Jason smirked, which earned him a playful cuff in the arm from the grinning girl.

"Young'uns, listen up," Nathan began. "This swamp is relatively narrow but miles long. We'll start on the eastern edge, but the dogs may find a coon on the far side. If'n that happens, we'll have to cross, as it would take too long to go around. But be careful where you step if we go into the swamp, as you can sink deep into the muck in some parts. Understood?"

The youngsters nodded and turned on their helmet lights.

The hunting party proceeded along the edge of the marsh with the frozen leaves making a crunching noise underfoot. As Arthur had described, many large, dead trees were sprinkled throughout the swamp. A cold breeze caused some branches to sway, as if the trees were beckoning the children to enter their realm.

Shining his light onto the swamp's surface, Bobby said, "That water *is* black, just like in Uncle Arthur's story!"

"I wonder why the water hasn't frozen over?" Tara whispered so only the other kids could hear. "It's been below freezing for a week now."

"Maybe young'uns' blood doesn't freeze so well," Arthur suggested, clearly hearing Tara's words even though several yards away.

"Uncle Art heard you!" Jason laughed with Tara as Bobby shook his head. "He hears a lot!"

Then Seth's loud bawl filled the night air. Moments later, Bill opened to confirm the ringtail's track.

"They found a coon!" Jason shouted.

For nearly ten minutes, the hunters listened attentively while the coonhounds continued the chase, headed due west. Then Seth and Bill began their chopping tree bark.

"They're treed, but they crossed the swamp as I feared they might," Nathan said, coursing his dogs' trek. "Looks like we'll have to cross it, too."

"What's this?" Tara knelt near the swamp's edge, looking at an imprint in the dark-brown muck.

"Very good, young lady." Arthur walked over, nodding with admiration. "You've found yourself a ringtail track there!"

"I did?" She beamed with her discovery. "I did!"

"That's the front paw," The Forest Ghost explained. "It looks very much akin to a human hand, doesn't it?"

"It sure does!" Bobby said, also studying the spoor.

"We'll make coon hunters of you yet," Nathan said with a grin. "Now pay attention—there's a decent trail across the swamp just up ahead. Walk where I and Uncle Art do. Like I said before, if you step off the path in certain places, you could end up in some pretty deep mud, real quick!"

"Understood, Mr. Ernst!" Jason acted as spokesman for the other kids.

Following the swampy edge for less than one hundred yards, Nathan found the trail that crossed the swamp, with Arthur walking just behind his nephew.

The preteens followed the adults, often with the dark water squeezing the pathway to little more than a foot wide. Even then, their boots made a sucking noise in the semi-firm muck.

After about ten minutes, Nathan stopped beneath a monstrous, but dead, spreading oak to listen to his hounds' continuing calls. A light wind whistled as it threaded its way through the skeletal tree's many holes.

"Where are we, Mr. Ernst?" Jason asked, looking at the skeletal tree.

"About halfway across," Nathan responded.

"So, we're in the center?" Tara asked.

"Thereabouts," the coon hunter replied.

"You mean," Bobby's voice came as a harsh whisper, "we're where the good wizard turned the bad wizard into an old, ugly tree— just like this one!" His light beam inched up the dead oak until it illuminated a large hole in the tree's trunk. There, the youngster saw a horrid, white countenance staring at him, and he screamed, "Aaaahhhh! *What's that?*"

Everyone shone their lights on the tree to see what had frightened the young lad so, but Arthur chuckled when he made out the face. "It's okay, young'un. That's just an ol' opossum looking back at you."

"Oh! Phew!" The redhead breathed a sigh of relief. "I thought it was the evil wizard!"

"Bobby, you scream like my little sister!" Tara smirked.

The boy's ego then blushed as red as his hair, while the other kids and adults laughed hard.

Reaching the swamp's far side minutes later, the hunters only had to backtrack a short distance to join the treeing hounds. They quickly spotted the ringtail near the top of a tall, leafless sugar maple.

"I'll let each of you take two shots at this raccoon." Nathan looked at the children. "Who wants to go first?"

"I do!" Bobby volunteered.

Jason piped in. "I'm second if he doesn't get him!"

"I guess I'll go last then." Tara smiled.

Unslinging the gun from his shoulder, Nathan loaded the .22 and handed it to Bobby. "Just look through the scope, put the red dot on the reflection of the raccoon's eye, and slowly squeeze the trigger. And always keep the gun's barrel pointed straight up, even after the coon comes out of the tree. Got it?"

"Yes, sir," the redhead confirmed. Raising the rifle and firing his two allotted rounds, both shots went wide. "Oh man! I missed!" The downcast boy relinquished the weapon to Nathan.

"That's okay, Bobby," Nathan replied. "There's a lot of air around a coon—even more when it's high in a tree." Handing the gun to Jason, he said, "You're next."

Taking aim, Jason's first shot impacted the branch where the raccoon perched. Unnerved, the ringtail moved a little and stared back into the hunters' lights. The second round also hit the branch, closer to the ringtail's head, but left the woodland critter unharmed. "At least I'm getting better!" He shrugged, carefully handing the rifle back to his mentor.

Smirking, Arthur added sardonically, "Only if'n your intent was to scare the raccoon to death."

With the .22 in hand, Nathan turned to Tara. "Well, that leaves you. Are you up for takin' the shot?"

"I've done a lot of target shooting with my dad," she replied, "but never shot at a live animal before."

Suddenly leaving Bill by the tree alone, Seth walked over to her. The hound nuzzled his large head against the girl's leg. She glanced down and smiled at the ebony cur.

"There's always a first." Nathan offered her the weapon.

The young girl accepted the rifle and to seated the gun's stock against her shoulder comfortably. Placing the scope's red dot on the amber reflection of the coon's eye, she slowly squeezed the trigger. Her shot was true, the bullet catching the raccoon in the head. The dead ringtail fell to the ground, and both hounds sniffed the vanquished prey.

"Well done!" Nathan accepted the rifle from the beaming girl.

"That was a perfect shot, Tara!" Jason shouted.

"Ah, it's just beginner's luck!" Bobby teased.

"Thank you," she said, smiling at Jason.

"Bobby and Jason," Nathan called out, "snap a leash on Seth and Bill. I'll skin this raccoon, and then we'll head to the truck. We can use the same trail to cross back over."

The two boys obeyed, with Jason putting his lead on Seth's collar, praising the hound for another job well done, while Bobby did likewise for Bill.

Walking over to Seth, Tara kneeled by the dog's side. "Thanks for the encouragement."

With a snort, the ebony cur licked her face.

Producing the short, silver chain—securing one end to a small sapling and using the ring at the chain's other end to hang the raccoon inverted by its rear foot—Nathan quickly skinned the furbearer. In minutes, he completed the task and placed the prime pelt inside his coat's game bag. "Uncle Art and I will take the dogs. Can you lead us back across, Jason?"

"Yes, sir!" the youngster replied proudly. "Follow me!" He turned and led the group back toward the way they had arrived.

When Jason had almost missed the trail, Tara whispered, "It's just to your right."

"She's correct, young'un," Arthur said from a considerable distance behind.

Looking back at the woodsman and then at Tara, Jason replied, "Thanks . . . to you both."

The youngsters hurried down the pathway, their youthful vigor soon leaving the adults far to the rear.

When they were over halfway across the swamp at a very narrow part of the trail, Bobby said, "Let me have a chance to lead."

"It's okay, Bobby. I got this." Jason gave Tara a furtive glance.

"Nah, let a real man show the way!" When the redhead tried to go around Jason, he slipped and fell into the black water. "Aaaahhhh! I'm stuck!" Bobby shouted, sinking into the mire nearly up to his chest.

"And you're still screaming like my little sister, goofball!" Tara laughed, but as she stepped out onto what appeared to be solid ground, the young girl also slipped deeper into the Black Swamp.

"Tara!" Jason shouted, jumping to her aid, only to find himself in the same predicament as the cold, smelly water seeped through his clothes.

Leading the hounds, the two adults soon came up from behind to witness the dilemma.

Arthur shook his head. "What the french fries are you young'uns doing now?"

Just about to address the youths, Nathan then turned to his uncle. "Wait, wait—did you just say, 'What the french fries'?"

"Yep!" The whipmaster beamed. "Been practicin' on tryin' not to cuss! How 'm I doin'?"

"Actually," Nathan gave a begrudged nod, "that's not bad. Not bad at—"

"Ahem!" Jason interrupted. "Could we get a little help here?"

"Well, lookee there, Nephew," Arthur chortled. "Looks like the swamp's growin' young'uns!"

"Sorry, Mr. Ernst," Jason said. "We weren't watching where we were going."

"There are consequences when we stray from the right path, children." The voice emanating beneath Nathan's headlight seemed older, deeper, echoing across time.

Noticing the slight yet familiar change in his nephew's voice, Arthur looked curiously at Nathan but said nothing.

Handing Seth's leash to Arthur, who still held Bill's lead, Nathan walked carefully over and extended his hand. The youngster quickly grabbed the proffered arm. With a mighty heave, Jason came out of the muck, sounding akin to water going down a sink drain as the swamp stubbornly relinquished its hold.

"We'll need to work together," Nathan explained. "Bobby is closest, so we'll pull him out next."

"Got it, Mr. Ernst!" Jason kept a grip on Nathan's arm and reached for the other boy. "C'mon, Bobby, take my hand!"

The redhead didn't hesitate to grasp his friend's hand. With some considerable grunting and groaning, Bobby finally came free of the dark mud.

"Now, step to your left and form a chain," Nathan directed the boys, "and we'll be able to get Tara."

"I'm lighter than you, Bobby," Jason said. "Switch places with me, and I'll reach for Tara."

Bobby readily agreed and firmly hooked Nathan's arm while reaching for his friend with his other hand.

Leaning toward her, Jason reached out. "Tara, take my hand!"

"No," she said, struggling in the mire. "I got myself into this mess, and I'll get myself out!" The feisty brunette fought the swamp's might, but after thirty seconds with no progress, she slumped, nearly exhausted, only to slide deeper into the stinking mud.

105

"Tara," Nathan spoke softly, "sometimes askin' for help is the hardest thing of all."

The young lady viewed the black water around her and sighed. Looking up at Jason, who was still reaching for her, she reluctantly took his hand. With several pulls, Tara finally made it to the semi-solid ground as the mud made a loud, protesting noise at its loss.

"My boot!" Tara glanced down. "It came off in the mud!"

Seeing her right, stocking-clad foot, Jason jumped past her to land on his knees. As the water seeped into the hole that had once held Tara, the would-be hero stuck his hand into the cold wetness. His cheek touching the water, he shouted, "I got it!" With a quick jerk, he extracted her rubber boot and held it overhead. However, his triumph was short-lived as the slime-filled footwear turned upside down and emptied its contents onto his face.

Seeing his now grime-covered countenance, Bobby and Tara couldn't contain their laughter.

"Here," Jason said, still kneeling and red-faced beneath the black muck. He then positioned her boot upright on the ground.

She slid her small foot into the boot, grinning so only Jason could see. "I'm going to beat you arm wrestling someday," she whispered, leaning in close to him.

They both looked at Uncle Arthur, who only smiled.

Jason felt a new warmth mixed with her familiar challenge, and the dark seemed friendlier.

Looking at the now shivering children, Nathan shook his head. "Well, I'd say that's all the coon huntin' we're going to get in for the night."

Nathan drove his young charges to their homes, first dropping Bobby off. When they came to Tara's house, he suggested Jason walk the young lady to the doorway.

"Sure, Mr. Ernst!" Jason responded, if a bit too eagerly.

The preteens quickly exited the warm truck cab. Although still wet from their dunking, they ambled in the freezing air.

"I had so much fun tonight!" Tara smiled as they walked up some short steps and stood before the front door.

"If you call taking a mud bath fun!" Jason said.

"Thanks for saving my boot." She laughed.

"My p-p-pleasure," he replied, with both youngsters knowing it wasn't the cold causing his stutter.

Clearly amused at his nervousness, she reached out and took his hand to give it a light squeeze. "I hope we can go together again soon."

"Me, too."

Releasing him, Tara turned the doorknob her father had left unlocked. She opened the door and smiled again. "Good night."

"Yeah, g-g-good night."

After she'd disappeared behind the shut door, Jason wasn't sure how long he'd stood there, perhaps hoping she might reemerge. A large hand gently touched Jason's shoulder, startling the young man as he looked up to find The Forest Ghost so close by.

Looking at the door and then back to Jason, Arthur nodded knowingly. "C'mon, young'un. It's time we got you home."

CHAPTER 9
When in Painted Post

January 1988

T he nearly two-month-old Tye growled in his puppy voice, playfully attacking his brothers and sisters in the winter morning cold. While his siblings frolicked on wobbly legs, Remmie lorded over them within the confines of the pen, content that her litter, even if already weaned, had focused on something other than her.

Lying on his stomach, Seth observed his progeny's mock battles through the wire mesh fence in the adjacent kennel.

Kneeling in the snow outside the whelping kennel, Tara also watched the puppies, mesmerized. "They're so cute!"

With their ungloved hands on the cold fencing, Jason and Bobby likewise beamed as they viewed the young coonhounds prance about.

Soon the litter noticed the ebony cur eyeing their every move, and the pups assembled as a gaggle to amble closer to their sire. All six of the little black and tans began barking as loud as their small frames could manage, focusing their attention on the large hound, who stood to rise high above the pups.

And then, Seth roared!

The children laughed as four of the puppies squealed in terror at the incredibly loud bawl and retreated to the safety of their mother. But both Buck and Tye, instead of running, barked back at their large sire.

"Would you look at that!" Jason pointed to the brave pups who refused to cower.

Seth cocked his head as his two sons came near. Slowly, all three dogs put their noses together through the mesh. Then the King of Hounds sat once more to watch the puppy antics begin anew.

"Mr. Ernst thinks this litter has the breeding to be great hounds someday," Jason said. "He says it's a lot of work to train a coonhound, too."

The woodsman's voice broke their preteen reverie. "Almost as hard as trainin' new coon hunters."

The youngsters turned to see Arthur, wearing his long, brown drover, with Nathan nearby, also dressed warmly, leaning on his oak walking staff.

"Are you going to teach us how to track today, Uncle Arthur?" Tara ran to the silver-maned man.

"We'll head into the woods for a spell, and I can show you young'uns a thing or two."

"What about you, Mr. Ernst?" Jason asked. "Will you be coming with us?"

"Not today," Nathan replied. "I'm certain Uncle Art could teach me a thing or two more about trackin'. Unfortunately, I have a tractor that needs fixin'."

When The Forest Ghost turned, the front flap of his coat opened slightly, revealing his bullwhip.

"Do you always carry that, Uncle Arthur?" Bobby asked, eyeing the braided coil hanging from a leather strap on the woodsman's belt.

"Pret' near," Arthur responded.

"Can you show us how to use that?" Jason asked, also studying the whip.

"Sure, young'un, I'll learn you someday." The whipmaster nodded with a smile. "But understand that it takes hundreds of hours of practice over many years to get good at it. Lord knows I've some scars on this ol' body to this day from first learnin' how to wield this." He patted the whip by his side.

109

"I heard how you earned some of those scars," Nathan said with a knowing grin.

"Your pa told you about that, did he?" Arthur winced.

Nathan's smirk grew wider.

"Well, what happened?" Jason caught the tacit exchange between the adults.

"That'd be a story for another time," Arthur replied quickly. "But I can do a little demonstration for you now. Jason and Bobby, I recall some old cans just by the barn door. Go fetch three of them, fill each with water, and put 'em on the posts over there." He pointed to the white fencing surrounding the graveyard of the Ernst family hounds.

At first looking excitedly at each other, the boys then ran to the barn. Inside the doorway, they spied a small pile of used dog food cans. Jason grabbed two of the tins, while Bobby took another. Using the faucet only a few feet away, they filled each container to the brim. Careful not to spill the water, they walked slowly to the fence and set each can on a separate post.

Nathan moved the children to a safe distance as his uncle took his whip in hand.

Rolling the bullwhip before him, Arthur made the slightest flick of his wrist, and the leather coil seemed to come alive. Slowly at first, he twirled the whip over his head with several rotations of his arm. His motions became faster. As the whip's tassels reached the end of each motion, the air boomed.

Wsssh-crack! Wsssh-crack!

Over and over in a flurry of lashes, the whipmaster adroitly worked the bullwhip like an extension of himself.

"That's so cool!" Bobby gawked.

Focusing on the first target, Arthur willed the leather viper forward, and its bite cut the can in half as both ends went flying in different directions. The second tin suffered a similar fate with an explosion of the metal and water scattering everywhere.

110

With one can left, Arthur intentionally cracked the whip just above his target several times. With a final lash, the coil reached out, and while the can's top careened away, its bottom remained perfectly still on the fence post.

The whipmaster brought the bullwhip to a stop, took a slight bow as the children clapped and cheered, and coiled the leather to hang it by the strap at his side once more. "Remember, young'uns, a whip is a weapon and not somethin' to be taken lightly."

Tara gave a little hop. "Can we go to the woods now, Uncle Arthur?"

"Certainly," the woodsman replied. "Are you ready?"

Both Tara and Jason nodded vigorously.

Seeing his two young friends smiling at each other, Bobby then looked at the ground. "Uncle Art? I want to learn to track someday, but I'd like to help Mr. Ernst with the tractor repairs, if you don't mind?"

Nathan and Arthur exchanged surprised looks, with the coon hunter speaking first. "Sure, Bobby, I could use a hand and much obliged for your assistance. Come with me then." He turned and walked toward the barn.

"I'll see you guys when you get back." Bobby beamed, but just before following in Nathan's wake, he gave a quick congratulatory wink at Jason, who returned a bemused look.

Hiking in the crunching, crusty snow past the cut cornfield, Arthur led his students up the steady grade to the edge of the woods. They stopped briefly to view the panorama of rolling, leafless, oak-studded hills. Except where coniferous hemlocks and white pines clustered as patches of green, they could easily make out ancient creeks, inexorably cutting their paths into the craggy hillsides.

"Even in winter, Painted Post is the best place on Earth!" Tara's pronouncement seemed to echo.

"Well," Arthur began, "I'm not sure there is a 'best place' on this ol' Mother Earth, but I'll give you this place is one of a kind."

He scanned the hills and slowly added, "There's certainly a magic here, if you know where to look."

"What are those, Uncle Art?" Jason asked, seeing some tracks in the snow nearby.

The woodsman quickly spied the spoor. "A gray squirrel made those. We're in an oak forest with plenty of acorns this year, so the squirrels will be frolickin' about. And that"—he pointed to a cluster of leaves near the top of an otherwise barren red oak—"would be a squirrel's nest. So, if'n you're lookin' for an animal's tracks, you need to understand that critter's behavior and habitat first."

The children followed the woodsman deeper into the woods. They came to a large area that had been churned with patches of brown, half-frozen leaves strewn everywhere atop the inch-deep snow.

"What did this? The wind?" Tara cocked her head.

Searching the edge of the jumbled leaves, Arthur spied a three-toed track making a crisp impression in the whiteness. "No. These scratchin's were done by a flock of wild turkeys. They'll dig a wide area when they're lookin' for acorns akin to the squirrels."

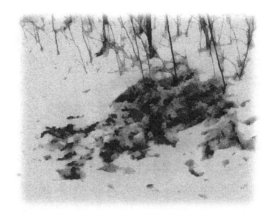

"I've heard the tom turkeys gobble in the spring!" Jason smiled confidently. "My pa says there's love in the air when they do, but I'm not sure what that means. Do you, Uncle Art?"

"Uhm, let's move on, shall we?" the whipmaster suggested hastily.

Ever observant, Tara spied something else, but it wasn't on the ground. "What about this?" She pointed to a nearby sapling, about an inch in diameter, with its outer layer stripped away to reveal the golden cambium beneath, with some shredded, gray strands of bark flowing gently in the wind.

"I know what that is!" Jason beamed. "That's a buck rub, huh?"

"Yep," Arthur replied, smiling. "Each autumn, whitetail bucks rub their antlers against sapling trees to remove the fuzzy velvet covering their horns. That allows the air to harden their horns and do battle with other bucks to win the affection of their ladies, the does."

"Is that back to love being in the air, Uncle Art?" Jason's face scrunched up. "What does that mean, anyway?"

"Uhm . . . that would be sorta like . . ." The confidence drained from the woodsman's face, hesitating before attempting a response. "Well, lad, it has to do with—"

Tara saved the moment, pointing at the ground. "What made these tracks?"

Breathing a sigh of relief, Arthur walked closer to examine the spoor in the snow. "Ah, these prints belong to a quill pig."

"Quill pig?" the children echoed.

"That would be a porcupine, young'uns." Arthur grinned. "Heaven help you if'n your hound ends up tanglin' with a porky. You could easily spend the rest of your night pullin' quills out of your dog as a result—a long and painful pursuit."

The kids let out excited "Oh's" as they studied the track, and their teacher pointed out not only the oblong paws and claw marks of the porcupine, but also places where the animal's spiny tail brushed the snow as it walked.

"What about coon tracks, Uncle Arthur? I want to see a raccoon!" Jason said.

"Well," the woodsman rose one eyebrow, "where do you think we should look?"

Before Jason could answer, Tara piped in, "Water! There are lots of creeks around here."

"Very good, young lady." The silver-maned man smiled. "You can't track an animal if you don't know where to look in the first place. Now listen." He shut his eyes.

The children were puzzled at first, but they mimicked Arthur by closing their eyes, trying to make out any sound. At first, only the soft, wind-driven clattering of the few still-clinging oak leaves made any noise. Somewhere in the distance, a crow cawed.

Jason solved the mystery. "I hear it! I hear a creek!"

"Me, too!" Tara opened her eyes to see Jason smiling at her.

"That would be Ryland Creek itself. Lead the way, young'uns." Arthur twirled his hand several times, showing the direction they should go.

At a near run, Jason and Tara followed the noise of the rushing water. Within five minutes, they were beside the gray slate-

114

bottomed, partially iced-over creek. Here, oaks, maples, and hemlocks grew with the latter arboreal species' boughs shading the area and causing the air to be colder than in the open forest. Arthur directed the children to walk on either side of the creek to search for coon tracks, and Jason gladly forded the stream at a shallow spot.

After a short while, Tara pointed to the ground once more. "Aren't these raccoon tracks, like those we saw in the Black Swamp?"

"Yep!" Arthur replied as he neared her while Jason splashed noisily across the cold water to join them. "Now follow 'em and see what they'll teach you."

Trailing the wood bandit's spoor, the young people often laughed, trying to course the critter's hectic circuit. When the snow yielded to hard ground, they lost the trail.

"Why does this coon go all over the place?" Jason scratched his head.

"You're reckonin' like humans do—who know where they want to go from the moment they start. But more importantly, you ain't thinkin' like a raccoon searchin' for a meal." When the boy looked down dejectedly, the woodsman-teacher quickly added, "Don't fret, young'un. I asked the same question when I was your age. So, unless'n the critter has climbed a tree or grown wings, his trail has got to be here somewhere."

Nodding, Tara then spied a nearby old log covered with green moss and snow. Searching the top of the fallen tree, she nearly screamed, "Here he is!"

"Wow!" Jason smiled. "That's very good, Tara!"

"You're a natural at trackin', young lady." Arthur smiled broadly.

Tara beamed at the compliment.

"Do you mean to tell me, Uncle Arthur, that Seth has to figure all this out each time he chases a raccoon?" Jason asked,

"And therein lies another lesson," the woodsman remarked.

"What lesson?" Jason shook his head.

"Appreciation," Arthur responded.

"Huh?" The right side of the boy's upper lip curled up slightly.

Gently nudging Jason's shoulder with hers, Tara said, "An appreciation for what a coonhound has to figure out each track, silly."

"Oh, I get it!" Jason said, his look morphing from puzzled to wonder.

For another hundred yards, they followed the coon's trek, often with Tara finding the way when the trail seemed hopelessly lost. Soon, they came to a set of picturesque waterfalls. The recent frigid temperatures had completely frozen the normally flowing water into a glistening wall of ice.

"It's beautiful." Tara spoke barely above a whisper.

"These falls hold a very special meaning for the Ernst family," Arthur replied, the melancholy in his voice clear. "My sister, Rose, would come here often with Jacob, Nathan's father, when they were young. It was their not-so-secret place."

"I wish I could photograph it, or maybe draw it." Tara studied it. Mesmerized.

"Yes . . . beautiful," Jason replied. But Tara turned away when her eyes met his, the boy looking directly at her and not the frozen falls. "You like taking pictures?"

"It is beautiful. Very much so," she finally managed to say, daring to look at him. "And I hope to be a professional photographer one day."

"Come along, children," Arthur said. "We can't stare at the ice all day. There's still a ringtail to find."

Scouring the ground after only a few steps, she shouted, "Here he is! Found him again!"

With that, the preteens began ferreting out the trail once more. Finally, the raccoon's long trek ended at the base of a huge, white oak.

"You've located his den tree." The woodsman pointed to a large hole in the tree's trunk about fifteen feet up. "He's probably snug in there and fast asleep."

The youths whooped at their success.

"It's close to noon," Arthur said. "You both gettin' hungry about now?"

"Oh, yes I am!" Jason shouted.

"You're always hungry." Tara laughed.

"I'm a growing boy!" Jason crossed his arms and asserted with a single nod.

"There's no denyin' that," Arthur replied.

As they circled back to the farm, the hunters came across their tracks in the field where they had first entered the woods.

"You have big feet," Tara said, looking at Jason.

"Hey—wait just a minute," Jason protested. "Those are Uncle Arthur's tracks!" Turning, he saw the mischievous look on her face and knew she had the better of him. He returned a wry grin.

Taking a few steps, Tara then stopped, seeing Arthur intently studying some other tracks in the snow close by. "What are those?" she asked, wide-eyed.

"Not again," Arthur muttered.

"What is it?" she repeated.

"Bear." The woodsman's voice seemed distant as he quickly scanned the forest. "A big one."

"I thought bears would be hibernating by now?" Tara asked.

"Sow bears pretty much sleep through the winter once they den up," The Forest Ghost replied. "Boar bears sleep for periods of time, too, but on warm winter days, they'll come out in search of food."

"It doesn't seem that warm right now," she said. "This bear must not think it's cold."

"No," the woodsman spoke slowly, "not this particular one."

Catching the warning in Arthur's voice, Jason's eyes went wide with a shared understanding. When the young man looked up,

117

Arthur gave him a furtive glance at Tara and quickly shook his head—a tacit command not to say anything more.

"It looks like that bear walked close to where we did," she noted, oblivious to the mounting concern of her companions. "But it's veering off and going another way."

In truth, the bruin's tracks *seemed* to wander away at a harmless, random angle apart from their footprints.

But the woodsman lifted a finger and felt the wind. "It's stayin' just downwind—easily able to track our scent if'n it wanted to," he mumbled low, as if talking to himself.

"Why would it do that?" Tara asked.

"No reason in particular, young lady," Arthur responded quickly. "Nothin' to be of concern. We should be headin' back now."

"Did you hear that?" Jason asked suddenly, his eyes shut tight as if trying to catch a noise again.

"Hear what?" Tara asked, straining to make out any sound out of the ordinary.

Opening one eye, Jason smirked. "I'm pretty sure that was a chocolate milkshake calling my name!"

Knowing this time the boy had the upper hand, Tara playfully cuffed his shoulder and then laughed. "Well, I'm hungry, too." She grinned. "And that was a *strawberry* shake you heard calling *my* name."

Jason smiled, listening to her wonderful laughter. With a quick look away from her, he gave the woodsman a hidden wink.

Arthur returned a nod of silent thanks at the boy's discretion.

They headed down the fields to the Ernst farm, with Arthur glancing back often, one hand on his whip, to ensure an unspoken threat did not follow.

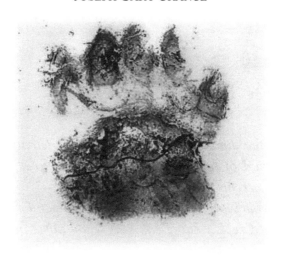

CHAPTER 10
A Menace Planned

On this late January day, it studied the activity of the farm below. A myriad of scents and sounds drifted to it slowly as the warming air currents flowed up the hillside.

Hidden from view, the Great Bear rested comfortably beneath one of Ryland Creek's many colossal white oaks, just beyond the edge of a cut cornfield.

Its stomach was full. Yet today it watched not for a meal but an opportunity.

It could wait.

Its long life had taught the bruin that patience was often the key to meeting its desired ends.

In its twisted mind, it sensed this day would be no different.

———— • ————

Mead hefted the .30-30 rifle in one hand. "So J.P. Smith just up and gave you these guns?"

Nathan nodded as he and his brother stood in the barn's doorway. "Yep. He reckoned I'd need 'em someday to shoot that nuisance bear."

"You're a coon hunter, not a bear hunter, Nate." The big man laughed.

"That's what I said," Nathan replied. "But I'll keep them nearby, just in case."

"Well, you never can tell. I've never known J.P. to be wrong about anything. Maybe he'll exaggerate on occasion—but wrong? No." He handed the weapon to Nathan with a conceding nod.

Accepting the firearm, Nathan set it on a rack inside the doorway that held the other rifle and the boxes of shells.

Both men looked to the far side of the barn to see Arthur lifting his grandniece so she could reach Butch's neck.

"Nice boy!" Lill stroked the mule's soft, brown mane.

The long ear brayed happily.

"I agree with you, little lady!" Arthur beamed broadly. "Butch truly is a good mule."

The faithful pack animal snorted, looking the woodsman in the eye—a shared history conveyed in the animal's warm stare.

"What do you say we let ol' Butch out so he can eat in the pasture and stretch his legs?" The silver-maned man smiled at the child in her pink-hooded coat.

Shaking her head vigorously, Lill shouted, "Good 'dea, Unc'a Art'ur!"

Setting the child gently on the ground, Arthur took her hand as they walked around the side of the barn. When Arthur had opened the stable door, Butch only needed a nod from the whipmaster to encourage it to trot outside. The mule paused, after taking several steps into the open air, to stand near the woodsman.

"We sure had some good times growin' up together, huh, ol' boy?" Arthur patted the mule's neck. "Wish Jacob was still here to reminisce about 'em."

Surprisingly, Butch seemed to snort in agreement.

While perhaps getting a bit too close, Lill walked forward to put her tiny hands on the long ear's front leg. The mule, however, knew precisely where the little girl was, and carefully sidestepped to ensure no harm would befall the gifted child. Arthur took Lill's hand and gently pulled her back. They watched Butch trot away into the pasture for a couple of hundred yards, stop, and begin to paw at the yellowed grass poking up through the thin layer of snow.

"Have fun, Butch!" Lill yelled, seeing the mule chomping at the vegetation.

"He's got somethin' to eat," Arthur said. "Now I think we should do the same. Are you gettin' hungry, young lady?"

"Oh, yes!" She raised both arms high.

"I heard that!" Nathan shouted as he neared them. "Let's go inside, and I'll make us some sandwiches. How does that sound?"

As fast as her short legs could move, the little girl ran into her other uncle's waiting embrace. Nathan lifted Lill to carry her into the house, with Arthur and Mead following in their wake.

In quick fashion, Nathan made a tasty lunch of homemade vegetable soup and cold roast beef sandwiches. The men's banter around the table focused on the continuing coon season and the upcoming perennial farming challenges of spring.

Also at the kitchen table, Lill doodled with some crayons and paper that her favorite uncle kept just for her. Sitting next to Nathan, who occasionally offered kind words about her artwork, she drew a bright-yellow sun with rays and a brown mule eating green grass. When she had finished her food and satisfied with her drawn masterpiece proudly presented to Nathan, Lill tugged on his arm with pleading blue eyes. "Cartoons, now?"

When Nathan looked for an explanation, Mead said, "This is when she likes to watch her cartoons."

"Of course!" Nathan smiled. He walked with Lill into the living room and turned on the television, changing the channels to finally find her favorite show. "All set?" He only received a curt nod from his niece, whose attention was already fixated on the screen. Before rejoining the adults, Nathan looked out the window to see Butch grazing contently in the upper field. Returning to the kitchen, he found the conversation between his uncle and brother had taken a new turn.

"So let me get this right." Mead slapped the table's wooden surface with one huge hand, sitting directly across the table from Arthur, who cradled a cup of coffee. "You believe it was the same bear that tracked Jason in the woods a couple of months ago, that also killed Welty's bull several miles from here, and then followed you and the kids while you were teachin' them how to track just last week?"

"Can't speak specifically to the bull and calf that Bill Welty lost, as I didn't see the tracks in that incident." Arthur leaned back in his chair, keeping one hand on his mug of coffee. "However, I did see the spoor left that night with Jason in the snowstorm and again with Jason and Tara on this farm a week ago. There's no question in my mind that the bear in those instances was Scar Paw."

Nathan sat at the table and joined the conversation. "Father Simmons reasoned that if animals have souls, then their souls could also be corrupted. But what could warp this creature's spirit so?"

"Hard sayin'." Arthur shook his head. "Perhaps it was wounded once by someone and seeks revenge."

"You're makin' this thing sound more and more human." Mead's face reflected his skepticism.

"More's the pity for that, Nephew, if'n animals should ever decide to pick up humanity's vices." Arthur grinned, taking a long swallow of his coffee.

The men could hear Lill in the living room, shouting the name of a cartoon character.

"She knows all the 'toons," Mead explained. "She repeats their names over and over so much that even I know all the cartoons."

Nodding with a smile, Nathan returned to the subject. "Pa always used to say—and J.P. Smith still does to this day—these hills hold a certain magic. As a kid, I thought that was just an expression, but I'm not so sure anymore. But it's still hard to imagine we have something lurkin' hereabouts that could cause such terror."

"Boys," Arthur smiled, "I have spent thousands upon thousands of hours over many years in the woods of Upstate New York, and I've seen things in the forests that can't be explained by modern man."

Lill giggled aloud, shouting another cartoon character's name.

"Really, Uncle Art?" Mead looked unconvinced. "Tales of bogeymen and monsters? Visions of ghosts in the mists? The Gandalark and some immortal Jesuit priest in these woods?"

"You know very well the tale of the Black Oaks that grow in this valley." Arthur countered with the local legend of some ancient, twisted trees said to capture the souls of evil men.

"Those are just tall tales!" Mead shook his head dismissively.

"Wouldn't be so sure those stories were complete fantasy if I were you, Nephew Mead." Arthur's tone underpinned his grave sincerity.

With a frown on her small face, Lill walked briskly into the kitchen and grasped Nathan's forearm. "Unc'a Nat'n? Butch! Butch! Butch!" There was no laughter in her voice nor in her frightened eyes.

"What's the matter, honey?" Nathan asked as she neared. Looking at his brother, he continued, "Is there a cartoon character called Butch?"

"Not that I recall," Mead replied.

The men shared a concerned look and then stood immediately.

Nathan took the girl's hand as they went quickly to the next room to discern what had so upset the child. Lill walked to the window, patting the glass rapidly with one flat palm, looking up the hillside, her voice growing frantic. "Butch! Butch!"

Following the child's gaze, the men moved closer to the window to see the long ear lying on his side. Butch made a feeble attempt to rise, but the old animal just dropped his head to the ground.

"What could be the matter?" Mead asked. "He doesn't seem to be hurt otherwise."

"Maybe Butch ate some jimsonweed," Arthur replied, referencing a particularly poisonous plant as he rubbed his chin. "If'n he did, that would disagree with his stomach somethin' fierce. I'll go up yonder and see what's wrong with the ol' boy."

The men walked to the front closet to get their coats as the little girl continued to stare out the window. Her breath fogged a white cloud on the windowpane, obscuring the landscape for a moment. She spoke in a low, soft whisper. "Bad bear. Very bad bear."

With his uncanny hearing, The Forest Ghost looked at the child and then turned to his larger nephew. "Does Lill's cartoon show have any bears in it, Mead?"

"Yeah. Quite a few," the big man replied. "Why do you ask?"

"Nothin'. Don't worry about it." Arthur's eyes narrowed as he gazed out the window again.

"Come here, dear," Mead said to Lill. "Let's get you ready to go outside."

The child obediently ran to her father, who dressed her in her warm, winter coat.

Heading out the front door to stand on the porch, the sound of Butch braying weakly drifted into the barnyard. They quickly descended the front steps, keeping their focus on the upper field.

While the mule's predicament might have been obscured from view, Seth emerged from his coop and immediately began pacing frantically in his kennel. The ebony cur threw his head in the air, as if catching a familiar scent on the wind, and suddenly let out a loud howl. Soon, the other hounds echoed Seth's concern. Even the puppies, particularly Buck and Tye, joined in the rising alarm.

"What's the matter, boy?" Nathan walked over to the cage as Seth jumped on top of his wooden coop and nearly climbed over the pen's wire fence. "

But the King of Hounds only howled louder. Fiercer.

"Calm down! Easy now!" Nathan commanded. Obediently, the dogs ceased their commotion, although Seth hopped to the ground, whined, and continued to pace back and forth.

"What do you suppose has gotten into them?" Mead set Lill down.

"Hard sayin'," Arthur began, "but I suspect they hear ol' Butch and think he's in trouble. I'll go up there and check him out."

"I go see Butch with you, Unc'a Art'ur?" Lill tugged on Arthur's pant leg.

"Not today, honey." The Ghost That Belongs to the Forest looked down at the tot and smiled. "It's best you stay here with your dad and Uncle Nathan for now. Your great uncle is goin' to see what's wrong with Ol' Butch and make everything all right."

She pouted and crossed her tiny arms across her chest.

"Go ahead, Uncle Art. We'll wait for your report," Nathan said and turned to his brother. "Can you help me with the tractor? I think there's a problem with the starter again."

"My pleasure, big brother," Mead grinned as the siblings walked toward the barn. "Lill, you can come watch Uncle Nathan and me fix the tractor. Would you like that?"

Looking disappointed, Lill reluctantly followed. The brothers and the child went into the barn's interior and disappeared.

Arthur looked up the hillside, one hand feeling the comfort of the bullwhip by his side. Walking around the corner of the barn and seeing the mule lying prone in the distance, he muttered, "Somethin' ain't right."

While Seth had watched his master disappear into the barn's interior, the hound's eyes now darted to The Forest Ghost, who heard the exceptional hound whined nervously.

"It'll be all right, boy," Arthur said, looking back at the anxious dog and then turning to leave. As he scanned the landscape, his keen eyesight only found an unnerving nothingness. He began the slow march up the field.

In just a few minutes of climbing the hillside, Arthur neared Butch. He could easily hear the mule's raspy breath, and the seasoned woodsman quickly spotted the discoloration of the grass around the long ear's body.

The wet, rusty color of the yellowed hay told of blood spilled.

126

Butch let out a soft bray at the familiar sight of the man. A delicate, red bubble grew from the mule's nose and burst.

"My God." Arthur stopped ten yards away from the stricken mule, his head shaking, burdened with pity, as his eyes fixated on the wounded animal. He then scanned the woods' edge once more.

"I know who did this to you, my old friend."

* * *

In the dim, single-bulb-lit interior of the barn, Mead nodded. "Yes sir, big brother, it's the starter, all right. I'll need a pair of half-inch wrenches. It should come off easily enough."

While both men focused on the faulty tractor part, Lill secretly moved toward the barn door entrance. Once certain her father and uncle were preoccupied, she slipped outside and began to run up the hill.

As the innocent ran past the kennels, Seth let out a short, loud bark, but the little girl continued, not heeding the hound's warning.

* * *

Arthur assessed the severe mauling the mule had endured. Slash marks to Butch's throat bled profusely, and another gash across the hindquarter had hamstrung the pitiful animal. There was one particularly vicious claw mark that raked the mule's ribcage.

"Easy now, fella." Kneeling, the woodsman gently stroked the long ear's neck. There was no more comfort he could offer. The mule's fate was certain.

A movement then caught the corner of his eye, and Arthur's hand reflexively reached for his whip.

"Hi, Unc'a Art'ur!" Lill managed, breathing hard after climbing the field's steep grade. "Butch, okay?"

"Stay right there, honey." Arthur motioned for her to stop. "You shouldn't be here now. Butch has been hurt very badly."

"I stay here." She nodded vigorously.

127

Upon hearing the girl's voice, the mule lifted his head slightly to see her and brayed sadly.

"You poor bas . . . ," Arthur started but caught himself in the presence of the little one. "You poor thing," he finally managed, offering some final solace to the quickly fading mule.

"Bad bear!" Lill shouted.

"You're right, dear." He kept his focus on Butch. "It was a bear what did this. If'n I were to make a bet, I'd say *which* bear done it."

"Bad bear! Very bad bear!" she repeated, but much louder this time, causing The Forest Ghost to look up to find the child pointing at the woods.

Immediately, the hairs rose on the back of Arthur's neck as he spun to stand, grasping his bullwhip.

It was too late. The bruin had planned its attack perfectly. The charging marauder was already upon the man as Arthur brought the whip into a backlash.

But Scar Paw was faster.

The rogue swiped with its massive paw. Arthur screamed as the bullwhip flew from his hand. The Great Bear then used its powerful jaws to latch onto the woodsman's arm. While the bruin might have been moderately surprised by The Forest Ghost's strength, a vicious shake of its head brought its intended victim to his knees.

"Aarrgghh!" Arthur shouted in as much rage as pain. He fought his way back to his feet, striking at the bear with his free arm. "Get out of here, Lill! Run to the barn!"

Standing on its hind legs to tower above the man, the Great Bear released Arthur's arm, only to slash the man with its sharp claws.

To his credit, Arthur never stopped punching and kicking the terror. But more of the yellowed grass on Ryland Creek became stained a wet crimson.

With a swipe of a massive paw to its prey's head, Scar Paw grunted victoriously as The Forest Ghost fell unconscious.

With their acute hearing, the coonhounds in their pens again raised the alarm.

Seth could no longer contain the driving urge. The hound inserted his paws into the wire mesh and carefully scaled the nearly seven-foot-tall kennel wall. Once near the top, he used his incredible strength to completely clear the hurdle and land on his feet.

Unconfined, the King of Hounds raced out of the barnyard.

The growing cacophony of the coonhounds' barking caught the brothers' attention as they stopped their work on the tractor to look at one another.

"What the heck do you suppose has gotten into your dogs?" Mead asked.

"Don't know," Nathan replied, but he also scanned the area for something he immediately noticed was missing. "Where's Lill?"

"Lill?" Mead called out. When there was no response, he shouted much louder, "Lill?"

The brothers shared an alarmed look.

Moving toward the barn door, Nathan saw Seth leap over the top of his kennel wall, and then he stood dumbfounded as his prized hound rushed around the barn to disappear. Instinctively, he grabbed one of the .30-30 rifles from the gun rack and took a handful of shells. Slipping out the doorway, Nathan began loading the weapon as he ran, following his dog's course. Rounding the barn's corner, the coon-and-not-bear hunter looked uphill and spied a large, dark form strike his uncle to the ground.

"My God, it's that damned Scar Paw!" Mead shouted, just joining his brother to see what was quickly transpiring before their eyes.

Jacking a shell into the rifle's chamber, Nathan lifted the gun to take aim at the enormous beast. But his tall sibling put one hand on the gun, forcing the weapon's barrel down.

"You can't shoot, Nate!" Mead motioned with his other hand. "Lill's in the line of fire!"

The malevolent thing focused on the man's exposed throat and opened its massive maw. Now, it would end the life of The Ghost That Belongs to the Forest.

But the struggle had brought the woodsman and Great Bear close to the fated mule. The loyal equine knew the precise location of the bear's head, and with all his remaining strength, Butch kicked with its unhurt hind hoof, striking the bruin hard in the face.

Had it been a normal bear, it would have run off into the forest.

Had the angle been right, the mule's powerful kick might have even broken the beast's neck.

But it was not to be this day.

Stunned by the brutal kick, Scar Paw shook its massive head. Its world dimmed for only a moment. Enraged, the huge bruin leaped onto the prone mule, using its sharp claws to rend the long ear's bone and flesh. In less than a minute, Butch went motionless.

Satisfied the mule finally dead, the Great Bear grunted. Breathing heavily, the beast turned back to the unmoving man. Now it could finish what it had planned and then hide in the forest once more.

"Bad bear!" Lill called out in her tiny, chastising tone. "Very bad bear!"

Turning to look at the intrusion, Scar Paw growled viciously. But the little one showed no fear. With its highly attuned abilities, the beast innately felt something more in this tiny human. The spirit of the land flowed within this forest child. Ryland Creek's aura radiated all around her.

No matter. Even this land's strange power could not protect her now. The little one would be an easy kill, and then it could return to finish the woodsman. Saliva dripped from its open jaws as it lumbered toward her, and the Great Bear made a sound so much like laughter.

"Huh, huh, huh!"

Then something—as black as the bruin itself—bounded high over the child's head, landing defiantly between the Killer of Mules and The Forest Child.

And Seth roared!

Startled, Scar Paw halted its advance. Once again, this troublesome hound had flummoxed its desires. But for the first time, the beast and its nemesis stood face-to-face.

So close. So very close now.

The bruin searched for a rising distress within the canine, the universal terror that had always emanated from every living creature it had ever encountered. The Great Bear paused to reach out with its heightened senses for that delicious feeling, and then it sensed . . .

Nothing. Absent was fear within the King of Hounds. Further, Scar Paw could not sense an uncontrollable rage akin to its own, but only the dog's staunch will to protect this child.

Seeing the beast hesitate, the ebony cur attacked. Sprinting forward, Seth sunk his sharp teeth into the brute. Despite the bear's thick hide, the powerful coonhound ripped a piece of fur away from the bruin's shoulder.

The Great Bear's anguished howl echoed throughout the forests of Ryland Creek. Once more, the amber grass became bright red. But this time, it was Scar Paw that felt pain and a burgeoning fear.

Now, Seth moved in rapid circles about the black bear, which vainly tried to match the exceptional hound's agility. Repeatedly, the hound struck fast, always drawing the brute farther from the wounded Arthur and Lill.

When Scar Paw finally faced his foe, Seth bawled mightily to keep the bear's attention. But as loud as the dog's howls were, the bear sensed something else. With a quick turn of its head, the bruin spied two more humans charging into the melee.

The exhausted marauder knew its designs were thwarted, and again by the dauntless hound. With the element of surprise lost, retreat stood the only option. It looked at its enemy and growled evilly at the unflappable King. Wheeling about, the beast made a mad dash for the safety of the trees.

With one last charge, Seth caught the brute in the rear quarter to tear another piece of flesh away. Scar Paw screamed in pain once more and vanished into the woods.

Out of breath, Mead immediately rushed to Lill while Nathan ran to Arthur's still form and kneeled.

Moving closer to his master, Seth turned to watch the forest, ever vigilant.

"How's Uncle Art?" Mead scooped up Lill in his arms and inspected her from head to toe. The giant breathed a grateful sigh of relief, as he could see no injury.

"He's hurt bad." Nathan, still holding the rifle, looked over his uncle's torn clothes and the multitude of claw and bite marks. "He's lost a lot of blood but still breathing. I think he'll be all right, but we need to call an ambulance now. How's Lill?"

"I'm okay, Unc'a Nat'n!" Lill shouted. "That was a bad bear! Very bad bear."

"And how, dear." Nathan sighed, hearing her voice.

"Doesn't look like Butch made it, though." Mead motioned with his head.

Turning around, Nathan could see the long-ear's eyes had already clouded over and the brutal carnage inflicted on the unfortunate animal. "No, he didn't," he said, quickly adding, "It must've been Scar Paw."

Walking over, Seth deposited a piece of black fur in his master's lap. The coon hunter put a grateful hand on his faithful dog's head.

Already facing downhill toward the farm with his little girl clutching him tightly, Mead said, "I'm goin' to call the ambulance. Don't like the idea of leavin' you two here alone."

Hefting the rifle to reassure his brother, Nathan replied, "We don't have much choice, and we can't move Uncle Arthur in his condition. But don't worry. We'll be safe with Seth nearby."

"You saw what Seth did for my little girl?" the giant's voice constraining ever so slightly, smiling gratefully at the hound, who bowed his head in reply.

"I did." Nathan nodded. "Seth must've known that thing was around. That's why he was barking the way he did—trying to warn us. Get a move on now. Uncle Art needs attention."

Carried away by her father, Lill gave her uncle and the ebony cur one last wave goodbye as Mead moved quickly toward the farmhouse and help.

CHAPTER 11
Something Unnatural

"But how?" The coon hunter's confusion bordered on anger. "How does Scar Paw always know where to find us?"

Nestling her head on his shoulder, Sharon watched a bright green leaf float gently across the pool below the waterfalls. "There are things, my love, that do not belong to the world of men. Things that go beyond modern man's understanding of nature. It's humanity's conceit, belief in their mastery, that has blinded so many such they cannot see what stands directly before them."

"See what?" Nathan sighed, her calmness flowing into him.

"There's a magic in these forests," she turned her head slightly to gaze at his face, "if you know where to look."

"I still don't get it." He shook his head slightly.

"You will, in time, my beloved," she promised. "Soon."

"But what does Scar Paw want?"

Sharon sat up, moving so their faces were near, and whispered, "That which you hold most dear."

Nathan stirred to the reassuring rhythmic "blip" of the heart monitor as he sat in the white, unnervingly sterile hospital room.

It was around noon on the second day after Scar Paw's attack. Arthur's prognosis was excellent, the doctors had said. While there were brief moments of consciousness, the wounded woodsman spent many hours asleep and had not spoken since.

Tucked beneath blue blankets, The Forest Ghost had several tubes running vital fluids into his body. The man's long, silver hair covered the pillow, and his breathing was steady while he rested. Often, Arthur would shift fitfully and moan in his sleep, and Nathan could only imagine his uncle was reliving the rogue bear's assault. About once an hour, a green-smocked nurse would come in to check vital signs and jot down some information on a chart near the foot of the bed.

Dozing off several times over the next few hours, Nathan startled when he awoke to find another visitor in the room sitting beside him.

"You snore, Seth's Master." Chief Gray Eyes sat comfortably, dressed in a brown, denim shirt and blue jeans. He wore an ornate necklace of feathers. On the floor by his side rested a large, tan leather pouch.

"How d'you know to find us here?" Nathan tried to shake the sleep from his waking mind. "Do you know what happened?"

"News travels fast from Painted Post," Gray Eyes responded with a kind look. "And yes, I know the creature you call Scar Paw has attacked The Ghost That Belongs to the Forest. Tell me more how this Great Bear fell upon my son."

While Nathan relayed the story of the bear's attack, Gray Eyes nodded pensively, with the chief taking considerable interest in the battle between Scar Paw and Seth. The coon hunter ended with a question.

"Could that bear have laid in wait for this ambush?"

For several moments, the sachem paused, drawing several deep breaths. "If this were any bear, I would think it had merely come back to defend its kill when my son went to see your dying mule. Instead, I fear this is no ordinary bear, Seth's Master, and I believe it possible the Great Bear planned this attack."

"How does it know where to find us? We seem to keep crossing paths with this thing—far beyond coincidence."

"Some of my peers believe a Great Bear is truly magical, neither confined to time nor space, and can appear or disappear at will. But I do not think this to be true. All bears have incredible hearing and smell—some say even better than dogs. Scar Paw may have become an even graver danger because its senses are so much greater than a normal bear."

"Enhanced smell and hearing?" Nathan searched for the words. "By some sort of magic?"

"No," the old chief scoffed, "just the luck of breeding and genetics."

"On a clear night, I've heard Seth treeing from over two miles away."

"Rest assured, Seth's Master, that Scar Paw's ears are much keener than yours."

Nathan's eyes widened. "That bear is following a coonhound's voice!"

Shaking his head, the Seneca looked disappointed. "I have something for you." He reached for the pouch on the floor, pulled out a long knife in a leather sheath ornately covered with multi-colored beadwork, and handed it to Nathan.

The coon hunter accepted the gift and pulled it from the sheath to reveal its gleaming silver blade. Nathan let the moment get the better of him. "Is this somehow magical?"

"No," Gray Eyes grinned, "it's very sharp."

"Thank you, Sachem. I shall always treasure this."

"There is more you must know, Seth's Master."

"Careful, Father," Arthur said weakly, opening his eyes and turning his head slowly. "You might be scarin' the young'un."

Rising quickly, Gray Eyes stood next to the hospital bed and beamed as he gently placed his hand on Arthur's shoulder. "It would seem no bear—not even a Great Bear—can kill the spirit of The Forest Ghost."

Grimacing, Arthur carefully sat up in the bed. "Scar Paw came a little too close for comfort in that regard, Father."

"It's good to hear your voice again, Uncle." Nathan moved closer. "What do you remember?"

"I recall that beast being on top of me, slashin' and bitin'. Then, nothing. Wait! I recollect Lill gettin' there just before the attack. She saw it—even tried to warn me—but I didn't understand what she was tryin' to tell me until it was too late. Is she okay?" There was a clear apprehension in the woodsman's tone.

"Lill's fine, Uncle Art," Nathan replied, and with no small measure of pride added, "Seth got there, and not a moment too soon. He stood between Scar Paw and Lill and then drove that thing back into the woods."

"Your hound did all that, did he?" Arthur asked, turning his attention to his Seneca father.

"Tell me more about the little girl," Gray Eyes began. "You say she saw the Great Bear before it attacked?"

"Yes, as if she were speaking to Scar Paw." Arthur nodded slowly.

With a solemn look, the sachem turned toward Nathan. "And Seth stood between the child and the bear, defying this beast?"

"Why, yes, Seth did just that." Nathan's brow furrowed. "Is somethin' wrong?"

"That is what you were tryin' to tell my nephew, wasn't it, Father?" Arthur interjected.

The chieftain opened his eyes once more, and the two longtime friends stared at each other for several moments before Nathan broke the silence. "Tell me what, exactly?"

Looking down, Gray Eyes took another deep breath. "Legends say a Great Bear is not only magical, but a vengeful beast. Your Seth foiled Scar Paw's intent, and this is only the first time we can truly know of. There may have been other encounters between this bear and your hound in the forest as well. It would explain Scar Paw's nearness to the black hound so many times."

"I understand." Nathan's eyes narrowed. "This thing isn't hunting *any* coonhound. It's hunting Seth in particular."

The wise sachem smiled at the younger man's epiphany.

"If this bear has been beaten, maybe it'll leave us alone now," Nathan said.

With a sad smile, the chief replied, "If Scar Paw were a normal bear, perhaps it would go away, never to be seen or heard from again. But you think like those who live in the world of men do. You must accept this, Seth's Master—the Great Bear will not stop until it finds the revenge it seeks."

The similarity between the chief's words and Sharon's warning in his dream momentarily caused Nathan to hesitate, but then his look hardened. "I don't run."

"So I have heard." Gray Eyes searched the other man's countenance. "So I have heard."

There was a rapid knock at the door. Before anyone could respond, a clean-shaven man in a crisp, green uniform, carrying a leather tote, walked into the room. Appearing not much older than thirty, he greeted the trio. "Good day, gentlemen. I'm Conservation Officer Steven Dolan from the New York State Department of Environmental Conservation—the 'DEC'—stationed in Albany. I hear one of you was attacked by a bear. A Mr. Arthur McCutcheon? I assume that would be you, sir?" Dolan looked at the bedridden, silver-maned man.

"Your powers of deduction are nothing short of amazin', Officer Dolan." The woodsmen smirked. "I'm Arthur McCutcheon, and this is Chief Gray Eyes and my nephew." He pointed to each man respectively.

"I see," the officer nodded politely. "Do you feel well enough to discuss the encounter with the bear, sir?"

"Officer," Nathan interrupted, "my uncle only came to a few minutes ago. Can this discussion wait?"

"And your name, sir?" Dolan asked.

"I'm Nathan Ernst. The attack occurred on my farm, and I witnessed it. If I may, how did you hear about the incident so soon?"

"Oh, that's excellent, Mr. Ernst! I'd like your take on what happened as well. And it's just dumb luck that I'm here. I was studying otters spotted in the Chemung River and overheard in a diner some folks talking about the assault."

With a conciliatory bow to the chief, Nathan said, "News *does* travel fast in Painted Post."

"Reckon I'm up for it, Officer Dolan." Arthur sat up a little straighter. "I can discuss what happened when the bear attacked—at least before I was knocked out."

"I sincerely appreciate you taking the time, sir." Dolan dug into his leather case to produce a notebook and pen and sat in the chair by the bed. When he found the other men staring, he said, "Please, just start at the beginning."

Stopping periodically to answer Dolan's questions, Arthur told the story, while Nathan provided additional details as the tale progressed.

When they'd finished, Dolan scratched his noggin. "That certainly sounds like abnormal behavior for a bear. But don't worry, gentlemen. The DEC will set traps, and we'll euthanize the animal once captured. Our traps are long, metal conduits that we bait. When the bear walks in and springs the trap, a heavy metal door then closes behind it, and it's caught, all nice and neat."

"Your devices," Gray Eyes shook his head, "will not work against this animal, Official Man from Albany."

"I assure you, sir, we shall catch this bear." Dolan looked somewhat offended. "We'll employ the considerable resources of the department to this effort."

"Money," the sachem spoke slowly, "only works as bait for men."

The official's countenance turned slightly red. "Sir, I personally have trapped three nuisance bears during my career."

Cocking his head, Arthur asked, "So, are you tellin' us that you're three for three in catchin' troublesome bears?"

"Well . . . uhm . . . I . . .," Dolan swallowed. "No, not exactly. There have been a few animals we were never able to catch. Several years ago, a large bear got caught inside one of our traps. But it broke out, though, leaving a chunk of itself in the trapdoor, as I recall."

Glancing at Gray Eyes and Arthur and then to the officer, Nathan asked, "By chance, was it part of the bear's rear paw you found in that trap?"

"Why, yes, it was." Dolan's eyes went wide. "How did you know that?"

With an intense focus, Nathan replied, "With all due respect, sir, you're not going to catch this thing."

Standing, the conservation officer didn't try to hide his indignation. "As I said before, Mr. Ernst, we *will* trap this bear." Dolan then thanked the men, placing his notes into his briefcase, and proceeded to leave. When he opened the door, three adolescents rushed into the room, followed closely by Beth Canton. The officer then exited, shutting the door.

"Uncle Art!" Tara was the first to make it to the bedside, but kept one of her arms behind her back with Jason and Bobby rushing to stand on either side of her. "How are you feeling? Does it hurt?"

The woodsman's face brightened at the sight of the children, and any sign of tiredness evaporated as he sat a little taller in his bed.

Holding a handled paper bag by his side, Jason asserted confidently, "He's gonna be okay 'cause his hair's silver." When the other kids looked at him with confused expressions, he grinned.

"You've got to have white hair before you die in the forests. Isn't that right?"

"That would be correct, young'un." Arthur chuckled. "My hair is silver!" With considerable bravado, he turned to Tara and smiled. "It's goin' to take more than that old bear to rid this world of me, young lady. What're you youngsters up to?"

Before her son could answer, Beth spoke up. "Today is Jason's birthday, and he requested we come see you as his gift."

"Yep!" Jason stuck out his chest. "I turned thirteen today! I'm a teenager!"

"Yeah, but you still have a lot of growing to do." Tara slapped the celebrant on the back.

The new teenager's ego deflated like a pricked balloon.

Pausing a moment, Arthur said, "Don't ever recall bein' someone's birthday gift before."

"Me, neither," the Seneca chieftain spoke, causing the children to notice the older man by Nathan's side.

"Kids, Beth," Arthur introduced, "this is my father, Chief Gray Eyes of the Seneca Nation."

Each youth, along with Beth, warmly greeted the chief, who smiled politely.

"A teenager now, eh?" Arthur asked Jason. "There are hideous monsters in the forests that wait until children hit their teenage years before they try to eat 'em! Isn't that right, Chief?"

"Thirteen." Gray Eyes looked up, searching the air. "Just the right age for those hungry beasts—not too tender, not too tough to chew."

"Hold on a minute!" Tara's eyes went wide. "I turn thirteen in about a week!"

"And my thirteenth birthday is at the beginning of next month!" Bobby quickly added,

Returning his gaze to the youths, Gray Eyes replied, "The terrible monsters in the forests of Painted Post will see you three, look at one another, and wonder who ordered takeout." He chuckled and then sat in a chair by the wall.

The youngsters gaped in silent, wide-eyed awe. Even Beth couldn't hide a snicker, seeing the youngster's reactions.

"If I recollect the calendar correctly, Nephew," Arthur said, "in nearly three weeks' time, that means we'll be huntin' with three teenagers!"

"God help us." Nathan smirked.

Then Jason looked at the coon hunter, who nodded a tacit approval. The new teen placed the large, handled paper bag on the bed.

"What's this?" Arthur asked. As he reached into the bag, his face showed immediate recognition as he removed his bullwhip. Any further words were firmly stuck in the woodsman's throat.

"Mead and I couldn't find your whip where you fought Scar Paw," Nathan explained. "So the young'uns volunteered to search the field. They spent the better part of an hour looking, but they finally located it."

"You can't be a whipmaster without a whip!" Jason smiled.

"Thank you," Arthur managed, his voice a bit choked. "Which of you found it?"

Smiling, Tara lifted one small hand and wriggled her fingers.

"Might've known." Arthur grinned.

Just then, the door opened, and a nurse in a green smock entered. The brunette wore a tag, blue with white letters, that read "Dolores." She walked to the foot of Arthur's bed, took one look at the silver-maned man, glanced at her watch, and then annotated several things on the chart in pencil.

"I'm conscious now." Arthur smiled, reading the nurse's nametag aloud. "Dolores?"

Forcing a smile that lasted a microsecond, the green-clad woman turned the clipboard, holding the chart so Arthur could see, and pointed to a mark. "I know. I marked it right here." Nurse

Dolores then replaced the chart at the foot of the bed and exited the room.

"Is this a hospital or a morgue?" Arthur asked, grinning wryly.

Touching Arthur's forearm, Tara said, "We also got this for you." She took her other arm from behind her back and presented a gift in a tall, brown box tied with a yellow ribbon.

Silent for a moment, The Forest Ghost untied the ribbon and removed the lid while the young people held their breaths. Reaching into the box, the woodsman lifted out a beautiful black fedora. He beheld the hat and beamed, carefully setting it on his head. "It fits perfectly, young'uns, but how d'you know what size to get?"

"We just asked the store clerk for the largest hat he had." Jason smirked.

"Reckon I had that one comin'." Arthur winced as everyone broke into raucous laughter. "Thank you very much, children. I shall treasure this gift forever."

"But something is missing," Tara continued, causing all to look at the young lady. Holding up a feather in her hand, she said. "I found this when we were searching for your whip. Is it from a turkey?"

"No," Arthur said, accepting the feather and examining it. "That's from a ruffed grouse."

"Maybe you could put it in your hatband?" Tara suggested.

All watched as The Forest Ghost paused, at first studying the plume, and then looking at Gray Eyes. "A long time ago—when I was just a little older than you are now—another young lady gave me a feather. It was white and from a crane. I haven't worn a feather in my hair since." Arthur looked at his adopted father.

With a solemn nod, Gray Eyes said, "She would approve of you wearing it again, my son."

The room remained silent, with everyone fixated on the feather in Arthur's hand.

"Uncle?" Nathan finally asked. "Who was this young lady?"

With a heavy sigh, The Ghost That Belongs to the Forest replied, "That would be a story for another time, Nephew." Again, he looked at his adopted father, a tacit history shared between them in that single moment.

Carefully, Arthur put the feather in the hatband, staring at it for several long moments. "Thank you, children. That'll do nicely."

CHAPTER 12
The Challenge

With a final smack of the long-handled mallet, Nathan drove the stake deep into the fertile soil of Ryland Creek. The name on the wooden marker read "Damned Mule." Burying Butch required Nathan to use a backhoe to break the frozen earth, and the work took the better part of the morning. The scarified ground stood in stark contrast to the other undisturbed, hallowed graves in the Ernst family's coonhound cemetery.

Now, the late winter sun hung high above.

Standing nearby, Tara and Bobby offered their silent final respects to the long ear when Jason spoke. "He was a good mule, huh, Mr. Ernst?"

"Yes, yes, he sure was." Nathan's sad smile grew. "Butch was certainly ornery, but I think Uncle Arthur would say that was part of his charm."

Bobby only grinned weakly. "Maybe that's why they liked each other so much?"

"I suppose they were kindred spirits of a sort." When Nathan looked up to find the youngsters' faces quite sullen, he added quickly. "Are you young'uns ready for lunch? We can go to Shirley's—my treat."

That did the trick.

"Yeah, Mr. Ernst, that would be great!" Jason piped up. "Can I get a hamburger and chocolate milkshake?"

"Me, too! But make that a double cheeseburger!" Bobby agreed.

Rolling her eyes, Tara's lips formed a smirk.

"Sure," Nathan chuckled at the growing boys' ravenous appetites, "get whatever you want."

The drive to Shirley's was short, and the kids piled out of the club-cabbed pickup, racing each other to select the table. Following in their wake, Nathan shook his head and chuckled again at their youth.

This time, the children selected a window booth. Upon seeing the crew, Danielle waved off another waitress about to serve the table where they'd sat. She handed everyone a menu, eyeing Nathan with a smile. "For a bachelor, you certainly have a lot of mouths to feed!"

Nathan mused for a moment. "I reckon I do."

Nothing if not efficient, Danielle took their order and prompted the chef to hurry for the "starving" youth.

When the food was finally served a short while later, Nathan stifled a laugh, watching the boys immediately begin to devour their meals.

Tara, on the other hand, ate much more daintily—almost reluctantly—and then said, "Mr. Ernst, will Uncle Arthur be okay? I mean, he seemed all right at the hospital yesterday, but will he be able to go into the woods again?"

"Uncle Art is a tough ol' bird," Nathan replied. "He'll come through this ordeal in fine fashion, you'll see."

She smiled, seemingly relieved by his assurances. Then Bobby let out an obnoxiously loud burp, and she swiftly cuffed the boy, not so gently, on the head. "Mind your manners!"

"Okay! Okay!" Bobby surrendered, rubbing his smarting noggin.

The hunters had just finished their meal when an expensive-looking car pulled into the diner's parking lot. The shiny, black limousine that caught their attention seemed out of place in their rural hometown. To their surprise, a well-dressed chauffeur exited and opened the limo's back door. A tall, middle-aged gentleman stepped out of the vehicle, appearing quite comfortable. He wore blue jeans, a camouflage baseball cap, tall boots, and a black leather coat. While the man could have passed for a resident of Painted Post, there was no evidence that dirt had ever touched his apparel.

When the stranger entered the restaurant, he immediately went to the main counter. Seeing Marty Rigby, the out-of-towner leaned over and spoke to the diner's owner. To Nathan and the children's surprise, Marty then pointed in the direction of their table.

"Are you Nathan Ernst?" the tall stranger asked as he neared.

"That would be me." The coon hunter looked up from his coffee at the newcomer.

"Are these your children?" he asked warmly, looking at the youngsters.

"Sort of." Nathan chuckled.

"Mind if I have a seat?" Before anyone could respond, the man pulled up a chair and sat close to Nathan.

"Can I help you, mister?" Nathan asked.

"As a matter of fact, you're the only person in this little town who can help me." The stranger grinned.

"Is that right?" Nathan cocked an eyebrow.

"My name is Edward Wellington. Most folks call me Drake." He offered his hand, and Nathan returned a firm grip.

"I've heard of you, Mr. Wellington," Nathan said. "You're a millionaire from Ohio who has some fine coonhounds, if recollection serves."

"Your memory is working just fine, young man." Drake smiled. "I have some of the best coonhounds in the country. Some would say *the* best. My walker hound—he's called Drake's Pride—just won the world hunt this past October."

"Well, congratulations, Mr. Wellington," Nathan replied. "That's quite an accomplishment to win that competition."

"Yes, it is." Drake beamed. "But word has reached my ear that there's a coonhound around these parts that's truly the best—a black

147

cur you own named Seth. Someone with my—well, let's say ego—won't let me call Pride the best in the country if, in fact, there's a better hound out there."

The children looked back and forth between the two men, but Jason spoke first. "Seth's the greatest coonhound that ever was, mister!"

"My, my, my! Aren't you the spunky one?" Drake smiled at the boy and then turned to Nathan. "Well, I gather you wouldn't be opposed to a contest between our hounds?"

Nathan shook his head. "Mr. Wellington, I don't do competition hunts. I've got nothin' against it, and I respect those who do. But it's never been an Ernst family thing to enter our dogs in a sanctioned night hunt. I'm sorry you drove all this way for nothing, but I must decline."

"I came here," Drake said slowly, "so I could hunt with your hound and know if my dog Pride could beat this Seth in his own territory."

"For braggin' rights, Mr. Wellington?" The disdain in Nathan's voice was unmistakable.

"You misunderstand me, young man!" Drake put his hands up defensively. "This is to be a private contest—just me and whomever you decide to bring along. I alone will know if Pride is the better dog, or not, than this Seth of yours."

"There's more you ought to know," Nathan said. "There's somethin' in these woods that's been causin' a great deal of trouble—"

"Yes, yes, I've heard," Drake interjected, waving his hands. "You have a nuisance bear—one that put your beloved uncle in the hospital. Black bear attacks happen throughout the United States every year, but this is of little concern to me. I'm willing to hunt in this town if you are."

"I'm impressed you know about Uncle Art, but you need to understand something else, Mr. Wellington," Nathan said, shaking his head. "This rogue bear might be homin' in on a coonhound's voice during a chase. Further, it could very well be this thing is after Seth in particular."

"Nonsense, young man," Drake replied. "That bear is probably over twenty miles away from here by now. Are you telling me that you'll never hunt your hounds in these hills—your home—ever again? Or are you just using that bear as a convenient excuse to not hunt against Pride?"

"Seth has nothing to prove." Nathan didn't let the snide remark rile him. "He's an exceptional hound, and that's good enough for me." He turned to his teenaged hunting crew. "It's time for us to go, young'uns." The children stood, ready to follow him to the front register.

Before they'd taken more than a few steps, Drake spoke up again. "Please let me get the tab for your meal." He then paused, glancing at Nathan. "I apologize, son, for being so rude. You see, it doesn't mean much to own the supposed world champion if a hound that never competed is, in fact, the better dog."

Turning to face the other man, Nathan replied, "Much obliged, Mr. Wellington, but the answer is still no."

"Regardless of who wins, I will pay your uncle's hospital bills in full," Drake added hastily.

The children's mouths went wide, gawking at each other. While they had no idea how much Arthur's medical care would be, they likewise suspected that bill wouldn't be cheap.

"No matter who wins?" Nathan stopped and turned back.

"Do it, Mr. Ernst!" Jason tugged on Nathan's arm. "Seth is gonna win anyway, and you'll take care of Uncle Arthur at the same time!"

"I agree with this youngster," Drake said. "And like I said, regardless of who wins, I'll pay all your uncle's medical expenses."

"Very well, Mr. Wellington," Nathan said slowly, nodding. "We'll hunt with you. My farm is on—"

"Ryland Creek." Drake smiled broadly. "I'll meet you at your place at sunset in two nights' time."

"Did your hound ride with you in that, Mister Wellington?" Tara looked curiously at the rich man and then at the limousine.

"No, young lady, Pride didn't accompany me on the way here. I wasn't sure if Nathan would accept my challenge, so now I have to go to my hotel and make a phone call to have Pride brought from my kennels in Ohio."

Walking over with the tab, Danielle was about to give it to Nathan, but the Ohioan snatched the paper from her hands. "I've got this, miss."

"Thanks again, Mr. Wellington," Nathan said.

"Please, call me Drake." As the out-of-towner read the bill, his eyebrows raised. "Who in the world ate four double cheeseburgers, two orders of chili-cheese fries, and two large chocolate milkshakes?"

Beaming, Jason and Bobby raised their hands.

"Where on earth do you two put all that food?" Drake laughed.

A suddenly mature Jason replied, "If you chased behind Seth in these hills, mister, you'd work up an appetite, too!"

Just as the sun slipped below the western ridge two days later, Drake arrived on the Ernst farm in a new, spotless pickup holding a gleaming aluminum dog box. Also as promised, the millionaire was alone. Once he'd parked his vehicle, the millionaire nearly sprinted to the back of his truck, lowered the tailgate, and opened the rearmost shiny box door. Atop the tailgate stepped Drake's Pride, a magnificent walker coonhound.

Once Drake had snapped a leash on the hound's collar, the walker jumped to the ground, looking about the farm like a lord surveying his servants' quarters.

150

While the three kids huddled around the kennels, Nathan walked over to greet his visitor. A few of the other Ernst hounds barked, and the puppies raced to the fence to view Pride.

Seth, however, just sat quietly on his haunches.

"That dog certainly is pretty—I'll give him that," Jason said sarcastically.

"Look at Pride!" Bobby also watched Drake's walker, his voice filling with awe. "Maybe Seth can't beat him."

"Bobby Bensen, how can you tell how good a hound is by only looking at him?" Tara cuffed the redhead, who winced. She then leaned closer to Seth. Putting her fingers through the wire mesh, she said in a low voice, "You're going to beat this Pride. I just know it."

Leaning forward to lick the girl's fingers, Seth looked at the walker and snorted.

"C'mon!" Jason motioned to the other kids. "Let's see what Mr. Ernst and Mr. Wellington are talking about."

The gaggle of youngsters ran over to the adults.

"Pride is a fine-lookin' hound," the kids heard Nathan say as they came within earshot.

"Fine looking *and* fine performing." The competitive edge wasn't absent from Drake's response. "This isn't an official competition, so let's agree to these rules, and I'll make it simple. The hound that trees the first two out of three raccoon wins, and the raccoon has to be seen to count."

"Seems agreeable." Nathan nodded. "Even though huntin' season is still open, can we agree not to take any raccoon tonight? Just tree 'em and let 'em go?"

"That works just fine for me," Drake replied. "I'm not here for fur or trophy."

"Well then, let's get this shindig on the road." Nathan then said to the children, "Jason, let Seth out of his kennel and load him in the truck. Do you want to ride with us, Mr. Wellington?"

"I'd as soon drive my truck, if you don't mind?"

"Suit yourself," Nathan said.

As Jason and Bobby ran back to Seth's cage, Tara went to Nathan's old truck, dropped the tailgate noisily, and opened the dog box.

"Here he comes!" Jason swung open Seth's kennel door.

Immediately, the black cur sprinted from his pen toward Tara but stopped just short to face the walker, still on his master's leash. Upon seeing Seth close up, Pride let out a low growl, but the heavily muscled King of Hounds only stared back. Under the weight of Seth's glare—with even Drake showing mild surprise—all watched Pride cower.

Seth then jumped onto the tailgate, gave the girl holding the door open another quick snort, and entered his dog box. Before she closed the door, Tara leaned close, and the hound brought his head outside the box. The young lady whispered, "You showed him!" She then added with a grin, "Now, let's prove who's the best coonhound in these woods."

"Harrumph!" Seth snorted, and then licked Tara's face just before she shut and secured the door's latch.

"Do we have all our gear?" Nathan asked Jason.

"Yes, sir, Mr. Ernst! Ready to go!"

However, Bobby looked downcast. "I sure wish Uncle Art were here to go with us."

Gently, Nathan put a hand on the redhead's shoulder. "We're doing this hunt *for* Uncle Arthur, remember?"

"Oh, yeah! That's right!" Bobby's face brightened.

"You're a goofball sometimes, Bobby Bensen." Tara shook her head.

"Let's load up into the truck, young'uns," Nathan said. "We've got a contest to win." He then turned to their guest. "Follow me, Mr. Wellington. Where we're goin' tonight will only take about ten minutes to get there."

"I'll be right behind you." Drake waved, loading Pride back in the dog box and then entering his truck's cab.

They traveled for several miles, heading deeper into the hills and valleys. Even with recent above-freezing temperatures, patches of snow still clung stubbornly to the forest floor. While ice was also prevalent on the stream banks, the wider parts of most creeks had open, flowing water.

Pulling his truck into a meadow at the head of a trail, Nathan and the youths quickly exited the vehicle. Parking his pickup nearby, Drake walked apace to lower his tailgate, opened Pride's box door, and snapped a leash on the dog's collar again.

However, when the Ohioan saw Nathan sling a .30-30 rifle over his shoulder, the millionaire asked, "That's a pretty big gun for hunting raccoon. Are the ringtails larger here in Painted Post? Besides, I thought we weren't going to shoot any coon tonight."

Looking into the forest and the surrounding hills, Nathan replied grimly, "It's not the raccoon around here I'm worried about."

Drake only nodded.

While Jason made it to the back of the truck first, Tara insisted on putting a leash on Seth. She then walked the ebony cur over near Drake and Pride, so the coonhounds stood close to each other.

"Ready to turn them loose?" Drake asked.

"We're ready if you are," Nathan replied.

Stepping to the side before the two hounds, Jason said, "Let them go on the count of three." Both Tara and Drake leaned over to grasp their hounds' collar with one hand and the other on the leash snap. "One. Two. Two and a half—"

"Jason Canton!" Tara laughed.

The teenager chuckled. "Three!"

With that, both handlers released their dogs, and the darkness soon absorbed the coonhounds.

"Let's go." Nathan waved one arm toward the trail

The hunters had not walked into the forest for more than three minutes when Seth's loud bawl filled the air and could be heard throughout the valley for many miles.

"Whoo-hoo!" Bobby shouted. "Seth's found a coon already!"

"Remember," Drake said, listening to the sweet melody of Seth's voice, "it's the hound that trees first. Getting the first strike doesn't count."

As Pride's voice also sounded in the night, Nathan shot a curious look at the other man. "We didn't forget the rules, Mr. Wellington—nor the agreement."

"Of course." Drake smiled as he heard Pride's trail bark again. "This is just a friendly competition."

The first chase was on. It was clear both hounds were trailing the same raccoon, but Seth soon outpaced the other hound. Drake fidgeted as the children exchanged nervous whispers.

Less than two minutes later, the ebony cur's voice switched over to his tree bark.

"Seth is treed!" Jason shouted. "We win the first chase!"

"Hold off, young'un," Nathan spoke calmly. "We have to see the coon in the tree before we can declare it's a real win."

"Yes, sir, Mr. Ernst," Jason replied. "I just got caught up in the excitement is all."

Pride began to tree alongside Seth.

"Well," Drake conceded, "at least my dog thinks there's a coon there, too!"

In less than ten minutes, the hunters were beneath a tall, leafless maple. Both hounds barked loud and rapidly, with their front paws firmly on that ancient tree's trunk.

"Right there's the raccoon!" Tara shouted and pointed, with all following her headlight's beam to see the curious ringtail peering down at the commotion.

"That ol' coon should count his lucky stars that we're not hunting for real tonight!" Bobby was nearly dancing with excitement.

"With the way you shoot, Bobby Bensen?" Tara replied, grinning. "That raccoon still wouldn't have anything to worry about!"

The red-faced redhead had no response as the two other kids guffawed, and even the rich man laughed.

"Seth won the first chase," Drake said. "Quite impressive, but let's see who gets the next two!" The Ohioan called his hound off the tree. "C'mon Pride, go find another coon!"

The walker obediently fell away from the tree at his master's command and disappeared into the dark woods.

"Seth!" Nathan shouted. "Den tree!" Like the other dog, the ebony cur quickly dropped to all fours and followed the other hound into the night's dark blanket.

"We'll head toward the creek." Nathan motioned with his headlamp in the general direction the hounds had gone. "We're likely to pick up another strike there."

The hunting party had not made their way a hundred yards when Pride began barking again. Directly behind them.

"Mr. Ernst, isn't Mr. Wellington's dog treeing from where we just came from?" Jason asked.

"It sure sounds that way." Nathan looked at the rich man. "I assume the rules are that you can only tree the same coon once for it to count."

"Quite, quite," Drake replied. "But we need to be sure Pride is on the same tree."

With a nod, Nathan led the way back to the beckoning walker. When they arrived, the hunters found Pride barking up an oak nearly next to the large maple where Seth had first treed. While there was a ringtail staring back at them in the oak where Pride was treeing, now the old maple held no raccoon.

"Oh man!" Jason shook his head. "That ol' coon just came down the first tree and ran up this one when Pride came back and treed it—again. That shouldn't count!"

"You can't say for sure it's the same coon," Drake said quickly.

"Mr. Wellington," Nathan began, "do you honestly believe these two coonhounds—one that has been officially dubbed the world champion—missed a second ringtail only about ten yards apart? Particularly when the raccoon that was in the first tree is no longer there?"

Then, Seth's loud voice then rang out again in the night, and Pride stopped to listen. The walker then dropped his paws off the tree and headed toward the sound of the other hound.

"We'll let you have that one, Drake," Nathan smiled confidently, "but I suspect this contest is about to be over in a few minutes."

The Ohioan's face waxed grim.

Turning off their lights, the hunters listened as Seth continued to work out the raccoon's trail. Pride also barked a few times, but it was clear the walker was far behind the ebony cur. A minute later, Seth switched over to his tree bark once more.

"Seth's treed again!" Tara shouted.

"Whoo-hoo! We win! We win!" Both Bobby and Jason shouted, jumping up and down.

Even Nathan winced when Jason added, "Hope you're getting used to being second, Mister Wellington!"

"Not so fast, boys!" Drake said. "You keep forgetting we have to make sure we can see the raccoon first."

"Mr. Wellington is right," Tara replied for her gleeful peers, who reluctantly nodded.

Working their way toward the beckoning hounds, the hunters found dog tracks in the snow.

Tara's keen sight first caught what all were seeking. "And here are the coon's tracks!"

156

Knowing the competition was likely all but over now, Drake sighed.

However, when the hunters made it to the tree where the two hounds were barking loud and rapid, hopes of ending the contest quickly faded.

"Looks like a den tree!" Drake couldn't hide his relief. In truth, the old oak had a large opening at its base, and no raccoon hung on the outside branches of the hollow tree. "The agreement was that we had to see the coon for it to count!"

"Ah man!" Bobby groaned. "But we saw the coon's tracks leading right to this tree and know that ringtail is inside that hole!"

The lad's shoulders slumped when Nathan softly said, "Rules are rules, Bobby. The understanding was that we had to lay eyes on the coon." Turning to the other man, he added, "Let's see if our hounds can't find one more tonight and end this contest."

"Agreed," Drake said.

Both men called their coonhounds off the tree, and Seth and Pride once more dashed out of sight and into the dark forest.

"We're not far from the creek," Nathan said. "I suspect they'll strike another trail soon."

Following Nathan's lead, the party made its way to the creek's banks in less than five minutes and halted.

"We don't know where the dogs are, Mr. Ernst." Jason shifted his feet, a bit antsy. "So, do we go upstream or downstream?"

Before Nathan could reply, Seth's bawl rang out once more in the hollow. He pointed his light's beam toward his hound's voice. "Seems like we're headed upstream."

Pride immediately sounded loud and entered the chase. This run, it was clear the hounds were neck and neck as they raced toward their quarry's sanctuary.

But then Seth's voice fell silent while Pride continued to sing.

"Mr. Ernst, where's Seth?" Tara craned her neck to hear something—anything—from the ebony cur.

157

"I'm not sure." Nathan shook his head.

"Looks like this contest may be coming to an end very soon." Drake smiled, looking at the two boys.

Racing into view of the hunters' headlights, Seth spun around, positioned between the children and the night's black veil, and growled fiercely.

"What's the matter, boy?" Tara kneeled next to the agitated dog.

Remaining focused on the dark beyond, Seth tensed his heavily muscled frame. His head shifted back and forth, trying to catch a scent on the wind. The King of Hounds took several steps forward.

And then, Seth roared!

Piecing together his faithful hound's behavior, Nathan's eyes went wide. "Mr. Wellington, call your hound back." With a single fluid motion, the coon hunter unslung the high caliber rifle from his back. "Call Pride back—now!"

"Not on your life, young man," Drake replied. "My dog just proved he truly is the world champion!" He quickly added, "I can't help it your hound suddenly became scared of the dark."

Turning his head, Seth growled at the millionaire.

Pride's distant trail voice switched over to a treed bark.

"I'd say this contest was over," Drake said, beaming broadly.

Before anyone could respond, Pride's tree bark became a long howl of pain and terror. And then silence reclaimed the darkness as the echoes of the walker's last cry faded.

"W-w-what just happened, Mr. Ernst?" Bobby spoke first, his jaw dropping.

"It's that damned bear again!" Nathan shouted. "We're leaving—now! Jason, put a leash on Seth. This hunt is over."

"Wait! Wait!" Drake said, frantic. "We can't leave my dog! Pride! Pride! Come, boy!" He continued to call out for a minute or so, but as Nathan herded the children toward the truck, he added, "We can't just abandon my hound out there!"

158

"Pride might've gotten away," Nathan replied, although he didn't sound hopeful. "We can wait by the trucks for a bit. Maybe he'll meet us where we began."

The march to their vehicles didn't take long, with Nathan staying in the rear, looking back over his shoulder often and listening. For his part, Seth constantly tested the air—ever vigilant.

But Pride never rejoined them. They waited another thirty minutes as Drake continued to call his dog's name into an indifferent night.

"Mr. Wellington, we can leave your coat where we parked." When the children looked at him for an explanation, Nathan said, "It's an old coon hunter's trick. A hound will make his way back and lay on a piece of clothing with his master's scent on it." He turned to their guest. "Hopefully, we'll find Pride here, safe and asleep on top of it come morning."

With a resigned sigh, Drake doffed his expensive leather jacket and placed it on the ground.

"Load Seth in the truck, Jason. We're going home," Nathan said. "Drake, you're more than welcome to stay at my farm tonight if you'd like."

"I appreciate the offer, but I will head to my motel for some fresh clothes. I'll meet you at your place bright and early tomorrow."

With their final goodbyes for the evening, they entered their trucks. Drake headed to his motel while Nathan and his young crew made the solemn ride back to Ryland Creek.

With the vehicles' retreating taillights still dimly illuminating the meadow, the darkness took a solid shape and stepped out of the forest just downwind of where the hunters had been.

Blood dripped from the beast's maw, staining the sacred ground of Painted Post.

Then came a sound—a deep, heavy grunt—that sounded eerily human.

"Huh, huh, huh."

The next morning came with the skies cloudy and gray, with Nathan accompanying Drake back to where they'd left the rich man's coat. To their dismay, not only did they not find the walker hound lying comfortably atop Drake's jacket, but the leather apparel had been shredded in several pieces.

Still carrying the .30-30 rifle, Nathan studied some tracks in the snow and quickly found the telltale mark. "It was Scar Paw, all right."

"I'll be damned." Drake made out the unusual bear's spoor. If there had been any hope of finding his champion hound, it melted away as Drake's shoulders slumped.

"Let's trace the bear tracks back." Nathan pointed with the rifle's muzzle. "That's where I suspect we'll likely find . . ." Unable to continue, he merely motioned with his head.

A short time later, following Scar Paw's trail backward, the men came to a behemoth, spreading white oak, its branches shaped like a cross. While there was no sign of the missing walker, the snow churned red screamed the story of Pride's fate.

Kneeling in the blemished whiteness—his face hidden and voice breaking—Drake's loss also bled into the soil. "I should've listened to you, young man, and never hunted here in the first place. But I got caught up in my ego, and now I've paid a terrible price for my foolishness."

"Mr. Wellington," Nathan began. "I'm terribly sorry for what's happened here, and if there's anything I can do to . . . ."

Remaining on his knees, Drake raised one hand, only shaking his head.

Nathan fell silent and numb.

CHAPTER 13

The Nightmare Realized

U ncle Arthur stood in a green gown. The silver-maned man leaned on a cane, and through the hospital room's window, he could see the surrounding, winter-held hills. The late afternoon sun glinted off the Chemung River, not far from its birth at the confluence of the Tioga and Conhocton Rivers in Painted Post.

"They tell me one more week, and then I'm finally free of this godforsaken place." Arthur's voice held hope.

"The doctors say they've never seen anyone heal so quickly." Nathan grinned at his uncle's impatience as he stood beside J.P. Smith, the only other person in the room.

"It must be all that fresh air around here." Arthur smirked, but then his look turned serious. "So, this Mr. Wellington lost a hound to Scar Paw, did he?"

"Yeah," Nathan replied after a brief pause.

Frowning, Arthur said, "It's a shame a dog had to die to pay my bills."

"That's not really how the entire story goes, though, is it?" J.P. interjected. "Mr. Wellington was warned of the possible consequences and accepted the risk. Had he not been told about that rogue bear, and how dangerous Scar Paw was, then it would be a different tale to tell."

"I suppose so," Arthur conceded. "Maybe the DEC will get lucky and trap that damned thing." When the other men looked back and forth, the whipmaster asked, "What's going on?"

"You've been cooped up inside this room for more than a week," Nathan began, "so you haven't heard the local scuttlebutt.

Seems the DEC set three bear traps—just like Officer Dolan said they would. And all three traps were torn to pieces."

Even as experienced a woodsman as Arthur was, he still made a whistling noise through his teeth. "That's one ornery beast."

J.P. nodded. "They're sure it was Scar Paw that destroyed at least one of those traps from some nearby tracks the conservation officers found."

"Is there any hope of riddin' this town of this scourge?" The Forest Ghost shook his head.

Looking first to Nathan, J.P. said, "Go ahead—tell him."

"This certainly is a day of mysteries!" Arthur laughed. "What is it you want to tell me, Nephew?"

"Mr. Wellington has put up a ten-thousand-dollar reward to the hunter who bags Scar Paw," Nathan replied.

"So there's a sizeable bounty on that bear's hide, huh? Wonder how the DEC will react to that? It's too bad our state doesn't allow bear to be hunted with dogs." Arthur moved close to his bed and sat at its foot.

"There have already been some rather unprecedented moves to see to this malevolent creature's end." J.P. smiled. "The DEC sanctioned a three-week-long, extended bear season in our area, and they're even allowin' the use of hounds to run bear for this special occasion. The hunters have to tree it, though. No taking a hibernating sow bear in her den."

Resting both hands atop his cane, Arthur grinned. "Sounds like Officer Dolan took the destruction of his traps sorta personal. When does this extended huntin' season start?"

"Tonight," Nathan replied.

"It's hard to believe." Arthur's eyebrows raised. "A special huntin' season, special provisions, the government bureaucracy reactin' so quickly . . . Appears the state is takin' this threat pretty serious."

"Many bears that aren't Scar Paw might be taken," J.P. mused with a sad look.

"I hope that all the bear hides and meat taken will serve many families," Nathan said

There was a moment of silence, broken by a loud knock at the door. A tall, thin man entered. He appeared several years older than Nathan and wore blue jeans and a dark-brown canvas jacket. The stranger looked directly at Arthur. "Are you Mr. McCutcheon? The gentleman whom everyone calls 'Uncle Arthur'?"

"One and the same, young man." Arthur smiled. "How can I help?"

"My name is Melvin Snyder. I used to live around here about ten years ago, but now I'm livin' near Syracuse. Rumor has it you have a bear problem down this way."

"A problem with a hefty bounty attached," Arthur said, and then introduced Nathan and J.P. Smith, who shook hands with the newcomer.

"I won't lie to you, sir," Melvin continued. "I've come back to Painted Post to gather that reward money. My hounds and I will take this bear."

"Please, call me Uncle Arthur. And if'n you can kill that beast, Melvin, then I say more power to you."

"I own some of the finest bear hounds in the state. With the DEC allowing this one time to use them to hunt and not just train, I assure you, we'll put this old bear up."

"Melvin," Arthur began, pausing as he stood a little taller.

"Please, call me Mel," the other man interjected with a smile.

"Mel," Arthur continued, "Scar Paw isn't your typical black bear. I have never come across its likes in these hills before. That thing planned its attack on me—of that, I'm certain. Further, from what my nephew here has told me, if his hound Seth hadn't intervened, that beast would have surely killed me."

"Well, I'm a bear man and not a coon hunter, but I've heard some grand stories about your coonhound named Seth." Melvin nodded at Nathan. "Why do you call it 'Scar Paw'?"

"It has a distinctive, somewhat diagonal mark on its left rear paw," Arthur replied. "You can't miss it."

"Ah, now I get it." Melvin smiled. "Wellington's ten-thousand-dollar-reward flyer mentioned the bear had a deformed foot. That's good to know, so we can be certain the bear we take is the one we're after."

"Findin' and then takin' that bear won't be easy." Arthur's voice grew grave, his blue eyes piercing.

"Not to worry," Melvin spoke with a clear certitude. "We'll get that old bear—you'll see—and even the score for you!"

"My uncle isn't exaggeratin'," Nathan replied. "I hunt raccoon. Bear are out of my league. However, there's something very unnatural about Scar Paw. Like my uncle said, don't mistake it for anything you've run across before."

"You, too? Don't fret, coon hunter!" Mel chided good-naturedly, putting a hand on Nathan's shoulder. "This is my area of expertise. Trust me when I say we'll get that ol' bruin for sure, put it in the ground, and then make a rug out of it!"

"If you make a rug out of it, Melvin, I suspect Mr. Wellington is going to want it," the heretofore silent J.P. Smith said with a smirk on his round face.

Melvin laughed hard. "For ten thousand dollars, sir, I'll have that rug lined with silk for Mr. Wellington!" He inquired into more details about the hunters' encounters with the wanted bear—times, circumstances, and locations. But Melvin's visage grew noticeably grim when Nathan ended with the story of the death of Wellington's hound, Pride.

"Gentlemen, thank you for your time and insight. You've been a great help," Melvin concluded.

"Good luck, young man." Arthur nodded.

"I'll be leavin', too, Uncle," Nathan said. "I have to buy some parts for the tractor, and Jason wanted to help me fix it tomorrow mornin'."

"Be sure to get what you need at my store!" J.P. added quickly.

"Tell young'un Jason I say hello." The whipmaster smiled.

Nodding, Nathan turned to their visitor. "I'll follow you to your truck, Mel."

They left Arthur's room and entered the elevator alone.

After pushing the button for the ground floor, and the elevator's doors had closed, Melvin confided to Nathan, "This Scar Paw is going to be a problem." His previous bravado shown before now absent. "Once a bear learns it can kill a dog, they become particularly troublesome."

"I hope we were abundantly clear about that when we told you about how dangerous that bear is."

"Yes, you were quite plain about the whole situation, and I thank you for that."

The elevator doors opened, and the men walked into the hospital's parking lot. Melvin's truck was parked close to the entrance, and Nathan noted how the red pickup was outfitted with a "six-holer" dog box mounted to transport the man's clutch of hounds.

The bear hunter continued as they stopped near his vehicle. "I hope Scar Paw will go up a tree with an entire pack of bear dogs trailing it, versus it just having to deal with one or two coonhounds as it did before with you and Wellington."

"Rest assured, Mel," Nathan warned, looking hard into the other man's eyes. "This beast is both trouble and a killer. Pray that it's you who finds Scar Paw and not the other way around."

———•———

Late the next afternoon, sitting on the barn floor, Nathan used an old rag to wipe the grease from his hands. The tractor repair had gone faster than expected, owing to Jason getting the right tools as Nathan called for each.

"How's Uncle Arthur doing?" Jason passed another wrench.

Accepting the tool, Nathan tightened the final nut. "He's recovering well and should be released soon. He said to say hello to you." The teen beamed at that news, but then a pensive look crossed the youth's countenance. Not more than a couple of feet away, the change caught Nathan's eye. "Somethin' on your mind?"

"Uhm, no," the teen, shaking his head free of the daydream, replied and then added, "Well, yes. I was thinking it was Tara's birthday tomorrow." He paused.

"Go on," Nathan encouraged as he stood.

"I'd like to get her a present."

"That would be a kind gesture."

"So, you think I should buy her something?"

"Certainly."

"But what?"

With an understanding nod, Nathan replied, "Your mother would probably be the best source for ideas in that department."

"Well, I . . . uhm. . . ."

"Didn't want to tell your mom?" Nathan completed with a curious grin.

"Yeah." Jason sighed.

"You should count yourself lucky to have your mom. Mine died when I was very young. I'd have been grateful to have her around to ask a question like that when I was your age."

"I suppose you're right." He smiled. "What was your mom's name?

"Rose," Nathan said, but then suddenly dropped the wrench. "Da-aaah! Dang shoulder!"

"You okay, Mr. Ernst?"

"I will be," replied, reaching into his shirt to massage his collarbone. "It aches from time to time, is all."

While continuing to rub, Nathan's shirt pulled back slightly to reveal a somewhat circular scar on his shoulder. The youngster caught his breath, spying the wound his mother had mentioned when Nathan was shot during an altercation with a dangerous man on the bridge over Ryland Creek.

"I bet you're hungry." The coon hunter broke Jason's thoughts.

"Yeah! How d'you know?"

"You and food are a pretty safe wager. Besides, it's close to dinnertime, anyway. Double cheeseburger at Shirley's?"

"I was thinking steak, actually." Jason smiled boldly.

"A steak?" Nathan laughed.

"Of course! I'm a growing teenager now!"

"I'll say. Sure—a big, juicy steak it is. It'll be my belated birthday gift to you."

They put the tools away and headed to get something to eat. The drive to their favorite diner was uneventful until they arrived at the parking lot.

"Whoa!" The teen's sharp eyes spied a particular vehicle, and his mouth stayed partially open. "Look at that truck with all the dog boxes on it!"

"That's Melvin Snyder's rig," Nathan explained. "He's the hunter I told you about who's goin' for the bounty Wellington offered for Scar Paw's hide."

"If he wants to get Scar Paw, Mr. Snyder isn't going to find that ol' bear in Shirley's!" Jason's eyes narrowed.

"Well, maybe he already got him." Nathan's tone indicated he was only half joking.

"I hope so, too!"

As they entered the diner, Nathan quickly spied Melvin sitting at the main counter and staring straight ahead, with both hands cradling a cup of coffee. The stools on either side of the bear hunter were unoccupied, so Nathan took a seat to Melvin's left while Jason sat on the right. Although the old seats squeaked loudly, the man from Syracuse didn't move or say anything.

"Mel?" Nathan asked after a few moments.

"It killed them all." Melvin's voice sounded hollow as he tried to raise the coffee mug to his lips. The man who had shown such confidence just the day before in Uncle Arthur's hospital room now could not control his shaking hands, some of the black liquid dribbling over the cup's edges onto the grayish counter.

"What killed whom?" Nathan spoke slowly, his voice low, while spying Jason watching intently.

"Never seen anything like it." Melvin stared straight ahead, speaking as if trying to make sense of his own words. His eyes darted back and forth, seeing a memory no one else could.

"Go on," Nathan coaxed.

"We came across Scar Paw's trail on the Johnson Road. We knew it was him by its track, just like Arthur McCutcheon said." Melvin forced a weak smile. "I had a pack of my five best hounds, and had two local boys, Ernie and Rick Heinz, accompany me. They're excellent shots, you know?"

"I'm sure they are," Nathan replied politely. "Please continue. Tell us what happened."

"My dogs struck in, and the boys and I were certain we were going to kill that beast once and for all. When we coursed my hounds, we figured we'd cut Scar Paw off as it crossed the Bells' cornfield. You know that big field by the river?"

"Yes, I know it. Did you make it there in time to get a shot off?" Nathan asked.

"We got there all right, and we could hear my hounds. They ran for over three miles, and we drove ahead of it and set up in the woods. By Bell's cornfield." He paused for a long moment. "My dogs kept pushing that bear closer to us. Even the wind was in our favor! We were so confident—just knew for sure we were going to take Scar Paw."

Melvin paused again, attempting to sip of his drink. He was only mildly successful this time, as more coffee stained the counter.

"Then what happened?" Jason prompted breathlessly.

Still looking ahead, Melvin leaned closer to the youngster. "That bear turned and went up a narrow ravine, away from the field, as if it somehow knew we were there—near Bell's cornfield. Like it just knew! It shouldn't have gone that way, even if it had known where we were." Melvin then looked directly at Jason. The man's eyes were wide, staring through the teen.

"Why not?" Jason gasped.

"It's a narrow gap. A bear knows it doesn't have the same agility as a hound, so it should have wanted to keep a large tree at its back to protect its flank or even climb a tree to escape the hounds. Instead, it moved into that narrow opening where it would lose any advantage."

"That sounds right . . .," Nathan began, but Melvin spun in his seat to put a hand down hard on the coon hunter's forearm.

"It knew *exactly* what it was doing!" Melvin's voice cracked. "It wanted my pack in that narrow place. And then that *thing* came down on my hounds, knowing the dogs also couldn't maneuver. From the sounds of the fight, it must have killed four out of the five of them almost immediately." Melvin's voice drifted off.

Nathan glanced down at the man's hand tightening on his forearm. Then he looked straight into the other hunter's eyes. "Please, tell us more."

"Like I was saying, we heard the battle between my dogs and that monster, so we ran as fast as we could." Melvin sounded desperate, pleading. "It couldn't have been over two hundred yards. We ran as fast as anyone could have! You gotta believe me!"

"I do," Nathan replied. "You said it only killed four of your hounds. What happened to your last dog?"

"Suzie was crying out in agony!" A tear streamed down the bear hunter's face as he put his cup on the counter. "I couldn't get there

169

in time to save her." Melvin's body choked back a sob. However, rage then replaced his pain. "It tortured my poor little girl! We shouted as we got closer, trying to scare it away, 'cause we didn't dare shoot. But it just stood there. Waiting . . ."

"Waitin' for what?" Jason dared ask. "And why didn't you shoot it?"

"It waited," Melvin shook his head slowly, "until I could see it. It wanted me to know it had my little Suzie beneath its paw, just holding her there. It could've killed her like the other hounds that laid dead sprawled around that place . . . that narrow place. Then that thing looked straight at me. I've never seen a bear that big in this state!" He paused and released Nathan's arm.

Neither Nathan nor Jason attempted to urge the distraught man to continue. Instead, they waited patiently.

Mustering his courage, Melvin continued, "Once that monster knew I could see, it clamped its teeth around Suzie and broke her neck! It was then that I raised my rifle and got off a potshot. My bullet hit the cliff near its face.

"But it didn't run! Not at first. It only grunted several times, like it was laughing at us!" The man's body seemed hollow as his spirit emptied. "Animals don't do that!" The bear hunter took a deep breath. "Before I could get another shot off, it ran up the gully to where we couldn't see it anymore—like it vanished."

After a few moments of respectful silence, Nathan said, "I'm very sorry for your loss, Mel." He motioned to the teen. "Jason, let's find a table."

"You're going after it, aren't you?" Melvin grabbed Nathan's forearm again.

"We'll get it." Nathan placed a consoling hand on the other man's shoulder.

Only the shell of a man responded. "I'd go after it, but I don't have any dogs left. That thing is pure evil! Your uncle was right!" Melvin's hands fell to the counter. "He was right."

"Sorry for your loss," Nathan repeated as Melvin released his grip.

Nodding slowly, the bear hunter turned on his stool and stared straight ahead. Motionless in pained silence, Melvin relived the nightmare.

Nathan and Jason sat next to a large window in the back of the little restaurant where they could see the river. Less than a minute later, Danielle brought glasses of water and a presumptive cup of coffee, which Nathan readily accepted with a thanks.

When Danielle had deposited the menus and left to serve another table, Nathan asked, "You doin' all right after hearin' what happened to Melvin's dogs?"

"I won't lie," the teen looked at his mentor with an appreciative smile, "that was a pretty scary story. But I'm not worried 'cause we've got Seth."

"Yes." Nathan smiled. "We have Seth." After a brief pause, he said, "My promise still holds for your birthday meal if you're up for it."

"Oh, don't worry, Mr. Ernst—even Scar Paw couldn't scare my appetite away."

"I imagine not," Nathan replied.

On cue, Danielle promptly returned and took their orders. When Jason had finished, she looked from her writing pad back to the youth. "You sure you can eat all that? A large ribeye, cooked medium rare and smothered in onions, a large serving of steak fries, and a monster chocolate shake?"

"Yes, ma'am," Jason grinned confidently.

"Don't be surprised if he orders seconds." The coon hunter smirked.

"All righty. By the way, I already made your milkshake as soon as I saw the two of you pull in." She smiled and then left to turn in the order to the fry cook.

When she'd left, Jason leaned closer. "Uncle Arthur once said ol' Scar Paw had an evil spirit. I figured that old bear was dangerous, for sure, but I thought he was only joshing about the evil part."

Taking a sip of his coffee, Nathan only nodded.

Jason sat pensively until Dannie soon reappeared with a large milkshake, breaking his reverie. The teen quickly poked the straw into the frozen treasure and took a slurp.

"Not too fast," Nathan warned. "You'll get a cold headache."

"Don't worry, Mr. Ernst," Jason said after another long draw through his straw. "My pa says I have a pretty thick skull."

Shaking his head, Nathan chuckled under his breath.

"Do you think it'll leave?"

"Scar Paw? Leave Painted Post?"

"Yeah, eventually move on to new territory or maybe just die of old age or something?"

"Hard sayin'. Bears can live for many years in the wild. But someone needs to stop Scar Paw before it leaves our hometown. That thing would only cause trouble somewhere else if it's not stopped here."

"I suppose you're right." Jason bobbed his head. "So, will you go after Scar Paw like you told Melvin?" His eyes went wide.

"It will hunt you with the same cunning you hunt it," Nathan said distantly, recalling Gray Eyes' prophecy. Noticing the teen biting the straw in his mouth and staring at him with a puzzled look, he replied, "I'm thinking there's no other choice."

CHAPTER 14
A Reason for Vengeance

The soothing sound from the gushing waterfalls of Ryland Creek filled the coon hunter's ears.

The rushing noise was always soothing in the dream.

"Sharon," Nathan shook his head, "I don't run from a fight. I never have. But me and my hounds hunt raccoon—not bear! This shouldn't be our fight."

Her impish grin returned. "In some Native American languages, the name given to raccoon means 'small bear.'"

She made him laugh as she could so easily do in life.

"Thanks for the history lesson," he replied, grinning.

"My love, there are many fights we do not choose. Things beyond our control that require our involvement all the same." Sharon smiled softly, her eyes looking deep within him. "It's not a matter of desire, but one of necessity."

"You're sayin' that I must go after Scar Paw." The coon hunter sighed heavily. "That I don't have a choice."

"Beloved," she leaned in closer, taking his hand, "the choice was never yours."

Unseasonably, four leaves floated on the stream's surface— turned crimson before their time.

Somewhere in the distance, a mourning dove let out its low, sad call.

Today Uncle Arthur would be released from the hospital sometime later that morning. Nathan stood on the front porch in the chilly mid-February dawn, the steam from his coffee gently wafting up to where he could see it and smell the delicious aroma.

Remmie sat lazily in the same pen with her litter. The coon hunter could spy and hear the nearly three-month-old puppies frolicking about as their mother watched. Nathan had spent the day before preparing some of the unoccupied pens to accept the pups. Tomorrow, he would separate them by pairs and place them into the open kennels.

Taking a sip from the warm mug, he scanned the hills surrounding his farm. These rolling forests were still his home, but the thought of a rogue bear lurking somewhere beneath the oaks preyed on his mind.

Over the first week of the special hunting season that the DEC had sanctioned, three bears were taken. Two bruins, one fairly sized, had been culled in the nearby town of Hornby. The other bruin had been taken in the village of Campbell while it had raided someone's garbage. Considering that many wildlife experts estimated a typical bear's home range had a twenty-five-mile radius, these animals had held a reasonable chance of being the culprit they sought.

Unfortunately, none of those bears had the telltale mark on its rear foot. Scar Paw remained at large. Only Melvin Snyder's hounds had located it that once—an encounter that had ended tragically.

"Where is it?" Nathan asked the trees of Ryland Creek, but the forests only responded with a light wind, something his senses could not interpret.

Looking at his watch, he realized it was time to leave to pick up Uncle Arthur. Nathan smiled, knowing the Forest Ghost would want out of that infirmary the very first minute allowed.

Going inside, he took the final gulp of his coffee, donned his fedora and coat, and grabbed his truck keys. Stepping outside, the hunter could make out Seth sitting on his haunches, watching his master with an occasional look back to the noisy, ongoing puppy battles.

Ambling to the kennel to kneel on one knee before his ebony hound, Nathan said, "You'll have to teach these pups—your young'uns—how to chase coon next season when they're old enough."

First looking at his progeny, Seth turned to his master with a confident expression on the hound's face.

"I'm goin' to get Uncle Arthur." Nathan stood, evoking a sudden tail wag from Seth. "I need to pick up some groceries, too, but we should be home around noon."

The powerful hound whined happily.

The coon hunter went to his truck, and soon his vehicle's taillights disappeared down Ryland Creek Road.

Hidden within the edge of the forest, something watched the Ernst farm.

This time, it used the soft breeze to its advantage, hiding its scent from the dogs below.

One hound in particular.

Drooling as it watched the man's vehicle drive away, the beast knew its patience had paid off again.

Soon now. Very soon.

In his hospital room with his muscular back to Nathan, Arthur was naked from the waist up. On the woodsman's left shoulder was etched an old scar, narrow if about three inches long. Reaching for an undershirt, he dressed, covering the wound.

However, Nathan was too curious. "That scar—the one on your shoulder—was that self-inflicted? The one I heard about from a long time ago?"

With a reminiscent look on his face, Arthur replied, "Yes, it was my fault for more reasons than one, I suppose. But if I hadn't earned that mark, you might not be here."

"Do tell." Nathan grinned as he sat back in the plastic chair.

"I was but a teenager." Arthur smiled, seeming to stare into the past. "I was with your father, Jacob. I must've been about fifteen, which would make your father about seventeen then. It was a warm August day, as I recall.

"I decided to show off with your grandfather Paul's whip," Arthur continued. "The problem was, I was only a novice with the leather then."

"Showin' off—in front of Pa?"

"Well, your mother, Rose, had just got her driver's license, so she dropped me off on your farm, but she stayed. Although your pa and I'd been friends for a little while, my sister had only known Jacob in school—and then from a distance. Your father was a man of relatively few words, even then."

"That was Pa, for sure," Nathan agreed with a smile.

"Then some other folks showed up to buy some hay from Paul, so I decided to give a little demonstration with his whip. As I said, I didn't know how to handle a bullwhip, and I paid the price."

"That scar?"

"Yep!" Arthur replied. "Now, don't get me wrong. While I couldn't make it crack, I had that whip just flowin' back and forth, winnin' the adulation of my sister and a girl who'd come with her father to buy that hay. But it was hot, and working that whip so made it even hotter. So, I took off my shirt."

"I can see where this is goin'." Nathan smirked as he leaned forward in his chair.

"Uh-huh." Arthur put a flannel shirt on and began to button it. "I got too cocky, and on one backlash, the whip bit me in the shoulder, leavin' this scar. Oh, how your ma and pa laughed as I danced about the barnyard, howlin'. I think that was when Jacob heard Rose laugh, and when he truly saw her for the first time, so to speak."

"And that's how my ma and pa started courting?"

"Yep." Arthur finished his last button and turned around.

"A little scar doesn't seem too high of a price to pay for startin' a marriage and a family."

"I got plenty more new scars, thanks to that bear! And, uhm, well . . ." He paused.

"Well, what?" Nathan cocked an eyebrow.

"I would earn one more scar from my whip that afternoon."

"Really? I only saw one scar. Was the other on your chest?"

"No." Arthur shook his head, closed his eyes, and sighed. "A little lower . . . and behind."

The coon hunter's eyes went wide. "Well, you had pants on during this—ahem—exhibition, didn't you?"

"Like I said, it was hot. . . ." Arthur's voice drifted off, but as his nephew started laughing, the woodsman added defensively, "I was wearin' some swim trunks!"

"Just how much lower is this scar?" Nathan guffawed, nearly doubling over.

Arthur didn't answer the question directly, but he also smirked. "That's exactly how Miss Stella Burns was laughin' at me, too."

"Miss Stella *Burns?* Would that be the current Ms. Stella *Wharton?*"

"Uh, yeah." The air seemed to escape Arthur's lungs, but as Nathan continued to laugh, The Forest Ghost started chuckling as well. "Go ahead! Rub it in!"

A pretty nurse then came into the room, hearing the ruckus. "It certainly seems like you're feeling much better, Mr. McCutcheon!"

"Why yes, I am, Nurse White." Arthur nodded gratefully for the intercession. "And you've saved my life once again, young lady."

She cast a sarcastic grin. "Okay, if you're ready, there's some paperwork you need to sign at the nurse's station before you go."

"I'll be there in a few minutes," Arthur replied.

She gave Nathan a short but approving look and then left the room.

Taking in the sight of his healed kin standing tall once more, Nathan said, "And I see you're growing a beard now?"

"Yep." Arthur rubbed his chin with its silver hair matching his mane. "How's it look?"

"It becomes you," Nathan replied. "I'll head down to the lobby and meet you there after you've taken care of the paperwork." He stood. "I'll take your suitcase." He reached for the blue luggage next to the hospital bed.

"Don't bother. I can manage," Arthur said. "I shall be downstairs in about five minutes."

"See you in a bit, Uncle." Nathan paused at the doorway, his smirk returning. "You realize, if'n you go after that bear, it'll be Scar Butt hunting Scar Paw, right?"

Moving hastily, Nathan immediately stepped into the hall just as a thrown pillow slammed hard against the closed door.

———————

When the elevator opened, Nathan entered the lobby. He was surprised to find not only Jason, Tara with her father, Michael, and Bobby waiting for him, but also Mead holding Lill in his arms.

"Wouldn't miss Uncle Arthur coming home for the world!" Jason said as soon as he spotted Nathan.

"The kids insisted I drive them here." Michael came over to shake the coon hunter's hand. "And it's good to hear your uncle recovered so quickly after that bear attack. Tara tells me stories about him, as well as what I've heard over the years. He's quite the character."

"Yes, Uncle Art certainly is many things." Nathan laughed. He then promised to get the children home. Michael thanked him, hugged his daughter goodbye, and left the gleamingly sterile hospital lobby.

Walking over, Mead deposited Lill, already reaching for her uncle.

"Well, hello, little lady." Nathan smiled, accepting the child from his brother.

"Morning, Unc'a Nat'n!" she said, hugging Nathan's neck.

"Tell Uncle Art we said hello. My lovely Sarah was up with John all night. My boy is runnin' a fever again. She wants me to go to the pharmacy and pick up some medicine. Can you drop Lill off after Uncle Arthur's welcome home party is over?"

"Certainly, brother," Nathan replied, never taking his eyes off Lill. "Are you hungry?"

"Yes!" The child in Nathan's arms bounced up and down.

"I already put her car seat in your truck," Mead said, grinning. "See you this evenin'." The big man leaned over to kiss his daughter and then left the lobby.

Turning his attention to the youths, Nathan said, "Uncle Arthur should be down shortly. And do I recall correctly you had your birthday yesterday, Tara?"

"I did!" The newest teenager beamed.

Not to be left out, Bobby piped in, "And my birthday is in twelve days, fourteen hours, and six minutes!"

"With Uncle Arthur coming home, and you all being winter's children, that sounds like pizza, doesn't it?" Nathan laughed.

The teens' approving cheer was so loud that nearby Nurse Dolores, who had been pushing a patient in a wheelchair, gave a disapproving look. Under her stark glare, the youths fell silent.

When the caretaker had wheeled around a corner, Lill said, "She not happy."

The teenagers snickered at the small child's insight.

"Can we see the puppies after lunch, Mr. Ernst?" Tara asked.

"That'd be fine," Nathan replied. "I'm sure Night wants to see you again as well."

"Puppies!" Lill raised her small hands overhead.

The elevator made a ringing sound as it reached the ground floor. The sight of Arthur stepping into the lobby, despite relying on a cane and walking with the slightest limp, caused quite the commotion. The woodsman held an unmistakable look of pride as he wore his new, feather-christened black fedora.

"Uncle Arthur!" the teens and Lill shouted.

"What's this I hear about pizza?" Arthur asked.

"You heard we were going for pizza from inside the elevator, old-timer?" Bobby cocked an eyebrow.

"I'm old, young'un—not dead." The woodsman grinned.

"Old-timer?" Tara shot the redhead a harsh look, which caused the remaining preteen to shrink slightly and say no more. She then turned to the whipmaster. "Do you like pizza, Uncle Arthur?"

"Young lady," Arthur quipped, "after nearly three weeks of hospital food, I could eat the cardboard boxes the pizza comes in!"

They laughed, but then Nurse Dolores reappeared, sans the patient in the wheelchair, pushing a cart full of meal trays. Again, her deprecating expression caused the young people to hush.

Seeing her scowl, Arthur smiled at the younger woman. "Except for the food you brought, Dolores. I found that to be quite tasty."

By the way she rolled her eyes, it was clear the nurse wasn't buying the suave, silver fox's story. Still, one corner of her mouth and an eyebrow raised ever so slightly. She then entered the elevator, and the stainless-steel doors closed behind her.

Hesitating momentarily to ensure the shiny doors wouldn't reopen, Arthur leaned forward on his cane, confiding to the youngsters. "In three weeks, that's the closest thing I've seen to Nurse Dolores smilin'. Now, I say pepperoni pizza with extra cheese!"

The teens cheered and turned to rush for the exit, with Arthur keeping pace.

Speaking to the child in his arm, Nathan asked, "Ready to eat?" Lill quickly smiled at her uncle's prompt. Staring at the growing wake of the eager lunch crowd, he shook his head. "I'm feedin' three young'uns, one toddler, and one huge kid."

⎯⎯⎯•⎯⎯⎯

The Ernst farm had been left undefended for nearly two hours before the menace came. It was Seth who first caught the slightest scent on the delicate wind, and his visceral growl alerted the other hounds in their kennels.

The dark marauder emerged from the woods and lumbered across the cut cornfields. It had watched the departure of the coon hunter. It knew the farm was unprotected.

Barking furiously, Seth ran back and forth in his pen. The other adult hounds likewise took up the alarm. Even the pups, catching the scent but naïve to the peril it posed, began yipping—part instinct, part fear—as the bruin came into the farmyard.

Scar Paw moved with purpose as the massive brute stopped several feet from Seth's pen. Separated by wire mesh, the beast sensed no fear in its nemesis, who stood defiantly, howling at it.

No fear—only the desire to warn and protect the others.

The bear then looked to the adjacent kennel. Brave Remmie also lunged at the wire door as most of the puppies scurried behind her. Walking over to the kennel door that barricaded the pups, the bruin took its first mighty swipe with its front paw. The entire pen shook, groaning under the powerful blow.

The King of Hounds quickly understood the beast's motive. Rushing to the wall separating his coop and the litter, the ebony cur bit down on the wire mesh and tugged.

Again, Scar Paw struck the pen door, and the metal framework shuddered violently under the onslaught. Remmie charged at the bear from the other side, but as ferocious as the defending mother's barks were, the bruin remained unfazed.

Four of the pups cowered in the corner, terrorized as the monstrosity outside the only home they had ever known struck again. Buck and Tye, however, joined their mother, adding their small voices against the threatening menace.

Seth's neck muscles strained, but the bottom of the old fence remained firm. Then, using his entire nearly one-hundred-pound body, the black cur grunted, pulling harder and harder. The base of the wire wall relented slightly.

The beast's next assault buckled one side of the kennel's doorframe. But the door's hinges held, and Remmie continued her screaming bawls. Like Seth, the mother hound knew, beyond doubt, the attacker's intentions.

With another firm tug from the ebony cur, the fence yielded some more—now a several-inch gap. He then released his hold and bit again into the mesh. Using his incredible strength, Seth pulled, and the weakened fence surrendered more—another inch.

The gate to the pup's kennel could withstand no more. The bear stood on its hind legs and hooked its front paws onto the doorframe. With one mighty jerk, the hinges broke, and the final barrier flew away.

Selflessly, Remmie attacked the dark marauder headlong to defend her litter. That had been the good mother's mistake, for the bear's size belied its speed. Scar Paw's colossal maw clamped down on her neck incredibly fast. With a brutal shake, the beast snapped Remmie's vertebrae, and her body slumped to the ground. Motionless.

Tye and Buck barked—their voices hinting at the barreled bawls they could have as adults. The bruin saw them only as a troublesome annoyance and no threat. Seeing the other pups in the corner, it charged.

Little Night, finding her sire's fearlessness, surged forward, leaping into the air. But with a quick swipe of its paw, the bear's strength flung her tiny body brutally into the wooden coop, and the pup fell to the ground, limp.

Still huddled together, the three remaining pups found no quarter from the murderous beast as it slashed and bit.

Under the brute's onslaught, the earth of Painted Post turned crimson once more.

Using his powerful jaws to clamp down on the wire once more, the King of Hounds' efforts finally yielded a six-inch hole. Seth barked furiously, catching Buck's attention. Seeing the gap, the smart little pup dashed through the opening into the temporary sanctuary of his father's pen.

Only Tye remained inside the coop with the terror. The youngling hound attacked Scar Paw's exposed flank. Normally, the bear would have hardly noticed a bite from such a tiny animal, its thick hide protecting it from the puppy's undeveloped bite. But the clever Tye found a chink in the marauder's armor—a wound not completely healed from Seth's battle with Scar Paw in the field from a few weeks before.

With a pained roar, Scar Paw tried to reach its little attacker. But Tye had locked his teeth, and his small body flew through the air as the beast spun about. It took the bruin three complete, rapid revolutions before the pup, still unharmed, finally released his hold.

While landing on his feet, Tye slid several inches in the pen's gravel due to the momentum. The little black and tan stood bravely in the pen's corner, facing the brute.

Angered but deliberately calculating, the brute moved slowly forward. To its surprise, the little hound didn't back down. Growling terribly, the huge bear raised its paw, ready to end the insolent nuisance.

Without warning, Bill lunged at the fence wall separating his pen from the whelping kennel. The walker's screaming bawl startled Scar Paw.

Using the diversion, Tye darted for the refuge of Seth's pen.

As Scar Paw recovered from the distraction, the little hound scooted beneath it. Spinning again with an uncanny agility for an animal so large, the beast chased after the pup.

But Tye ducked through the opening to the safety of his sire.

The menace stopped short of the fence. Although separated by the wire mesh, the Great Bear and the King of Hounds were mere inches apart. The rogue paused. It could yet sense the need to protect from the dog, who stood boldly between itself and the remaining pups.

Again, to its bitter disappointment, no delicious fear flowed from the ebony cur.

None. Nothing. Whatsoever.

But Scar Paw perceived something new. Now, there was rage within its nemesis.

If not fear, then rage would do.

Hopping three times on its front paws, it grunted low, *"Huh, huh, huh."*

Then all became silent—the fateful calm in so many battles just before the end. No dogs barked. The bear didn't growl. And the wind did not blow.

Scar Paw's massive brawn tensed for its final assault on the flimsy barrier between it and victory. But then the beast froze. The hiatus in its attack had been fortunate, for its keen auditory sense could now readily hear the man's truck approaching, if still more than a mile away.

Growling a last time at its fearless ebony foe, the Killer of Puppies turned and sprinted out of the farmyard and toward the edge of the forest. Once more, the hillside absorbed the monster as its bulk faded silently into the cover of the dense oaks.

———— ◆ ————

The sky had filled with dark clouds as Nathan pulled his fully occupied truck onto the Ernst farm. Even before he'd parked the pickup, the previously cheering teens were now horrified into silence upon seeing the carnage.

Only Arthur spoke. "Oh, my God."

Giving his kin a glance, the coon hunter shoved his truck's transmission into park. "Take care of Lill, Uncle Arthur." Nathan sprinted from the vehicle to finally stop and kneel at the cooling body of the courageous Remmie.

The teens raced to Nathan's side, with Arthur following behind, carrying Lill. The whipmaster stopped far short of the massacre, though, and turned his back, not wanting the child in his arms to witness the murderous aftermath. Searching the ground, the woodsman found the telltale mark of Scar Paw's left rear foot.

With a glance at the adjacent pen, Nathan expressed a moment of gratitude at seeing Seth, Buck, and Tye, all safe.

Walking slowly to the pen, and placing her hand on the twisted metal fencing, Tara's shattered voice kept repeating the whisper, "What happened?" A weak whimper came from the side of the pen, and she rushed over, her knees firmly planted on the ground. She gently lifted Night to cradle the small pup in her arms. Tears formed in the girl's eyes as the puppy moaned softly, looking up.

Then Night exhaled her final breath.

"No, no, no!" Tara screamed. "This can't be happening!" She fell forward, her body an ineffective shield to save the lost soul.

The girl's pain coursed through the ebony hound. Seth turned and rushed to the far side of his cage, as close as his confinement would allow him to reach the forest's edge.

And Seth roared!

185

The pained bawl from the King of Hounds caused every living thing within earshot to pause until Ryland Creek finally absorbed the unusually long echo.

Stunned, Jason and Bobby remained motionless. They saw Nathan, his fists shaking at his side, as the coon hunter tried to control his growing fury.

When the first drop of cold rain hit the rim of his black fedora, Arthur hugged Lill closer and knowingly looked up into the sky with a slow, reverent nod.

The deluge came.

And Painted Post wept.

The echo of the hound's bawl reached Scar Paw, and the beast, like all other wildlife on Ryland Creek, stopped to listen. In its nemesis's voice, it could feel the delicious, satisfying sorrow.

The Great Bear searched again for fear in the dog's cry, and it sensed. . . .

No fear. Nothing. Whatsoever.

But there was something else in the ebony hound's voice that caused the bruin's massive frame to shudder involuntarily. For there, intertwined with the noble sire's pain, was a threat—a vow—that the beast and hound would meet again.

The marauder grunted heavily and proceeded deeper into the forest as the rain fell.

Soon now, it knew.

So very soon.

They'd watched Nathan dig. Each time, his shovel bit savagely into the hard earth of the Ernst family's graveyard for their beloved hounds. All the while, the coon hunter said nothing. He then gathered the bodies, one by one, and carefully positioned them in

186

the earthen depression—the brave mother surrounded by her slain innocents. Nathan then shoveled the last of the nearly frozen, wet dirt onto the mass grave.

Seth and his sons, Tye and Buck, stood nearby stoically, unmoving, watching the ritual they instinctively understood.

"Why did that thing do this?" Tears flowed freely down Tara's face as she kneeled by the grave's side. "Why'd it kill puppies? I helped *name* these puppies!"

Moving quickly over to the bereaved girl, Seth nudged her, and Tara wrapped her arms around the hound's neck, her sadness wetting his coat.

While Jason stared at the grave, Bobby looked up at the adults, searching for an answer.

Leaning on his walking staff, Arthur's long silver hair was tossed by the cold, soft breeze. The whipmaster only offered a deferring nod to his nephew. But Nathan remained quiet.

In her bright-pink coat, Lill approached the newly dug mound. She carried a small pinecone, the best she could do in the absence of springtime flowers. All watched as the little one walked to the edge of the churned soil, kneeled, and placed the cone on the grave, delicately patting it.

Joining the child, Buck and Tye took several steps forward to place their tiny paws on the fresh dirt. Their acute olfactory ability could detect the scent of their mother and siblings in the earth. Looking at the sky, they let out surprisingly loud, mournful cries. Gently, Lill pet both pups on the head. She then pointed to the field beyond, speaking more to the young hounds than to anyone else. "There they are—your mommy and your brother and sisters—right there!"

The puppies seemed to follow her finger and wagged their tails at ghosts unseen.

All silently watched the precious tot. Arthur stared intently at the child's quixotic behavior and then smiled with some peculiar insight but said nothing.

When Tara released her hold, Seth turned away to look up the hills, past the fields, and into the forests. His keen senses told him that his enemy was no longer present, but the King's body tensed as if willing the forest marauder to return one last time.

Still sobbing, Tara stood, and Jason put his arm around her shoulders. His eyes widened slightly as she accepted the chaste gesture. The teenage boy's head dropped, hiding a tear that escaped down his cheek.

With Tara's earlier question unanswered, Bobby asked, "Mr. Ernst? Why did Scar Paw do this?"

After several moments, Nathan spoke softly for the first time since setting foot on his violated home. "I don't know why tragedies occur in this world. It's something I've asked myself many times before and never found an answer. If circumstances were different, I suppose my pa would say Scar Paw was only doin' what bears do, and takin' its life in anger would be wrong."

He paused. All eyes—human and canine—were on him. An old, familiar rage welled up within him, and the coon hunter remembered the dream with Sharon that had started this day.

"I never wanted this fight, but now I'm certain of one thing." When Nathan next spoke, his voice held a coldness that made February's icy wind warm by comparison. "I don't know how, or when, or where, but that bear needs killin'."

CHAPTER 15
Beginnings, Old and New

March 1988

Affixed to the hay bale, the black-and-white target with its red center, one of four spaced evenly apart and over seventy-five yards away, appeared small. Further, the target already held some telltale signs of the shooter's earlier attempts and progress made.

Lying prone in the cold field, the teenager concentrated on the bulls-eye, allowing the front sight to blur a bit before he squeezed the trigger. The Ernst farm seemed to tense for the next shot, even the wind momentarily halting, as if Painted Post were holding its breath. Just like he'd been told it should, the .30-30 rifle's loud report surprised Jason when the weapon fired.

"Not bad shootin', young'un!" Arthur exclaimed, one hand on his walking stick, studying the target. "You nearly clipped the bulls-eye that time—less than a half inch to the left."

Bobby and Tara cheerfully applauded while Nathan, viewing the same shot through a set of binoculars, motioned his approval with the slightest of nods at Jason's performance.

While the constellation of holes in the target from his earlier attempts was not necessarily brag worthy, Jason beamed, as there was little doubt about his marked improvement.

Ten feet to Jason's left, and holding the other .30-30, Tara chimed in, "It's my turn!" She also lay supine on the frigid ground, keeping the weapon's muzzle carefully pointed down range.

"Anytime you're ready, Tara," Nathan said, focusing his spyglasses to view her target.

190

Seconds later, the bark of her rifle sounded throughout the hillsides.

"Congratulations!" Nathan then let out a low but approving whistle as he studied the target through his binoculars. "You shot dead center."

"I just imagine it's Scar Paw's head," her reply came as cold as the melting winter snow flowing in Ryland Creek, "and what I'll do to him for killing those puppies—*my* puppies."

"Whatever works for you," Arthur replied solemnly.

Tara fired the rifle four more times, loaded another five rounds, and then emptied the rifle's magazine once again. She couldn't keep her broad smile back. A comparison of her and Jason's targets showed a distinction, with the young lady's pattern being more accurate and precise. Of her ten shots, only one round had fallen outside the two-inch red center—and then not by much.

"My turn!" Bobby, ever the competitor, kneeled to tap Jason's shoulder.

With a quick roll, safely keeping the firearm pointed toward the targets, Jason handed the rifle to the redhead. "I loaded five rounds, but there's no bullet in the chamber right now. It's all yours."

"Thanks!" The redhead accepted the gun, but as the newest teen tried to load his first shell by rotating the trigger guard down, the weapon jammed.

"Remember, Bobby," Nathan spoke calmly, "you have to take the lever through its full range of motion to load and eject the shells properly."

"Right, Mr. Ernst. I apologize." Bobby's face flushed slightly, his shoulders slumping beneath the weight of his mistake. He then worked the lever correctly and successfully loaded the bullet into the firing chamber.

"Nothin' to be sorry about, young'un." Arthur likewise softly schooled, "You can't get better without practice."

With a smile, Bobby settled down, the ground a bit warmer due to Jason having been there moments before. Aiming carefully down the barrel, the youngster jerked the trigger. "Did I hit it?" he asked, looking up at the coon hunter, who intently studied the target through his binoculars.

Lowering the glasses, Nathan replied, "If by 'it' you mean the hay bale, yes. But you missed the paper completely."

"Well, if it had been Scar Paw, I'd have still got 'im!" Bobby's deflated voice sounded more than a touch defensive.

"Only because Scar Paw is as big as a house." Tara smirked.

"There's nothin' more dangerous in these woods than a wounded bear, children," Arthur said. "Take your shootin' seriously."

"Got it," Bobby replied. He fired nine more times, with his last round hitting the middle of the black ring. The onlookers, including Tara, cheered his final shot, and the redhead stood prouder.

"Load each rifle with five rounds," Arthur instructed.

Per the woodsman's request, Bobby loaded one weapon while Tara loaded the other, as Jason handed the correct number of bullets to each.

Once Tara finished loading, Arthur traded his walking stick for her rifle. "Ready?" The Forest Ghost asked, bringing the first .30-30 to his shoulder.

Nathan cocked a knowing eyebrow. "Ready."

Aiming at Bobby's target, Arthur emptied the weapon's rounds in less than ten seconds as he worked the lever action flawlessly, and the spent brass went flying into the field.

The target's center was destroyed entirely—five perfect bull's-eyes.

Handing the gun back to Tara, Arthur motioned for Bobby's weapon. Receiving the other rifle from the redhead and concentrating on the fourth unused target, the woodsman once again rapidly discharged the weapon with another flawless display of marksmanship.

"Not bad shooting for an old, silver-not-white-haired guy." Jason grinned.

"Hah!" Arthur responded with a gleam in his eyes.

Leaning in, which caused the other two teenagers to huddle closer, Tara whispered, "What does having white hair mean again?"

With his chest slightly out, Bobby replied, "If your hair turns white, you'll die in the forest."

"I wonder what happens if you go bald?" Jason snickered.

"If that occurs," the Forest Ghost intoned, somehow instantly behind them, "you get sunburnt on top of your head if'n you're not careful."

Despite themselves, the teens startled as one, proving that while Arthur McCutcheon may not have healed completely, there was no damage to his stealth.

"Tara and Bobby," the coon hunter then called out, "please help pick up the brass casings on the ground. That's a lot of money to leave here in the field. Jason, would you please give me a hand to move the bales over to the fence line?"

"Sure thing, Mr. Ernst!" Jason replied.

Walking to the bales, Nathan and Jason tore the targets from the hay and put the holey paper aside.

The teen looked back when he heard laughter from Tara and Bobby as Arthur pointed to the ground several times while the kids ferreted out the used casings. Jason put his hands beneath the parallel bale twines and hefted the nearly 60-pound load, if with some effort. "Mr. Ernst, can I ask you something?"

"Reckon you just did." Nathan laughed as he, too, grabbed a bale.

As they carried their loads to the barbed wire fence about fifty yards away, Jason cast another look at Tara. She, Bobby, and Uncle

Arthur had apparently found all the spent brass and were now ambling toward the farmhouse.

With a nod, Jason began, "Did you know when it was right? I mean," he hastily clarified, "did it feel right when you met . . . your girl?" The teen paused, searching his mentor's face.

At first, Nathan didn't respond but looked down. Had the coon hunter just heard a beautiful laugh in the soft wind or the echo of a memory? For a moment, he no longer stood in a field on a chilly March day. The frigid winter landscape melted away, and the warmth of a bygone July bloomed. He could see a pretty face, surrounded by flowing hair, suspended before him in the tepid water of a swimming hole, and an impish grin framed by wet locks in the warmer shallows that turned into an uncontrollable laugh. And then there was a petite hand holding a small rock.

At a swimming hole on Ryland Creek—a lifetime ago.

The scene evaporated as Nathan shook his head, unable to will the vision to stay, wondering if he had also spoken her name aloud.

"Mr. Ernst?" the teen prompted.

Still looking at the ground, Nathan finally smiled. "Yes, you'll know for certain if'n she's the right one."

"Tara's very pretty." Jason's words spilled out all over Ryland Creek, and he blushed.

"Pretty is maybe what first gets your attention," Nathan's eyes narrowed slightly, "but you soon realize looks are only skin deep."

"I'm the only boy in school who can beat Tara arm wrestling!" Jason grinned.

"You'll grow stronger, yet." Nathan stopped, holding the bale of hay, which caused Jason to halt as well. "But you must only use your strength to protect her."

More seriously, the youngster nodded. "Yes, sir, I will. And I know my pa would whoop my butt for sure if I ever hurt a girl."

"You've got a good father there." Nathan smiled as they resumed walking with their loads. At the fence line, they stacked the bales—Jason's load on the bottom, Nathan's bale positioned on top.

"I wonder if she'd go to the show with me. Tara said she likes movies." Jason blurted out. "There's the usual Saturday matinee this afternoon in town." The theater had a name, but he didn't have to mention it since Painted Post only had one movie house.

"You'll only know if'n you ask."

"Yeah, I suppose. I bought her a belated birthday present. It's in my coat that I left down by your house before we began target shooting today." The teen then looked down dispiritedly. "But it doesn't matter about going to the movies anyway, because I don't have much money right now."

"Here." Nathan reached for his wallet and then opened it to hand the youth a twenty-dollar bill. "I've been meanin' to pay you for your help tending my dogs."

"Oh no, Mr. Ernst! I couldn't!" Jason waved his hands. "We never agreed that I'd get paid for taking care of the hounds. I can't accept it."

"Take it. I'm thankful for what you do. I'm sure Uncle Arthur feels the same way."

Reluctantly, the youngster accepted the money, stuffed the bill into his shirt pocket, and then beamed. "Thank you, Mr. Ernst—that means a whole lot. I just hope she'll go with me."

"The trick isn't gettin' her to go," Nathan said as they started to cross the field toward the remaining two hay bales. "It's convincin' her to stay."

"But how will I know if she'll stay?" The teenager was back to being a teen again.

With a smile, Nathan replied, "You will hear it in her laugh. You'll see it in her eyes. And you'll know because she will show you when she's ready."

195

"But when will that be?" Jason's pace slowed a bit, scratching his head.

With a helpless shrug, the coon hunter walked by the bewildered teen, who then hurried to catch up as Nathan grasped the closest hay bale by its twine.

With a firm grip on the last bale, Jason asked, "But how should I act in the meantime?"

"Always be a gentleman and treat her like a lady." Nathan lifted his load.

"Did your father teach you all about girls, Mr. Ernst?" A smirk grew wide on Jason's face.

With a chuckle, Nathan replied, "There were some trails Pa let us figure out for ourselves." Then the hunter stood back, assessing the teen as if it were the first time he'd seen Jason in months. "You're getting taller."

"That's what my mom said." He beamed. "She says I'm growing out of my clothes faster than she can buy 'em!"

"I'm forced to agree." Nathan laughed.

They deposited the last two hay bales next to the others and walked down the field

Once back at the farmyard several minutes later, Jason quickly spotted Tara and Bobby inside the coonhound pen with Buck and Tye, while Uncle Arthur rested comfortably in a rocking chair on the front porch, with one of the .30-30s across his lap.

Leaving Nathan's side, Jason ran to the kennels. Bobby sat on the dog coop with Tye in his arms as Tara knelt beside Buck. "Hey, you two! Would you like to go to the movies this afternoon? I'm buying!" He then named the features playing at the movie house, and the other teens nodded vigorously.

"Oh man, wait!" a crestfallen Bobby suddenly recalled. "I promised to help my dad work on our truck. I can't go with you."

"Well," Jason said and then hesitated. Bobby had been his anchor. Now cut loose, he floated adrift in his teen angst, nervously adding, "Tara, would you alone go me with. . . . I mean, this afternoon going with me movie to. . . ." The sheer amusement that came over Tara's face as she playfully tousled Buck's ears didn't help. He sighed. "I mean, w-w-would you—"

"Jason Canton," she made no effort to hide her smirk, "are you asking me out on a date? And one that's not in the forest and without any coonhounds running around?"

Swallowing hard, Jason began, "I . . . uhh . . . uhm . . ."

"Yes." Tara rescued the floundering boy. "I'd love to go to the movies with you."

"Ahem," Arthur spoke loudly from the front porch. "Be sure to call your folks so they know your whereabouts."

Looking up, the youngsters saw Nathan standing near his uncle on the porch, with both men smiling.

"Yes, sir!" Jason shouted. "We will!"

The teenage herd ran past the men and into the house to make their phone calls. Thankfully, both sets of parents agreed to the impromptu date. Another call to the cinema determined the next showing of the double feature began in about an hour.

Redonning the light jacket he'd taken off before their target practice, Jason reached into his front pocket to ensure the little package remained where he'd put it. He then rushed by Nathan and Arthur on the porch to catch up with the other teens, who were already running hard toward the truck.

As he made his way to the porch steps, Nathan looked back at Arthur, who remained in the rocking chair and still holding the .30-30 in his lap. The woodsman scanned the forests, as if expecting something to appear. "Would you like to join us in town, Uncle Art?"

"No," the woodsman replied, not taking his eyes off the surrounding hills. "I'll stay here if that's okay by you."

"Sure, no problem. Is there anything you need?"

"Nothin' time and a clear shot won't heal," the silver-maned man finally said. With a sigh, Arthur then stared at the nearby Ernst family hound—and one damn mule—cemetery.

"It wasn't your fault when we lost Remmie and her pups," Nathan said, studying his uncle's now bearded visage.

Not speaking for a moment, Arthur replied, "Best you get the children to their movie so that they won't be late."

"Mr. Ernst!" Tara shouted from the truck. "Can we take Seth into town with us?"

As he descended the porch steps, Nathan simply gave an affirmative wave, and the young lady left the boys and ran to the kennels. When she opened the pen door, Seth jumped up, placing his paws on her shoulders, and licked her face.

"Oh, y-y-yuck!" Tara giggled as she turned toward the truck.

"I don't think she likes kissing!" Bobby whispered, leaning closer to Jason.

While Jason reflexively punched his friend hard in the shoulder, it was Jason's face that flushed red. Laughing, Bobby opened the truck door and jumped in, with Seth leaping into the front seat.

"What was that about?" Tara asked as she neared, obviously seeing Jason hit the redhead.

"Nothing," Jason spat out quickly. "You know—it was just Bobby being Bobby." Thankfully, his explanation seemed good enough for the girl as she climbed into the truck. He then joined her in the club cab's rear seat.

With Seth sitting stoically next to him, Nathan drove down Ryland Creek Road.

They first dropped Bobby off at his house with the redhead waving goodbye and saying, "Have fun!"

The movie theatre was only fifteen minutes away. As they pulled to a stop in the parking lot, Jason could see the large, plastic, black-lettered titles of the double feature prominently displayed on the white marquee. There were only about a dozen vehicles nearby.

"Thanks for the ride, Mr. Ernst," Jason said as both teenagers exited the truck.

"My pleasure. Do your parents know when the show's over?"

"Yes, sir," Jason responded. "My mom is going to pick us up in a couple of hours."

"Okay. Enjoy yourselves." Nathan smiled as his loyal hound whined.

Hearing the ebony cur, Tara stopped, leaning back into the truck cab, rising on her tiptoes to hug the dog. "You be a good boy." Seth sat motionless for a moment as she embraced him, but then he licked her across the face. "Ugh! Not again!" She giggled, wiping off the slobber.

"See you soon," Nathan said. As Tara took a few steps away, he looked directly at the young man with a reminder. "Always treat her like a lady."

"Yes, sir, I will," Jason replied with a smile and then shut the door to run and catch up with his date.

Akin to doting parents, the coon hunter and coonhound watched the two youngsters make their way into the theatre safely. Shaking his head, Nathan turned the key to start the engine. As he was about to shift the vehicle's transmission into drive, Seth growled ominously. Following his dog's gaze, Nathan saw Terry Wilkerson walking briskly across the parking lot in the wake of the two teenagers. The hunter couldn't be fooled, quickly recognizing a predator on the track of its prey.

Seth whined anxiously, looking from Terry to his master and then back at the villain, who slunk into the movie house.

"I see him," Nathan said.

———•———

There was no one in line, and Jason walked up to the ticket counter and purchased the tickets. The proud teen then went to the concession stand where he bought two large sodas and popcorn, with lots of butter, per Tara's request.

A twenty-something-year-old with a name tag labeled "Patrick" courteously heaped the popcorn into a big bucket and put the sodas into a cardboard cup holder. Jason picked up the drinks and the snack.

"You're getting taller," Tara suddenly noted, her voice somber with a hint of admiration.

Feeling close to six feet in height at that moment, Jason beamed and then reached into his coat pocket to remove a small, white box wrapped with a pink ribbon. He then handed it to her.

"What's this?" she asked.

"I wanted to give it to you for your birthday." He avoided her gaze. "It's a little late, but now seems as good a time as any."

With a smile, she pulled one of the ribbon's ends and opened the box to remove a silver bracelet that read "TARA."

"Do you like it?" Jason looked up to see her mesmerized by the gift.

"It's absolutely beautiful," she replied, if not much more than a whisper. "Did it cost a lot to get my name engraved on it?" The young lady shook her head. "I'm sorry. I shouldn't have asked that."

"It's all right," the simple boy said, "but if your name were any longer, I would've had to split another cord of firewood for Mr. Ernst."

"Goofball." She laughed softly. "But thank you, very, very much. This is so kind of you. Can you put it on my wrist?"

He did, fumbling only slightly with the tiny hasp to secure it.

Holding her hand up to admire the present, Tara then fixed her deep brown eyes on Jason, who felt a strange but somehow comfortable warmth well up within him.

They walked back to a small counter, situated before the last row of seats, to get drinking straws and some napkins. Jason put the snack tray and bucket of popcorn on the counter.

The lights began to dim in the small theatre when an all-too-familiar voice surprised the young man.

"It's been a while, cousin, and this time you're not with Nathan Ernst or that old man, Arthur McCutcheon." Terry Wilkerson snickered. "Who's the pretty girl?"

———•———

Nathan parked his pickup near the cinema's entrance. Another car drove into the lot, coming to a stop not far away, and the coon hunter saw none other than J.P. Smith behind the driver's wheel. But Nathan knew there was no time for pleasantries with Painted Post's resident storyteller. He had to get into the theatre and quickly.

Looking at his agitated hound, he said, "Calm down, boy. I'll be back soon."

As the door shut, Seth moved quickly to the driver's side to watch his master depart.

The faithful dog's loud bark caused Nathan to stop and walk back. With their faces only separated by the truck door's window, he said, "Easy now, Seth. I promise I won't be gone long."

The man's comforting tone did little to mollify the ebony cur, who whined nervously while watching his master open and step through the theatre's glass doors to disappear within.

———•———

"Leave us alone, Terry." Jason said, unmistakably seething.

"No, I don't believe I will. We're kin, as it is." Terry laughed and reached with his grimy paw to take a handful of their popcorn.

"Oh, that's so gross!" Tara watched the man shove the popped kernels into his face, not entirely closing his mouth with each chew.

"C'mon, let's leave this loser." Jason motioned to the concession stand. "I'll buy some more popcorn."

"Not so fast!" Terry quickly reached for Jason but, in the dim light, accidentally grabbed the girl by the wrist and pulled her closer.

201

Even when he realized his mistake, the bully didn't relinquish hold of his unintended hostage. "Don't you walk away from me, son! I wasn't done talkin' to you yet."

There was no warning. Instead, Jason struck his third cousin, by marriage, square in the face. He felt sure that's what Mr. Ernst would have done.

While he absorbed the teen's punch, Terry was surprised by how hard the youth hit. Reflectively, he cocked his free fist back to retaliate. But the quick-thinking Tara, still in the villain's grip, brought the heel of her boot down on the top of Terry's instep. The ugly little man shrieked in pain, released the girl, and hopped several times on his unwounded foot. It only took a few moments for Jason to position himself in front of Tara before Terry regained some semblance of composure.

Now, heads in the theatre had turned about to see the commotion. Another pair of teens, a vaguely familiar boy and a girl not much older than Jason and Tara, stopped to watch the spectacle.

If there was anything Terry Wilkerson hated most, it was being shamed in public. He'd show this insolent pup, family relation or not, that nobody could get away with embarrassing him—not now or ever. He lunged at his defiant cousin and was almost upon Jason, but then it happened again, similar to that day several months ago in Shirley's diner. Something stole the villain's momentum and viciously spun him around like a top.

There was no, "I warned you once," or, "I told you to leave him alone." Jason had been right—that wasn't Nathan Ernst's way.

Unprepared, Terry Wilkerson took a brutal hit to the face. The theatre's darkness seemed closer and swooned about him. Years later, the villain would recall that punch as the second-hardest punch he'd ever taken in his entire life.

The hardest came a few seconds later.

The coon hunter's second strike caused the curtains to fall on Terry's consciousness. Had it not been for Nathan quickly grabbing the man's shirt, the antagonist would have dropped unceremoniously into the waste receptacle, as appropriate as that may have been.

Lifting the unconscious man by the shirt, Nathan set Terry in a sitting position against the wall. To the astonished look on Tara's face and Jason's approving smile, he said, "You two can enjoy your movie now."

"We will." Jason smirked. "Now."

Nodding his goodbye, Nathan began to leave as the theatre lights were then completely turned off. A preview of coming attractions lit the main screen while a narrator's loud voice hyped an upcoming action feature.

Quickly stepping forward, Jason placed his hand on Nathan's forearm. There was no "Thanks, Mr. Ernst" spoken aloud. There was no need. One coon hunter had helped another, and it was as simple as that. A silent gratitude shared.

In the darkened hallway, Terry revived, shaking his head. No one noticed the bitter little man stand in the theatre's flickering light. He reached into a pants pocket and removed a switchblade. The rising volume of the movie trailer masked the spring-loaded noise of the blade ejecting from its hilt. Taking several quick steps forward, the villain aimed the knife at the unsuspecting coon hunter's back.

The razor-sharp blade was in motion. Only six inches away.

Their vision had not adjusted to the darkness, so they couldn't see clearly.

With the knife's tip less than three inches away, Terry sneered, certain he would have retribution this day.

In that instant, Jason saw the blade's silver metal catch a glint of light from the theatre's lobby, but it was too late. The teen's eyes went wide, and the words froze in his mouth.

Now, the blade was only an inch from Nathan's back.

Then something emerged from the hallway's blackness. Something capable of seeing in the darkest hollows of Ryland Creek. Its white fangs gleamed in the shadows and clamped down on Wilkerson's wrist with excruciating pressure. The momentum of the large hound's body drove Terry to the hard floor.

The would-be villain screamed in agony as Seth's jaws tightened harder, and with his powerful neck, shook the man. Terry's hand opened, and the knife dropped noisily onto the tiled floor.

When Seth had finally stopped jerking him about, the miscreant clenched his free fist to punch his canine attacker. But as he tried to strike, a boot came down hard on his forearm. Between the leather shoe and the fangs, Terry lay stymied and helpless. The King of Hounds then placed his huge front paw on the little man's chest, firmly planting the villain to the floor.

"Get off me, Ernst!" Terry screamed. However, when he looked up, he found that the boot pinning him to the ground belonged to Jason Canton.

"I saw what Terry just tried to do, Mr. Ernst," Jason said. "But I couldn't warn you in time. My sorry excuse for a cousin almost stabbed you in the back."

With a thankful nod to the teen, Nathan knelt. He leaned in close to the trapped man's face, with the nearness erasing all ambiguity. "I truly didn't care much for you botherin' your cousin, but I promise you this—I'd have taken it *real* personal if'n you'd hurt my hound."

Certain retribution would follow, Terry closed his eyes, waiting for the inevitable blow that would relieve him of his senses. Instead, he heard several footsteps, and then an entire bucket of popcorn, with lots of butter, rained over his face.

"You forgot your snack," Tara said.

Wagging his tail, Seth released his hold on the man's arm, looked at the girl, and snorted.

Nearly out of breath, J.P. Smith came rushing around the corner. "Oh, there you are, my heavens! I'm so sorry, Nathan! I saw Seth out in the parking lot, acting all excited. When I opened your truck to calm him down, he jumped out and ran straightaway to the front doors. He got inside when some other patrons entered the cinema before I could catch up."

"That's quite all right, J.P. It turned out for the best just the same," Nathan replied. Focusing back to Wilkerson, the coon hunter's eyes hardened. "I highly recommend you go. Now."

Jason removed his boot from his cousin's arm, allowing the shamed bully to stand. As Terry tried to leave, the younger man quickly grabbed the other's shoulder. When the villain looked up, the teen said, "After today, we're no longer kin."

With his head down, Wilkerson ran out of the movie house.

The teenaged couple who had watched the spectacle unfold also started snickering. The other young man turned to his pretty date. "This show is going to have a hard act to follow!"

"I'll get us some more popcorn," Jason said to Tara.

"Patrick," J.P. called to the theatre employee behind the white counter, "there's a spill here that needs cleaning." The resident storyteller then said to Jason and Tara, "Let me treat you to some snacks from the concession stand."

"Thank you, sir, but you don't have to do that," Jason said.

The local purveyor winked. "No, no—it's my pleasure, son. And thanks to you and Seth, I get to watch this film vermin-free."

Nathan laughed while Jason grinned.

"I love you!" Tara shouted happily.

For a moment, Jason's heart leaped, but when he turned, he saw his date leaning over, planting a kiss on Seth's large crown.

"If I'm going to play second fiddle," the teenaged boy muttered, "it might as well be on account of Seth.

In his truck, convinced Wilkerson had truly left the premises, Nathan paused before shifting the transmission into drive.

The King of Hounds sat stoically in the front seat, staring out the truck's windshield as if nothing extraordinary had just happened.

"That's twice you've saved my life," Nathan said to his trusted companion.

Upon hearing his master's voice, Seth looked nonchalantly at Nathan, turned back to stare ahead once more, and gave a quick snort.

"Guess it's just all in a day's work, eh, boy?" He smirked, but the ebony cur only continued to peer out the window. Regally.

But then again, it was Painted Post after all.

———— ∘ ————

"Do they remind you of anyone?" queried the young woman with the forever impish look as she sat beside the waterfalls.

In the slower moving water, two bright-green, upturned leaves swirled such that their stems crossed to float gently on the pool's surface.

"Jason and Tara?" Nathan asked, sitting close to her.

"Yes," Sharon replied.

With a grin, he softly admitted, "Yeah, they remind me of us."

"Now do you understand?" Her eyes narrowed.

The sing-song melody of a scarlet tanager momentarily interrupted the coon hunter. He listened to the bird's soft twittering. After a few moments, Nathan responded honestly. "Understand what?"

Sharon grabbed his face with both hands, bringing him closer to kiss him, her warmth cascading through him.

When she released him, their faces still so close now that her hair brushed his cheek, the pretty ghost slowly shook her head, laughing and sighing. "You are hopeless, my love."

CHAPTER 16
Cat and Mouse
Late June 1988

For a time, the forests of Ryland Creek breathed deeper, more naturally again. There had been no sign of Scar Paw for over two months. Its last known encounter, much to the chagrin of Officer Steven Dolan, was the destruction of yet another DEC bear trap in early April.

But then—nothing. The cunning beast seemed to have disappeared as insidiously as it had appeared.

At a local fire department one warm Monday afternoon, with nearly fifty residents attending, Officer Dolan proudly droned on about the statistics of the special bear season. With some fancy slides displayed on an overhead projector before rows of gray, metal folding chairs, the officer recounted that six bears had been taken. Another bruin had been caught near a dump and relocated to the Adirondacks.

Standing, Arthur McCutcheon said, "None of those bears killed—nor the one you trapped and moved—were the one that's caused all the trouble." The crowd turned to see the silver-maned man, the local authority on the forests, and who'd come closer than anyone to the beast in question.

At first, Dolan seemed indignant until he recognized the no-longer-bedridden speaker. Keeping his voice measured, the state official said, "Well, it's possible, Mr. McCutcheon, that the nuisance bear may have died of old age."

That response evoked a wave of snickering from the attendees.

"That's more likely what *will* happen one day," a woman in the back shouted, "because you ain't the one who's goin' to catch 'im!"

The crowd laughed again—only harsher.

To his credit, the young man from Albany, with his face turning light red, then suggested, more humbly, "It is possible the bear moved on—maybe into Pennsylvania."

Bill Welty, the farmer who had lost part of his herd and prized bull to the rogue, then stood. "Did you think to call the Pennsylvania Department of Wildlife to tell them this theory of yours?"

Before Dolan's deepening embarrassment would allow him to respond, the local Forest Ranger, likewise in a green uniform, spoke up. "I have been in routine contact on the subject with my counterparts in Pennsy, Bill. I've also asked them to let me know if they take or trap any bear with Scar Paw's markings."

"Thanks, Gary." Bill gave a satisfied smile.

"Steve," the Forest Ranger continued, "why doesn't Albany extend the special hunting season? Same rules as before—no shooting a bear if you see more than one at a time or a yearling, which will prevent taking a mother or her cubs, and focus on the bear we're looking for."

Leaning closer so his uncle could hear, Nathan said, "At least one government official has their act together."

Arthur nodded in silent agreement and sat once more.

"I'll see what I can do, Gary. In the meantime, we'll continue to set our traps," Dolan replied but couldn't hide his waning confidence.

With the meeting finally ended, the local citizenry grumbled and emptied the fire department.

With a sigh, Nathan said, "If'n you don't mind, Uncle Art, I'm going to head to Addison for a bit. I need to think."

Since they had come to the meeting in separate vehicles, Arthur waved goodbye. "I'll meet you at the house. I feel like making spaghetti and meatballs tonight. Dinner should be ready around six o'clock."

"I should be back by then." Nathan smiled.

The drive to St. Catherine's church in Addison only took about ten minutes. The tall, red maples circling the church's parking area were adorned in their summer bright green and shaded the coon hunter's short walk.

Nathan stepped into the house of worship through large wooden doors and sat down in a dark-brown, oaken pew. The sun remained high in the sky such that the stained-glass windows' filtered light gently flooded the interior. The Stations of the Cross lined the walls, seven on either side of the church. There were pastel yellows and blues everywhere, with a faint smell of incense and candles permeating the place with a blessed solitude.

Two life-sized statues were at the front, gracing both sides of the altar. Mother Mary, in a brilliant-blue dress, held the child Jesus in one arm. The other statue was of an adult Christ, adorned in a magnificent, ankle-length, white cloak, with a bright red sash draped over one shoulder, both hands reaching upward. There the statues stood—from east to west, the birth and the resurrection, the alpha and the omega.

He was alone, or leastways, there were no other people there. The coon hunter sighed softly, remembering the many Sundays and holy days of obligation—a content recollection of the sermons and lessons learned.

As he closed his eyes, memories flashed before him. Nathan could see his father, Jacob, and Mead, when his sibling had been the happy-go-lucky child. Smiling, he recalled a teenaged Sharon, as if she sat next to him now, her angelic face as she kneeled quietly, praying. He then imagined Lill giggling and skipping through a field, trying fruitlessly to catch yellow-winged butterflies, as he and Sharon had once attempted to put fireflies in a jar—a long time ago.

Then there was the image of Seth, as a young hound, running through the forests, taunting his sisters to keep up, which made Nathan smile. Even as a pup, the ebony cur had shown extraordinary speed and agility. Furthermore, the dog embodied a nobleness foreign to most men. The hunter said a grateful prayer.

Darker thoughts found their way into his consciousness. Memories of two coffins, on separate occasions, being lowered into the ground. There was the harsh sound of his shovel biting into the cold earth of Painted Post. More images—those of the final clod of dirt landing on the cold mounds—the graves—as he buried the mule, Butch, and Remmie and her slain pups.

In Nathan's mind flashed Jason's saddened countenance.

Bobby holding back tears.

Tara's shattered spirit.

And tiny Lill placing the pinecone on the wet earth.

Then he was in the hospital, beside Uncle Arthur's bed, and a false memory born of fear emerged as his uncle's heart monitor went from a comforting blip to a steady, flat tone.

Then came a vision of the beast, Scar Paw, in all its unholiness. A malicious look crossed the beast's face, the abomination that threatened Painted Post. It stood before him, defiant, only the hunter and animal. It charged, but neither in life nor this vision could he turn away.

And then that horrid, mocking sound.

Huh, huh, huh.

The coon hunter's teeth clenched, and his fists trembled, the manifestation of rage that came so naturally all his life with the constant struggle to contain his temper. His hands were not his own, audibly pattering the wooden seat. A sense of guilt filled him. How could he bring this anger into such a holy place? The hunter, eyes still closed, tried to abate his feelings.

A warm, soft touch suddenly rested atop his right hand. The sensation should have shocked Nathan, being caught wholly unaware. Instead, his fury flowed away, and his mind calmed. He opened his eyes to peer into the gentle face of Father Simmons.

210

Just sitting there, the priest, dressed in black with a white collar, smiled. Intuitively, the retired cleric waited for the younger man to speak.

"I'm sorry, Father." Nathan began his confession.

Shaking his head slightly, Simmons raised a finger to his lips, and sat back in the pew that creaked noisily in the mostly empty church. His eyes were drawn to the same statues that Nathan had focused on earlier.

The coon hunter sat dumbfounded, waiting.

Finally, after nearly an eternal minute, the cleric spoke. "I often find, in the tranquility of this place, the answers come to my mind. I'm likewise certain those thoughts are not entirely of my own conjecture."

Nodding, Nathan replied, "I feel likewise. There is peace here."

"I remember watching you, Mead, and your father every Sunday, sitting in these pews." The priest laughed. "Your brother would fall asleep sometimes during my homilies." He straightened in his seat again. "Those were innocent times."

"What I'm wanting to do now isn't exactly innocent." Nathan spoke slowly. Upon seeing the surprise on the priest's face, he hastily added, "Is revenge always wrong, Father?"

"It's the thoughts and schemes that vengeance stokes that often lead to the committal of grave sin." His smile remained friendly, and he continued after a slight pause. "You're going after that bear—the one the people here call Scar Paw—aren't you?"

With his jaw dropping, Nathan looked up, wondering if something divine had not imparted his inner thoughts.

"I was at the meeting with Officer Dolan, too." Father Simmons grinned. "I sat in the back."

Lowering his eyes, Nathan smirked at the revelation. But then his face grew grim. "That bear mauled my Uncle Arthur, nearly killin' him. It came onto my farm and slaughtered my hound Remmie and four of her pups, and it also killed Butch, our mule."

"Understandably, you're upset," the priest acknowledged with a nod. "And the state of New York and the people here share your concerns. Most believe this rogue animal won't stop its killing. Perhaps it cannot stop." He paused. "Do you think it will strike again?"

"That's all true," Nathan replied. "And yes, I believe Scar Paw will attack once more."

"I am not trying to rationalize anything about this situation, my son. Yet often, the *reason* we do something can be the difference between sin and virtue."

"I've been struggling about whether I should even try to hunt this . . . this thing. I'm not sure I'm up for the task."

"Some of the greatest prophets and saints were also some of the most unsure and reluctant individuals." The priest nodded with a pensive look. "This little church's patron, Saint Catherine, once noted that if people could overcome self-doubt, they need fear no other enemy."

A balm entered Nathan's soul. The last bulwark of hesitation in his heart collapsed.

"I will stop this bear from doing anymore harm." The coon hunter's eyes then peered through the priest. "I will defend my family and my home."

———— • ————

The huge bruin slumbered in the growing, dusky shadows of The Black Oaks of Ryland Creek. Here, it felt comfort beneath these ancient and twisted trees that purportedly trapped the souls of nefarious men who died in this woodland. Since it had been a cub roaming the forests of Painted Post, Scar Paw had known the legends about the Black Oaks were not simple human fantasy. The fettered evil that emanated from this place permeated the bear's mind and body.

212

An image of the ebony hound then formed in the beast's unconsciousness. The sleeping brute let out a growl loud enough that it caused several whitetail deer, over a hundred yards away, to bound deeper into the forest.

A mosaic of images became connected, integrated into its deep torpor. Scar Paw breathed a heavy grunting noise.

"Huh, huh, huh."

It would attack once more.

And with pure malice, it would destroy the heart of Painted Post.

Late June perennially brought final exams at the end of the school year. Maintaining high grade point averages, Jason, Tara, and Bobby were already looking forward to the fall's hunting season.

For now, it was summer, and the teens helped Nathan ready his haying equipment, huddling around the tractor in the barnyard on this bright sunny day. Thankfully, the alfalfa was tall this year, for spring had brought plenty of rain. Now, a soft wind tickled the green fields, with the tall grass heads undulating in response.

Handing Nathan a wrench, Jason asked, "Did you hear the DEC extended the bear season for another month just to catch Scar Paw?"

"Yes, I did." Nathan accepted the tool and placed it atop one particularly stubborn nut.

"Do you think that ol' bear is still around, Mr. Ernst?" Tara asked. "Might it have moved on?"

"Could've," Nathan groaned as he applied pressure to loosen the nut. "It's been a while with no sign of that thing." The coon hunter didn't mention, though, his fears that the bear remained in the forests, watching and waiting.

The doors to the farmhouse were open, so when the telephone rang inside, all could hear.

"I'll answer it!" Bobby gave a short jump.

"Thanks, young'un." Nathan smiled, and the redhead turned and sprinted to the house.

"Where's Uncle Arthur today?" Tara asked.

"He went into town to get us some parts," Nathan spoke, his last word sounding more like a grunt as the nut finally relented.

"Something is always breaking on a farm, huh, Mr. Ernst?" Jason waxed philosophical.

With a nod and a laugh, Nathan said, "Certainly seems that way."

"How are Tye and Buck doing?" Tara stole a glance at the beautiful black and tan pups, each in their separate kennel. While their frames had not filled out yet, Seth's sons were nearly as tall as he was.

"They're doin' well." Nathan handed the wrench back to Jason. "I'm eager to start their training."

"Do you think they'll be as great as Seth someday?" Jason asked.

"Good, maybe. But as good as Seth?" Tara interjected, sounding more than a little doubtful and casting a quick look at the ebony hound, who sat on his haunches.

Well within earshot, The King of Hounds snorted.

"Mr. Ernst!" Bobby ran onto the porch. Whether he was out of breath from the earlier run or excited, no one knew. "It's Mr. Welty on the phone! He said a huge bear just killed one of his calves, and he can still see it in the upper part of his field! He's sure it's Scar Paw!"

The teens stared at the coon hunter, who at first only remained silent, motionless. Nathan finally spoke. "Bobby, tell Bill I'll be right over." The redhead disappeared back into the house. "Jason, fetch me one of the .30-30s. There's a backpack with some extra supplies just inside the doorway—bring that, too. Quickly now."

"Yes, sir, Mr. Ernst!" Jason sprinted away. In less than two minutes, he returned with the gear as Tara and Nathan finished putting the tools away.

"Should we wait for Uncle Arthur?" Tara asked.

"Uncle Art would certainly be a big help, but I don't know when he'll return. By that time, Scar Paw might disappear back into the woods." She nodded, and he continued, "Load Seth in the truck. There's a lot of bad blood between those two, and I think he'll understand we're huntin' Scar Paw today."

"You're taking Seth?" Tara's eyes grew wider, and her worry crystal clear.

"I won't let him off my leash," Nathan promised. "Now go."

Five minutes later, Seth was loaded into the truck. Jason held the backpack as the two other children watched Nathan put the rifle into the back seat.

"I'll drop you off at your homes. I don't want you in the woods when we know that bear is around."

"Mr. Ernst, we're going with you." Jason's tone was firm, acting as advocate for the other young people.

The determined look on the teen's face almost made Nathan laugh. "It's too dangerous, and your parents would never agree, and further—"

"My pa said there's no safer place in the woods than with you and Seth." Jason spoke up quickly, the first time he'd ever interrupted Nathan. "And like you said, if we wait too long, Scar Paw might be gone."

"My dad says the same thing!" Tara nearly shouted.

All eyes turned to Bobby, and the redhead grinned. "Eh, what my parents don't know won't hurt 'em."

"I'm not so sure," the coon hunter said, hesitating.

"There's no time to lose, Mr. Ernst," Jason persisted. "If you drop us off, Scar Paw might disappear into the forests for another couple of months."

The youngster's logic was hard to refute.

"It's against my better judgment, but all right," Nathan finally conceded, surveying the teenage wall of resistance. His jaw then tightened. "And this time, we hunt Scar Paw and not the other way around."

———— • ————

The conversation between Nathan and Bill Welty was short, for in the upper field about three hundred yards away, all could easily see the beast's massive form while it gorged on its kill.

"I'd go after that monster myself," Bill said. "I could sure use that bounty money, but these old bones aren't good for much anymore. And wouldn't you know it—the DEC has one of their traps in my upper field. But instead of getting caught in it, that durn thing goes after another of my calves!"

Nathan and the boys stood around the truck. Tara held Seth on a leash nearby.

"We'll do what we can do, Bill," Nathan replied. "Young'uns, we will follow along the hedgerow." He pointed to a row of trees, mostly tall, mature, shagbark hickories that separated two of the farmer's large fields. "We'll sneak along the far side to hide our approach. If we can make it within a hundred yards of Scar Paw, I should be able to get a clear shot. We need to stay quiet, okay?" The coon hunter stared at his hound. "That includes you, too, boy."

Seth snorted.

"Mr. Ernst," Jason grinned, "sometimes I think Seth understands English."

Nathan stopped to give a short laugh. "Better than I do, most days."

Seth snorted again.

"I'll carry the backpack," Jason volunteered as he put his arms through the 20-pound sack's straps.

"Thanks," Nathan said. "Now follow me and remember to stay quiet."

"Good luck killing that monster!" Bill waved as the hunters departed.

Thankfully, the hedgerow, so key to their strategy, began near the base of the steep hillside. The hunting party waded their way through nearly seventy head of Welty's cattle. While the cows had likely congregated by the barn for refuge from the bear, the herd now helped mask the hunters' movements.

"Oh man!" Bobby moaned, stepping into a giant pile of cow droppings.

"Hush!" Tara whispered harshly, justifiably swatting the redhead's shoulder. "Besides," she grinned, "the manure will help cover up your smell."

At first, Jason worked hard to stifle a laugh. Stealing one last glance as they made it to the thick hedgerow, he whispered, "It's still there, and it doesn't look like Scar Paw has seen us yet."

Nathan only nodded as they continued to move uphill quickly but silently.

The leafy hickories were interspersed with white dogwood bushes. While the heavy foliage hid the hunting party's approach, it likewise prevented them from seeing the exact whereabouts of the beast.

After what seemed forever, Nathan held up one hand, holding the .30-30 with his other, and spoke just above a whisper. "We should be close. Stay put. All of us goin' through the bushes at the same time will make too much noise. I'll go it alone now."

The kids nodded silently, with Seth only making a low, anxious whine.

Painstakingly, Nathan worked his way through the bushes. If he were right about their location, they should still be slightly below the bear, downwind, and within a hundred yards. The hunter wished he had his uncle's stealth, but there was little other choice at this point. Controlling his breathing, he moved through the thicket, step by slow, cautious step.

It seemed the longest ten feet he'd ever spanned, but finally, the rifle's barrel cleared the other side of the brush. Immediately, he spied the sightless eyes of the mutilated calf staring at him less than seventy-five yards away. Emerging from the dogwood, Nathan quickly brought his rifle up to take aim at . . .

Nothing. Scar Paw was nowhere in sight.

"You're nearby, aren't you?" Nathan muttered low, silently vowing he wouldn't fall for the evil bear's trick that had nearly killed Uncle Arthur. The coon hunter kept his weapon ready. "Young'uns," he whispered just loud enough for them to hear. "Cut through the bushes. Quietly now. I don't see Scar Paw, but it could be close by."

While not speaking, the teenagers unfortunately made more noise than Nathan had hoped. When they finally emerged, Tara still held Seth's lead.

"Where is it?" Bobby asked.

"Not sure," Nathan conceded. "It's unlikely it caught our scent since the wind is in our favor. But with this bear, all bets are off. Let's go."

The hunting party walked across the short-cropped grass to the half-eaten calf.

"There! Its tracks!" Tara quickly pointed. "And they lead farther up the field."

As the sharp-eyed young lady had said, the bloodied paw marks traveled uphill. Adding to the mystery of the bruin's whereabouts, their view was blocked by another thick row of trees about fifty yards away that ran perpendicular to the hedgerow they had followed. Where the two tree lines nearly merged was a small opening, just large enough to allow Welty's tractor into the uppermost field. The bear's path suggested it had passed through that gap.

"Scar Paw might be waiting for us right on the other side of those trees!" Bobby's voice trembled.

"Tara," Nathan said, "let me have Seth now." She walked over and handed the leash to him. "Come now, boy, nice and easy," he murmured to his hound. He then walked toward the opening, with the teenagers following closely, casting wary looks about as if expecting the bear to appear at any moment.

With his nose to the ground, Seth let out a low growl. While the bear's footprints were no longer visible—the grass wiping the unfortunate calf's blood from the bruin's feet—the exceptional hound could not be fooled, knowing exactly where Scar Paw had passed through the pasture.

When they reached the opening between the fields, Nathan paused.

"Is everything okay, Mr. Ernst?" Jason asked. "Do you think that bear is waiting for us on the other side?"

"No." Nathan sounded disappointed. "Seth would be much more excited if it were nearby."

Despite their mentor's assurance, the teens held their breath as they walked through the gap. Instead of seeing the ruthless marauder bearing down on them, they spied something strange but man-made.

"What is that?" Jason pointed to a long, silvery tube mounted on a four-wheeled axle not far away. The contraption was about forty inches in diameter. One end of the pipe was welded shut, while the other side had a thick, rust-colored iron slab with metal rails to guide it, positioned directly above the opening.

"That would be Officer Dolan's solution," Nathan began, but the youngsters' confused looks caused him to continue. "It's a bear trap. There are likely donuts and bacon grease on the inside meant to lure a bear into the tube. Once inside, the critter will trip a lever, and that door will come slammin' down behind it."

"Donuts?" Bobby sounded hopeful.

"Not for you, knucklehead," Tara said, her glare enough to make the boy wince.

Tugging again on the leash and with his nose still to the ground, Seth knew precisely where Scar Paw's trail led. Nathan let his hound gently pull him up the long field with the teenagers following close. When they came to the forest's edge, the ebony cur confirmed the rogue had taken a narrow path deeper into the woods. While there was also the scent of a raccoon here, the exceptional hound obeyed his master's desire to follow the renegade bear.

They continued, slowly, beneath the full, early summer green canopy of red and white oaks. In some places, the grade was steep. Nearby, a small runoff stream popped and gurgled.

After nearly ten minutes of walking in the growing heat, Jason whispered, barely loud enough for all to hear. "Can we take a rest, Mr. Ernst?"

With a nod, Nathan said nothing as Jason removed the backpack and set it beside the base of a spreading red oak. The coon hunter was lost, deep in thought as the youngsters milled about before him.

They'd walked several hundred yards, and the position of the sun had changed. Now, they were circling back toward the Welty farm. The hill on their right, to the west, gently sloped above them. The wind no longer favored them, and Seth would be scent blind, unable to detect the bear's spoor in the breeze.

A memory forced its way into the coon hunter's mind.

"You must know this truth, Seth's Master," Nathan said low, repeating Gray Eyes' warning. "This creature will hunt you with as much skill and cunning as you hunt it."

"Mr. Ernst?" Jason asked with the same puzzled look as the other teens.

Years of communing with the forests of Painted Post had honed Nathan's awareness like a knife's edge. Without a word, Nathan wheeled about to face behind them, bringing the rifle to his shoulder and firing the weapon almost instantly. The subsequent explosion seemed even louder, echoing in the tight forest.

Less than fifty yards away, the bullet struck the trunk of a black oak, missing the waiting Great Bear's head by less than an inch. So close had the near-fatal shot been that sharp splinters from the twisted tree drove into Scar Paw's face, and small steam of blood flowed down the monster's cheek.

Caught off guard, the colossal bear let out a shocked roar.

"D'Aaahh!" Nathan screamed as he jacked another shell into the gun's chamber, aiming the weapon, praying for just one more chance.

But Scar Paw was faster. The beast vanished into the forest's greenery.

After several tense moments, Nathan finally lowered the gun but kept his eyes focused on where Scar Paw had escaped in the vain hope the bear might reappear.

The young people stood, dumbfounded. It had happened all too suddenly—never even giving them a chance to scream—but they had seen where Nathan had aimed and watched as the beast spun about and disappeared.

Also realizing the missed opportunity, Seth let out a loud growl, understanding the marauder's tactics.

Jason was the first to find his voice. "How . . . but how did you know Scar Paw was behind us, Mr. Ernst?"

"Because that's how I'd have hunted my prey." Hope bled from the upset hunter. "We missed our chance to kill that thing. We won't see it again today. Hopefully, there'll be another chance." Nathan sighed. After several long moments, he said, "Let's head home."

Forming a single line of disappointment, they began the long walk back.

After traveling nearly three hundred yards, they reached the upper end of the field when Jason stopped. "Oh, Mr. Ernst, I left the rucksack in the woods! I'm sorry!"

"It's all right, young'un." Nathan turned and chuckled. "I should've noticed you weren't wearin' it. Guess I was a bit down about not killin' that bear. But I remember where you left it. I'll go back with Seth and retrieve it." Far below, they could see the safety of the Welty farm. "We'll meet you kids at the truck. Just head downhill—you can't get lost."

"Do you think Scar Paw is still around?" Tara asked.

"No," Nathan replied. "With our luck, that bear is probably in Schuyler by now." The coon hunter mentioned the neighboring county nearly twenty-five miles away. "Scar Paw is a hideous thing, but I don't reckon it's *that* clever to try and attack again today."

"Okay, Mr. Ernst." Jason nodded. "You be careful, and we'll see you down at the truck."

"Remember—no dillydallying—straight back to the farm." Nathan turned with Seth at his side.

"Will do!" Jason said, and the teens watched their mentor and his loyal hound disappear into the lushness.

The kids walked and laughed, talking excitedly about the bear chase. They stopped for a moment near the DEC's silverish trap with its artificial maw beckoning and noticed the elongated metal tube had many holes drilled in it.

"I bet that's so a bear can breathe easily once it's trapped," Tara said, pointing at the perforations.

"I'd bet you're right," Jason replied.

Continuing again toward the narrow opening, the teens hadn't gone ten yards when something large and black suddenly filled the hedgerow's gap. The menace that stood on four legs, staring directly at the children, let out a low grunt.

"Huh, huh, huh!"

Jason nearly screamed, "It *is* that clever!"

The bear ambled toward them, less than a hundred fifty yards away.

"What do we do!" Tara grasped Jason's nearest arm.

222

"The trap!" Bobby shouted. "If we get inside it, then we can close the door behind us, and Scar Paw won't be able to get us!"

As if time had suddenly stopped, Tara turned to Jason. "Bobby actually had a good idea for once."

"Let's hope it's not his last!" Jason replied. "Go!"

The teens turned and ran as the huge bear continued after its fleeing prey—but not at a run, overtly confident in the outcome.

Reaching the trap first, Jason helped Tara get inside.

The bear lumbered on. Fifty yards away now.

Next, Jason grabbed Bobby, who clambered into the opening but then stopped, blocking the entryway.

With a quick look back, Jason found Scar Paw far too close for comfort—and coming nearer. "Bobby! *What are you waiting for!*"

"But it's dark in there!" the redhead moaned.

"For Pete's sake!" Jason placed his hands on Bobby's butt to jam the hesitant boy into the tube and then scrambled inside behind his friend.

The rogue menace was only ten yards away.

"The lever!" Jason yelled, seeing the nearing monstrosity's drool escape its open jaws. "Pull the trip lever!"

Only five yards short, the bear with the bleeding cheek stopped and breathed heavily again, *"Huh, huh, huh."*

"Where is it?" Tara asked.

"Pull *anything!*" Jason was beyond exasperation.

At the edge of the trap door, Scar Paw rose on its hind legs, with its giant front claws reaching.

"Got it!" Tara shouted victoriously, and the heavy iron slab fell noisily to seal the tube from the outside, leaving about a one-inch gap at the door's bottom.

For the briefest of moments, the beast paused just beyond the rusted metal barrier between itself and the children. It then roared terribly and struck at the door again and again.

The entire trap shuddered against the brute's rage. The teens screamed, with Bobby shrieking the loudest. They jumbled about inside the tube, climbing over one another as the bear's pounding continued.

Through the tube's many holes, they could glimpse the movements of the beast outside. For nearly five minutes, Scar Paw would randomly charge the trap, its battering almost capsizing the tube. Several times, it stuck its nose up to the holes, sniffing deeply, sensing the adolescent's terror, smelling their hopelessness, and even catching a slight whiff of cow manure.

Then the assault stopped.

Quiet, but for the teens' labored breathing.

Sunlight poured into the trap in colander fashion, and Tara realized she was hugging Jason. She wasn't sure how or when they had embraced each other, but in the silence, she relaxed in his arms.

"Do y-y-you suppose it's gone?" Bobby asked in the semi-darkness.

"I hope so," Jason said, still listening keenly.

"Do you think Mr. Ernst and Seth will find us?" Tara asked.

"I don't know," Jason replied.

After a pause, Bobby asked, "Are there any donuts left?"

They started laughing, but then detected the slightest of noises outside. Something once more broke the daylight filtering into the tube as it traversed from one end of the trap to the other.

Suddenly, fingers reached under the small gap below the trap door, and the metal doorway made a grating sound as it moved noisily up the rails.

A large, black head appeared in the trap's opening and then glared at the youths.

"Seth!" Tara nearly burst into tears.

Opposite his loyal hound, Nathan leaned inside the darkened tube and peered at the scared-witless teens. "Awww sheesh! They're just cubs." He glanced over at his ebony cur. "Reckon we'll have to let 'em go."

The King of Hounds returned his master's gaze and snorted.

CHAPTER 17
Something Exceptional

"I do not want this pain for you, my beloved." Sharon sat on a rock near the base of the waterfalls, her face only inches from her lover. Tears formed in her eyes.

She had never cried in the dreams.

"Today?" Nathan asked.

She nodded, sitting beside the stream that was Ryland Creek.

She nodded between the streams that ran down her cheeks. "Yes, this day."

"If it's my time, then so be it," Nathan said, trying to interpret her tears.

"This day, you will lose, my love." Sharon's voice spilled over with sadness. "Steel your heart."

Her voice had never been sad in the dreams.

A large raven alit on a branch in plain sight from the falls, cawing raucously several times. Nathan looked up at the carrion bird with its dark eyes focused on him.

He turned his attention to her and spoke slowly. "There can be no other way. Scar Paw has killed ruthlessly. It might leave us alone someday, but then it'll just as likely become someone else's concern. That's not our family's way—to pass on a problem."

"No, no, it is not," Sharon conceded, managing a smile. "The Ernsts have never backed down from a fight."

The midnight bird cawed again with its gaze still set on Nathan. Angered, the coon hunter reached down into Ryland Creek and found a large stone. With all his might, he hurled the gray rock at the annoying avian. The stone came close to striking the feathered antagonist and even hit the branch it perched upon. But the bird, unusually ugly for its kind, glowered. Mocking and daring.

Three brown-grayish starlings appeared—a raven's mortal enemy. The smaller birds screeched noisily at their larger foe. A fourth starling landed silently behind the malevolent avian.

Even so, the dark foe remained, taunting.

Then, a fifth starling darted out of the sky, viciously raking the black bird across the head. Outnumbered, the carrion eater flapped its large wings several times, preparing for flight.

But the raven paused for one last glance at the coon hunter, screeching horribly before it finally bolted into the air with the starlings in close pursuit.

"When?" Nathan asked, looking at his lover.

Sharon responded with only a short promise. "Soon now."

"I'll do what I must." Nathan looked back to the sky, seeing the starlings in aerial combat with the raven, diving and turning in a graceful, combined effort.

"You have no choice, my beloved." Sharon took his hand to refocus his attention on her. "You never did."

———•———

Nathan's dream-filled eyes fluttered open. He'd fallen asleep, fully dressed, on the large sofa in the living room. The nearby clock on the wall read a little after seven in the morning. The sun was already climbing high into the blue sky. He mentally chastised himself. Rarely did he "sleep in." Why should this day be any different?

It had been three days since the latest incident with Scar Paw on the Welty farm. In his waking mind, Nathan tried to sort out the meaning of the dream.

Arthur's voice startled him. "She comes to you in your dreams, doesn't she, Nephew?"

"Who comes to me?" Nathan looked over to find Arthur sitting comfortably in a chair nearby.

The woodsman turned his head slightly. "Sharon—the girl you lost the day that you and she were to wed."

"Yes, yes she does." The younger man swung his legs over the side of the couch to sit. With an incredulous look, he asked, "But how do you know?"

"You talk in your sleep." Arthur smiled slowly. "You honor her memory, but you're caught up in the past, Nephew, and not the present. Be mindful of where you are and live your life."

"I'll take that to heart." Nathan nodded, recalling similar advice he'd once given to Jason.

"And I assure you—Sharon is much more than a dream." The Ghost That Belongs to the Forest then smiled. "This is Painted Post, after all."

There was a loud knock at the front door.

"You best see who's come a callin'." Arthur's eyes gleamed. "If'n it's Stella Wharton, tell her I went for a long walk in the woods, and I didn't say when I'd be back."

"Don't worry." Nathan chuckled. "That would be the young'uns. I told them to arrive bright and early so we could begin hayin'. They don't disappoint." He stood and walked to greet their guests. When he opened the door, Jason stood with Tara and Bobby flanking either side. They all wore jeans and short-sleeved shirts, their enthusiasm to begin the day on their faces.

"Morning, Mr. Ernst! We're ready to help with the haying!" Jason said.

Before Nathan could greet them, Arthur's gruff voice came from behind. "First things first, young'uns! Have you had breakfast? There's no hayin' on empty stomachs."

Nathan stepped to the side to allow the children to see the silver-maned man with the now matching beard.

"I haven't eaten yet," Jason replied.

"Me either," Tara said.

Bobby grinned. "I already ate, but I could certainly eat again."

"How do pancakes and sausage sound?" Arthur suggested.

"Oh, sure!" Jason smiled broadly.

"I'll help," Tara said, and the two other teens just stared at her in unashamed disbelief. But the tough country girl added, "Yes, I can cook, too. But don't think for a moment that I can't still kick your butts!"

Nathan laughed. "All of you can help Uncle Arthur make breakfast. I'm going to take a shower and be back in a jiffy."

While large and strong, it had been no match for the Great Bear. Looking at the carcass of the slain creature, the bruin clamped its powerful maw around the lifeless neck. Using sheer brute strength, Scar Paw lifted the considerable dead weight and carried the unfortunate victim, first very near the Ernst farm and then beyond.

The marauder finally deposited the load precisely where it would give it a tactical advantage—the upper hand needed to defeat the man and his black hound, who would surely come after it now.

Unburdened, it ambled back for nearly a mile to the edge of the field where it had slain the mule. A light breeze blew over it, and the beast knew it would be only a short while before the wind alerted the ebony cur to its presence.

Precisely as Scar Paw hoped.

With his hair still damp, Nathan came downstairs to find the kitchen table laden with victuals. His uncle and the teens sat patiently, obviously waiting for him to make his appearance. The tempting smells of the sumptuous breakfast promised that Arthur and Tara had proven their culinary skills.

"Well," Nathan smiled, "what are you waitin' for? Dig in!"

The teenage boys needed no further prompting, as both used their forks to spear the still-steaming stack, each securing three pancakes.

Tara carefully forked one pancake and put it on Arthur's plate.

"Why thank you, young lady," Arthur said, watching Jason and Bobby in their feeding frenzy. "With those two, I was beginnin' to wonder if'n the rest of us were goin' to get anything to eat."

"Haying is a lot of work!" Bobby managed with a full mouth of pancake and syrup. "Besides, Jason and me are still growing!"

"No denying that." Nathan laughed, watching the food rapidly disappear.

Talk of the day ahead quickly ensued. Nathan explained what needed to be done and their roles. The hunter-farmer would drive the tractor and bale the hay. After swapping the bailer with the wagon, Nathan would drive through the fields as Jason walked alongside and lifted the 60-pound bales into the wagon, where Bobby and Tara would then stack the rectangular loads. Together, they'd unload each wagonful into the barn's loft and start the process anew until the field was clear of the newly baled hay.

"While I'm baling," Nathan continued, "you can take care of the hounds and help Uncle Art clean the kitchen. How does that sound?"

Jason spoke with a smile. "Sounds good, Mr. Ernst!"

"You're never short on enthusiasm, are you, young'un?" Arthur nodded with a sly smirk.

"Nope!" The teen grinned.

"Okay, that's the plan," Nathan said.

"Dishes first!" Arthur said, and the teenagers stood and began clearing the table.

Leaving the kitchen flurry behind, Nathan smiled as he heard the youths' laughter. He donned his fedora and light jacket, then stepped out the door onto the front porch.

Outside, the forest greeted him. The air had grown warm, likely already in the upper sixties, promising a hot afternoon. The trees in the surrounding hillsides were lush green, overshadowing all manner of wildlife beneath their canopy.

Then, the coon hunter turned to see the rows of raked alfalfa waiting to be baled. Drying in the sun for several days now, the cut grass had turned a golden brown. He ambled down the steps and toward the field, wanting to be sure any morning dew had evaporated so as not to bale wet hay. As he approached the first row, Nathan kneeled and stuck his hand into the hay. To his delight, it was dry. He started to inspect the next row, but a sound arose from his dog kennels.

Seth let out a long, deep howl.

Listening closely, Nathan detected alarm in his beloved hound's voice. The warning from the ebony cur prompted his dream with Sharon to the forefront of his thoughts. He stood, scanning his fields and the abutting tree line, but saw nothing unusual.

Seth's continued bawling encouraged the other hounds to join in, their voices lifted into a cacophony. An urging.

Something was amiss.

Then, the coon hunter detected the slightest of movements at the forest's edge but couldn't determine what had caused the motion. The wind? Or something else?

At the slam of the front porch door and the clamor of boots on the porch's wooden floor, Nathan turned around to spy the teens, who were pointing at the excited coonhounds. Looking up the field, Jason spied him and waved. He motioned for Bobby and Tara to follow. They ran toward the coon hunter, who turned back to stare at the tree line.

"What's gotten into Seth and the other hounds, Mr. Ernst? Did you see something?" Jason, nearly out of breath, gasped when he and his friends neared.

The former movement Nathan had searched for then emerged from the woods, taking shape, and standing boldly in plain view. Its mammoth bulk, even at the distance of several hundred yards, was keenly apparent.

"Scar Paw," Nathan only half-whispered, but the teens heard him readily enough, following his gaze and immediately recognizing the menace from just a few days before on the Welty farm.

"Is it really him? Here? Now?" Tara asked, albeit with a slight tremble.

"Can't be sure at this distance, but it's certainly a huge bear." Nathan put a hand on his Jason's shoulder, and then turned back to watch the bruin. "Fetch me one of the .30-30s and the backpack inside the barn." He motioned to Tara and Bobby. "Go with Jason. I'll stay and keep an eye on it."

Without another word, the young people raced to the barnyard, passing the excited hounds, whose warning barks seemed to grow even louder.

Hanging on the wall rack were both high-caliber rifles with the pack directly below. Jason removed one gun and scooped up the backpack. "C'mon. Let's get back to Mr. Ernst!"

As they started out, Arthur appeared on the porch.

The woodsman's questioning expression prompted Jason, running with the other teens in tow, to shout, "We think it's Scar Paw, Uncle Art, up on the edge of the field. We can see it!"

"Good God!" Arthur replied. "Let me grab my whip, and I'll be right there." The silver-maned man disappeared into the house.

The kids sprinted to Nathan, still focused on the forest, but the bear had vanished.

"Is it still there, Mr. Ernst?" Jason wheezed, handing the gun and sack to Nathan.

Accepting the gear, Nathan placing the backpack on the ground. He opened the pack, removed a box of shells, and immediately

232

loaded the weapon. "Before you made it back, it looked like it was digging for grubs."

"That seems like a strange change in Scar Paw's preferred diet," Bobby said.

"It might be another bear," Nathan replied, "but somethin' tells me it's our Scar Paw all right."

"Why do you think it's him?" Tara's brow furrowed.

Glancing at his kennels, Nathan said, "Because Seth thinks so." He reached into the pack once more, pulled out a long knife in a sheath covered with ornate beadwork, and secured it to his belt. "I'm going after it."

"All alone?" Jason protested. "No way! We're going with you!"

"No, not this time!" Nathan's sternness caused Jason to recoil slightly. He then added, much softer, "I almost lost all of you on the Welty farm three days ago. I won't repeat that mistake. Stay here and let Uncle Art know where I'm headed."

Looking downtrodden, the teens only nodded.

"Wish me luck." Nathan then smiled, gripping Jason's shoulder, attempting to cheer the lad. "There are some hunts where we have to go it alone."

Suddenly orphaned, the young people watched as the dauntless hunter began walking away at an oblique angle—a path that would take him quickly into the woods and several hundred yards below where the bruin had first emerged.

Two minutes later, reaching the forest's edge, Nathan turned and waved once at the staring teens.

And then he disappeared into the oaks.

———————

The young people must have stood there for five minutes, silent, anticipating the report of a large caliber rifle, the thunderous announcement of Scar Paw's demise.

Even the hounds had hushed, with Seth studying the forest and pacing in his kennel anxiously.

No birds sang or squirrels barked. The wind did not stir. Not a sound could be heard. As if Painted Post held its breath.

"Where's Nathan?" The Forest Ghost, bullwhip in hand, startled the children from their reverie.

They turned about as one, with Bobby replying, "He went after Scar Paw all by himself."

"We should be helping him!" Jason insisted.

"No," Arthur said, shaking his head. "Nathan won't risk your lives again. Further, you young'uns would make far too much noise to sneak up on a bear—especially *that* bear. He's done the right thing in goin' after it by himself. All we can do is wait and see."

Sighing heavily, Jason replied, "Okay, Uncle Art, if you say so."

"C'mon now, young'un." Arthur tried to lift the boy's spirits. "There are hounds care for. Rest assured, Nathan will return soon enough—successful or not in killin' Scar Paw—and want to get some hayin' done today. Everyone agreed?"

With a collective nod, the teens reluctantly walked back to the kennels.

Close to the field's edge, Nathan worked his way through the trees. The slight grade uphill helped conceal his approach, and the lack of any wind served to hide his scent. Rendering only the slightest of sounds, the coon-now-bear hunter edged closer. He estimated he was less than ninety yards from where he'd seen Scar Paw last. Coming to the base of a huge red oak, he put one hand on the tree and slowly peered around its thick trunk.

There stood the beast, digging determinedly at some tufts of green grass beneath a slight opening in the leafy canopy.

Nathan couldn't believe his good fortune and brought the rifle up to his cheek to take aim at the mammoth brute. He gently pulled the weapon's hammer back, and his finger began to squeeze the trigger. . . .

Without warning, the formerly preoccupied bear wheeled about and disappeared into the thick forest cover.

"D'Aaahh!" Nathan cursed his change of luck. He ran to where the bear had been foraging, hopeful for another chance to take a shot. Perhaps, he prayed, the unsuspecting bruin could still be taken by surprise.

But therein lay the coon hunter's fatal flaw.

For Scar Paw had known exactly where its enemy had been the entire time.

———————

Seth's acute senses caught the story on the wind.

The bear—his foe—remained nearby.

His beloved master was in the forest now, facing the sinister rogue alone.

And that would not do.

———————

"I got the feed!" Bobby shouted.

"I'll get the water," Tara said.

"Ugh." Jason wrinkled his nose. "I guess that means I get to clean up the you-know-what." The other teens laughed, almost desperately, as if trying to will away the angst they felt with Nathan's absence.

"There are worse jobs, young'un." Arthur chuckled.

"Oh, really?" Jason reached for the shovel designated for the cleanup task. "Like what?"

"Like . . . like," the woodsman stammered. "Well, just trust me, there are." The teens laughed and went about their chores while Arthur returned to the porch and sat in his rocking chair.

While the other dogs wagged their tails, eager for their food, Seth continued to pace nervously, constantly looking uphill and into the forest.

Scooping the feed in each hound's white plastic bucket, Bobby measured out the required amount, while Tara went to the barn to turn on the spigot to the water hose. When the redhead had fed all the other dogs, he finally walked to Seth's kennel. Reaching to open the gate, Bobby saw the large hound on his haunches near the rear of the pen. "Good morning, boy," he soothed. "I didn't forget you."

Surprisingly, Seth remained sitting instead of rushing to greet the teenager as he normally did. Thinking nothing unusual, Bobby opened the gate to leave it ajar.

Precisely as expected.

As the unsuspecting youth entered the kennel, the large coonhound used his powerful limbs to launch into the air. The ebony cur caught Bobby in the chest, causing the youth to fall backward to the ground. Seth stopped for a moment to lick the boy's face, which yielded a "Yuck!"

Then, through the open pen door, the hound bounded away to freedom.

Looking up, Jason yelled, "Seth, come back here!"

But the loyal dog continued to charge out of the barnyard.

"Oh no! What have I done?" Bobby was on his feet immediately. Turning to Arthur, he shouted, "Seth's getting away!"

"Too late to catch him now," The Forest Ghost said, standing on the porch while watching the magnificent hound drive hard toward the wood's edge.

"But what should we do?" Tara, seeing the whole spectacle, nearly panicking.

"Nothin' anyone can do about that now," Arthur spoke slowly. "Seth'll find Nathan, and I suspect both of 'em will be back home soon. Don't you worry. Finish up your chores in the meantime."

Reluctantly, the teens obeyed and resumed their tasks, while Arthur continued to scan the forest where Seth had entered and then disappeared.

———•———

The tracks didn't make sense.

For nearly a mile now, Nathan had been trailing the beast. He'd immediately followed the bear's spoor from where he had almost been able to take a shot. However, the path that led away wasn't footprints on the forest floor. Instead, a broad swath of churned leaves clearly showed the direction Scar Paw had taken.

It was easy to follow the beast's trail. *Too* easy.

As he continued on, the hunter reflected on the encounter with the bear several days before. Instead of just receiving some splinters from the oak where it had lain in ambush, had his shot perhaps directly hit Scar Paw on the Welty farm? It hadn't seemed so. Neither Nathan nor the kids had seen much blood after his quick shot at the brute, so he assumed he'd failed at making a fatal wound. But now, the trail seemed to indicate Scar Paw had dragged itself through the forest, as if badly hurt.

Catching the slightest tinge of red on some leaves, Nathan bent over to touch the foliage. Turning his hand over, he studied the wetness transferred to his fingertips.

Blood! I must have hit it that day on Welty's farm after all.

Now, Nathan knew he was tracking a wounded bear—the most dangerous thing that could ever befall the forests of Upstate New York. Further, it was Scar Paw, which promised the way ahead would be even more treacherous.

The coon hunter moved deeper into the woods of Ryland Creek.

———•———

Seth charged up the hill, still hot on his master's track. He arrived at the place where Nathan had first stopped by the ancient red oak. With little difficulty, the ebony cur followed Nathan's familiar scent and came upon the swath of churned foliage on the forest floor that led into the depths of the hollow.

The hound took in the smells of the man, the marauding bear, and a new odor—that of death. Seth read the different scents and understood. Yes, the dog knew what the rogue had precipitated, the true reason for the path of upturned leaves.

The King of Hounds set out once more at a fast run, knowing, more than ever, he had to reach his master first.

———————⊶⊷———————

When they had finished their chores, Jason put his finger to his lips and gave his other teenage compatriots a tacit look not to say anything but to follow him.

"Uncle Art!" Jason shouted.

"What is it, young'un?" Arthur, in his rocking chair on the porch, folded down the morning's paper he'd been reading.

"Mr. Ernst asked us to gas up the tractor before we started haying. We'll just be in the barn if you need us."

Nodding, Arthur replied, "Okay, do what you have to do."

"C'mon!" Jason whispered, and his curious companions followed. Once inside the doorway, he grabbed the second .30-30 rifle and box of shells, and then loaded the rifle quickly. "We're going to help Mr. Ernst with Scar Paw." He then put some extra shells in his pocket. "We can't let him and Seth face that thing all by themselves. But we can't tell Uncle Arthur, 'cause he'll just try to stop us for sure."

The other teens smiled broadly in agreement.

Slipping out the barn's back, using the building to hide their exodus, the would-be rescuers quietly made their way toward the forest.

———————⊶⊷———————

Nathan couldn't believe what he was seeing.

Since detecting the bear's blood, the coon hunter had traveled another quarter mile, uphill by a steep, but familiar, embankment. Nathan then spotted the large but unmoving bulk only fifty yards ahead. The brute lie sprawled on the ground near the cliff's edge with its head facing the opposite direction. It did not move, nor did it appear to have heard the man's approach.

Was the beast attempting a ruse to bring the man in closer and then attack? This unnatural creature had proven itself cagey many times before, but the skilled hunter could detect no heaving of the animal's torso. It wasn't breathing—of that, he was confident.

Scar Paw's trail had been so easy to follow, Nathan reasoned, since the rogue had been mortally wounded. It had dragged itself through the forest, collapsed, and then died from the effort.

Perhaps it was finally over, but the coon hunter approached the unmoving bear with his rifle ready, leaving nothing to chance.

———⋅———

Arthur's lessons in teaching Jason and Tara how to track was quickly paying off, for they soon found Nathan's footprints in the field and followed them into the woods.

"Whoa!" Tara said as they came upon the churned leaves. "If this is Scar Paw's trail, anyone could follow it through the woods."

"You're the expert tracker." Jason beamed, still holding the .30-30. "Lead on."

"Let's go!" Bobby brimmed with excitement.

Moving quickly to catch up, they followed the path into the forest.

———⋅———

The teenagers had been quiet for some time.

"How long does it take to fill a tractor with gas? Kids these days," Arthur muttered to himself. "Children!" he shouted from his rocking chair. When there was no response, he stood and descended the porch steps.

"Jason, Bobby, Tara!" the woodsman called out, walking through the barn door. The tractor was parked where it always had been, but the youths were nowhere in sight. Looking behind, he immediately saw the missing rifles.

"What the flapjacks!" Arthur shouted and then smiled. "Hah! Nathan's got me not cussin' even when the young'uns aren't around!" He ran to the barn's back door. The woodsman easily made out the tracks of the teens headed toward the woods.

"Oh, no," the Forest Ghost said, shaking his head grimly. "What have you young'uns done now?"

———————

Nathan moved forward stealthily. Although he still had not detected any movement from the beast, only twenty yards away, something wasn't right. Leaving nothing to chance, he aimed his rifle at the bear and fired a bullet into the bruin's side.

And then . . . not a thing.

Scar Paw hadn't even flinched. The terror was truly dead, for no bear—uncanny or not, supernatural or not—could have withstood that punishment without some reaction.

"It's finally over." The coon hunter leaned the .30-30 against a nearby tree and walked toward the corpse. He was still naturally cautious, though, moving around to see the bear's head. To his relief, Nathan saw the clouded-over eyes of the giant bear.

There was no doubt. Scar Paw was gone from this world.

Kneeling beside its head, he observed the hole his bullet had left in the bear's rib cage, indicating that his precautionary shot had likely passed through a non-beating heart. Up close for the first time, he said, "I thought you would've been even larger than this."

Peering down at the bear's skull, Nathan spied flecks of blood against the black fur. Placing his hand on its head, he felt multiple holes formed like a crown.

"Bite marks! The mighty Scar Paw attacked by another animal!"

An unnatural cold caused him to involuntarily shudder—the sense of something amiss. The coon hunter vividly recalled the nature of the trail that had led him to this spot.

As if something had been dragged.

Stepping to the bear's hindquarters, Nathan lifted the lifeless form's left rear paw. Another chill coursed through him, for the mark on its footpad that had been the beast's namesake was missing.

Then he understood the trail he'd followed, hearing Gray Eyes' warning clearly in his mind like several days before.

This bear will hunt you with as much cunning as you hunt it.

There came the slightest of movements behind him, and Nathan looked up to see the lethal menace of a very much alive Scar Paw between himself and his rifle.

The beast let out a deep grunt. An almost human laugh.

"Huh, huh, huh."

———————

Hearing the gunshot ring out, Seth stopped abruptly. The weapon's report helped determine his master's whereabouts, further confirmed by the scent drifting on the air currents. The King of Hounds also found the rogue's telltale smell.

The coonhound was still more than a quarter mile away. There was no time to lose with his master's life at stake, and the loyal dog surged ahead, using every ounce of his strength.

The ebony cur ran like the wind.

Like the speed of destiny.

———————

241

The teens were nearly out of breath when they heard the shot. The rifle's report echo faded, stealing their voices as they wondered what the sound meant.

"Do you think Mr. Ernst got Scar Paw?" Jason asked.

"Maybe!" Tara's look of confidence grew.

"All right!" Bobby echoed hopefully. "Maybe we came all this way for nothing!"

"No sense in trying to be quiet now." Jason urged them forward. "Let's keep going."

They set out faster than before at a near run.

———————

Scar Paw let loose a savage roar, which had always intimidated the beast's prey or challengers. It expected the man to run, and then it would quickly mow down and slay its victim with ease. But the Great Bear soon shook its head, confused, for instead of fleeing, the human reached to his waist and pulled a long, silver knife from its beaded leather sheath.

"I don't run," Nathan seethed, holding the glinting blade before him.

Sniffing the air to its disappointment, it sensed no fear in the man's heart. But that didn't matter now. It was certain this encounter would end as it had planned.

The bruin lunged.

Anticipating the frontal assault, Nathan took one step forward, then immediately sidestepped. With a downward slicing motion, he swung the knife that Gray Eyes had gifted him at the brute's neck.

The beast had not foreseen its opponent's tactic.

But it was fast. Very fast.

Just in time, Scar Paw dropped its head, protecting its windpipe. While the knife might have missed its intended target, the razor-sharp blade sliced off the top of the marauder's left ear. Howling wildly, the terror let every creature in the forest know its rage.

Spinning around to face the man again, the beast shook its massive head.

Calculating his next move, Nathan watched the bear. In terms of size, he was outmatched more than four to one. Slowly, moving closer to the cliff's edge, the hunter hoped for a chance at victory if Scar Paw would just attack again in the same manner—another charge.

But this was the *Nyah-gwaheh*, the Great Bear, and not so foolish as to be predictable. It approached deliberately, cautious now, with a rivulet of blood from its damaged ear streaming down the side of its face.

With another step back, Nathan felt his left boot heel rock gently over the cliff's edge. The coon hunter need not look, knowing the land well, with the nearly thirty-foot drop, steep but not wholly vertical. A towering, white pine stood only four feet to his right, growing just on the precipice's ledge.

The unholy thing approached to within a few yards of the man but stopped. It knew its prey was cornered with nowhere to escape. The ebony cur's beloved companion was trapped, and the Great Bear would kill the man and be done with it.

Hope drained as Nathan sensed the pause, fearing the bear would not charge as it had before. He did the unthinkable, rushing forward, and caught the brute off guard. The desperate tactic was his last, best chance. Bringing the knife down quickly, Nathan aimed directly for its right eye.

But Scar Paw was faster.

The bruin moved just enough to have the weapon miss harmlessly. It then swiftly swiped with its sharp claws, raking the man's leg.

The coon hunter screamed as the bear's counterattack drew blood, but he managed to pivot to face his enemy. Growling ominously, the terror raised on its hind legs to tower over him. Still in motion, Nathan turned the blade to bring it back for another thrust.

Had the angle been right, the knife would have penetrated the beast's heart.

But again, Scar Paw moved far too fast, shifting its mass just enough so that the blade's cut, while painful and slicing through its thick hide, was not fatal.

Spinning, Nathan punched into the beast's face, channeling all his rage.

The power of the man's blow caught the bear unprepared—only the mule had ever hit it so hard. Its mind spun hazily under the weight of the man's punch. Shaking its massive head to regain its senses, the beast countered with a vicious swipe of its paw, catching Nathan in the chest.

The bear's counterblow hurtled Nathan backward through the air toward the cliff's edge. Propelled helplessly by the Great Bear's raw strength, his body impacted hard against the white pine, his head striking its trunk. Unconscious, the coon hunter slumped to the tree's base.

Scar Paw grunted, knowing victory was one final bite away, closing the short distance between itself and the unmoving human.

It was over. . . .

Or so it thought.

A tremendous roar, an unmistakable challenge, filled the woodland hollow.

The Great Bear turned to find its forever nemesis.

For only a few feet away, the King of Hounds stood defiant.

———— • ————

The familiar bawl met the teenagers. They were sweating now in the rising summer heat. Their clothes clung to their bodies, but the thought of stopping never occurred.

"That was Seth!" Tara shouted. "They can't be far ahead—maybe a hundred yards at most!"

"Let's go!" Jason started to run, but his foot caught a tree root, and he fell forward as the .30-30 went flying away.

──── ● ────

Dropping to all fours, the bear moved toward the dog. Scar Paw seethed, its hate for the hound eclipsing all else. This day would see the end of any that dared oppose it.

The Great Bear growled viciously and charged with its unnatural speed, reaching for the hound's head with its snapping maw.

But the coonhound used his natural agility to flank the brute. Then, Seth's powerful jaws sunk into the bruin's side, deep into the flesh of the Killer of Sheep.

──── ● ────

The teens scrambled, and Jason recovered the weapon.

Again, they heard that bear's terrible growl, confirming they were so very close now.

The young people said nothing and ran headlong toward the sounds of battle.

──── ● ────

Scar Paw became pure agony as the powerful dog's bite drew blood. It swung its massive bulk around, hoping to throw its attacker off.

Releasing his hold, Seth used the momentum of the bear's maneuver to land on his feet and face the Great Bear again.

With an uncanny agility of its own, the beast turned while simultaneously swiping at his enemy's head, grunting evilly, assured that the canine's life was its for the taking.

But for all the Great Bear's might . . .

And for all the beast's speed . . .

Seth was faster.

Seeing the opportunity, The King of Hounds charged below his foe's outstretched arm and sunk his teeth into the Scar Paw's rear leg, rending a large piece of flesh away from the Killer of Bulls and Calves.

———●———

Running hard, the young people came to a recent wind-fallen oak. Through its many branches, still thick with leaves, they could see a flurry of movement on the other side. They were so near now they could feel the struggle.

Then the sound of Scar Paw's brutal scream split the air, and they stood paralyzed.

———●———

It had never felt such acute pain.

Although wantonly familiar with the color crimson, fear seeped into the brute as it realized the sanguine wetness staining the ground belonged to it. The resulting anguish caused too much distraction, and the beast turned defensively, uncoordinated.

Seth immediately surged against Scar Paw's exposed side and again bit down, and with a vicious turn of his head, tore hide from the Killer of Bear Dogs. The ebony cur paused, tired from both the run to his master and the fight. Still, the otherwise unscathed hound faced the slow-moving bruin, barking and taunting, drawing it farther from the unconscious Nathan.

The Great Bear caught the scent of more humans, but it could only afford to keep its focus on the canine. With a feeble attempt, yet again, the bear struck at its enemy.

But Seth easily outmaneuvered the bruin's pathetic attempt. The King of Hounds—with a preternatural strength driven by vengeance—then bit hard once more, ripping muscle and sinew from the flank of the Killer of Mules.

246

Coming to their senses, the teens dashed around the fallen oak. Only seventy-five yards away, Jason could easily see the melee, the tumultuous battle between the titans. Instinctively, he knew the situation was all wrong. He couldn't use the rifle for fear of hitting Seth.

"There's Mr. Ernst!" Bobby pointed at the motionless form against the tall pine. Nathan's head was sunk to his chest, his fate unknown.

They watched as the ebony cur viciously tore away a hunk of Scar Paw's rear leg, and the bear's right side collapsed. Seth then positioned himself just beyond the reach of the wounded bruin, daring it to chase him.

The deadly marauder looked at the hound and quickly glanced behind to where Nathan lay. The brute understood its enemy's tactics.

"Huh, huh, huh," Scar Paw grunted, and spun about. It didn't care about its exposed flank, instead moving toward the helpless human.

Today, Evil would have victory over Man, one way or another.

Terrified, Jason raised the rifle.

"You can't shoot!" Tara shouted.

Time stopped for all of Ryland Creek.

The terror was close to Nathan. So very close.

There was never any hesitation about what Seth must do, never questioning whether he should or should not.

That's not how a dog thinks.

Scar Paw rose on its rear two legs. It was malice. It was hate.

There was only his beloved master's life hanging in the balance in that stalled moment in time—nothing else mattered.

The dark-souled creature angled down toward the unmoving human. The Great Bear opened its huge maw.

It was pain. It was death.

The selfless purpose for which the ebony cur had been born—the entire reason for his existence—culminated in this moment.

For the love of a man, The King of Hounds lunged, moving faster than he ever had. Seth leaped into the air, his powerful jaws clamping down on the throat of the Killer of Puppies. The ebony cur allowed his heavily muscled body to swing over the cliff's edge.

The bear's gravely wounded side collapsed.

Scar Paw's fierce, shocked roar reverberated as the dog's momentum carried both beast and hound over the cliff.

And then they were gone.

It had happened all too fast—and the wide-eyed teens stared incredulously at the emptiness that had been both threat and salvation only seconds before.

Tara's cry echoed through the hills.

"Seth!"

"Wake up!" Sharon screamed, grabbing him hard by the shoulders.

"I want to stay here with you," Nathan groaned between gritted teeth. Never had he felt pain in the dreams, but now, an intense misery coursed through his body.

"Wake up! It's not dead!" she persisted, shaking him harder.

"What are you talking about?"

"Scar Paw isn't dead! It lives! Wake up!"

"I want to stay here," he repeated.

"It will come for the children! You must wake up! Wake up now!" Sharon's face faded into Jason's alarmed visage, shaking Nathan's shoulders. "Mr. Ernst, please wake up!"

In the world again, Nathan tried hard to focus. "Jason? Bobby? Tara? What happened?"

"You were knocked out, Mr. Ernst!" Bobby replied. "Seth and Scar Paw fought, and they both just went over the cliff!"

"Seth? Seth was here?" Nathan's mind cleared as he grasped Jason's arms.

"Yes!" Tara cried now. She couldn't help herself. "Scar Paw was headed straight for you, but Seth dragged him over the edge! I can't see either one of them at the base of the cliff, but they must be dead!"

Spying his rifle nearby, Nathan tried to rise and retrieve it, but his wounded leg gave way, and he fell back against the pine's trunk. He turned to Jason. "Listen to me, son. Scar Paw is *not* dead!"

"How do you know that?" Jason looked doubtful.

There was no time to explain. Nathan spoke louder. "I just do—you have to trust me! I can't make it down the side of the cliff in time with this leg, but you can. Go over about fifty yards—you can climb down safely that way. Seth might still be alive, too, but kill that bear! I know you can do it, Jason."

"I will, Mr. Ernst." Jason reached for his rifle. Before he could grasp it, though, Tara snatched the weapon and ran to where Nathan had indicated. She slipped over the cliff's ledge.

"Tara!" Jason and Bobby shouted.

But the young woman had disappeared.

———————

Scar Paw woke. The fall had left it unconscious near the cliff's base for only a few minutes. The bruin's keen nose quickly read the story floating on the wind. The humans were still atop the steep hill, but it could neither see nor sense the ebony cur.

Was its mortal enemy finally dead?

The monster looked up, intent on retaking the cliff. It would end the life of the man and the children. The beast rose, weak and slow, and began to move uphill. It hadn't taken more than a few steps, its terrible wounds causing it to hobble, when it heard something scuffle to its side.

And Seth roared!

There, not far from the Great Bear, the hound crawled on his front legs, dragging his hind legs. But the fall had not crushed the hound's spirit. The brave coonhound howled again and continued *toward* the beast, taunting the malicious thing while also warning his master above.

Slowly, the brute limped nearer the canine. Killing the severely wounded dog would be easy now. It ambled closer, only ten feet from the coonhound, who howled defiantly once more. The brute raised a paw, intent to bring its sharp claws down on the hound's head. The long vengeance would finally be realized. It was over.

Then, from its side, without a sound even the Great Bear's supernatural hearing could detect, something stepped between the monster and the King of Hounds.

"Remember me?" The Forest Ghost smiled.

The beast grunted, shock registering on its face.

With bullwhip in hand, Arthur's arm shot forward, and the leather braid—an extension of himself—reached out and struck the terrible bear's right eye.

Scar Paw roared in pain, rising on its hind legs, vainly hoping to intimidate The Ghost That Belongs to the Forest.

Instead, the whip cracked again and again as the whipmaster expertly lashed out at the beast. Each time, the leather viper bit into the bear's hide, drawing blood, and removing fur. Dropping to all fours, the Great Bear attempted to brave through the leather fury, but a well-aimed lash to its sensitive nose sapped its will.

The menace that had terrorized Painted Post for so long now felt unadulterated fear. Its many wounds caused blood to flow down its face. The bear raised a paw to strike, and the leather then furled around its limb. Only out of reflex, the bloodied monster drew its arm backward quickly, tearing the bullwhip from Arthur's grip to fly away and land somewhere behind the marauder.

Holding on to his whip too long, Arthur lurched closer to the beast. Had it not been so wounded, the bear's subsequent strike would have been fatal. Instead, the Great Bear struck slowly at the whipmaster, and while its claws drew blood, it was only a glancing blow.

"Aaarrgh!" the now-weaponless woodsman shouted stepping back, holding his bleeding arm.

Instinctively, Scar Paw sensed the human and the severely wounded canine were defenseless. Finally, the odds were in its favor, and the unholy creature growled low and wicked.

Seth whined, looking up at Arthur.

"Well, Seth, ol' boy," Arthur said, unmoving as the bear closed in. "Reckon if'n I must die this day, I'd just as soon leave this world with you."

Lulled into confidence by its stationary prey, the beast limped closer. When only a few yards away, it stood once again on its hind legs, releasing its ferocious growl, and began its final pounce with murderous intent.

The Ghost That Belonged to the Forest screamed in defiance.

The fearless Seth's roar echoed throughout the valley.

And a rifle, not a whip, boomed in the forested air.

It had only been the luck of the terrain—the bear stepping into a slight depression—that caused the bullet to miss its intended, mortal target. Instead, the bullet drove into Scar Paw's already-wounded shoulder, and the beast collapsed under the impact.

Tara looked above the sights of the .30-30.

Any other woodland creature would have run away, but the severely injured Great Bear screamed furiously. The most dangerous animal in the forests of Painted Post roared, focusing its attention on the young woman and lumbered at her with all the speed it could muster.

Quickly, Tara worked the rifle's lever action. But in her haste as she watched Scar Paw charge, she didn't work the lever correctly, and the gun jammed. The rogue bruin was nearly on her—but ten feet away.

Then, another explosion sounded, and a second bullet ripped into Scar Paw's neck. The round missed its spinal cord only by fractions of an inch. Once again, the terror collapsed to the forest floor.

Only a few feet from Tara, Jason looked down the metal sights of the .30-30 rifle's blue-black barrel. The young man worked the lever action, aiming once more, but the bear offered no parting opportunity.

For this battle was over, the marauder knew. There was only one craven path remaining—to escape. It rose and scrambled ingloriously from the cliff's base, ignoring the excruciating pain of its many wounds, fleeing past the hound and whipmaster to vanish into the greenery of Ryland Creek.

A noise caught Jason's attention. The young man looked uphill to find a wounded Nathan, leaning on Bobby, as they slowly made their way down the cliff's side.

"Nice shooting, the both of you," Nathan managed through gritted teeth.

"Thank you, Mr. Ernst." Jason's chest swelled.

However, Tara said nothing, turned, and ran to kneel beside Seth.

Likewise, Arthur knelt by the dog as the King of Hounds lie sprawled on the ground. The brave hound moved his head weakly to lick Tara's hand.

Now with Jason's support, Bobby helped Nathan down the remainder of the incline. Within a minute, they reached the others.

Still holding his wounded arm, Arthur stood again, silently studying the prone dog,

With her face buried against Seth's neck, Tara's body convulsed in rhythmic sobs. Jason left Nathan to stand near her and gently place his hand on her shoulder. Bobby retrieved Arthur's bullwhip and returned it to the silver-maned man.

As Nathan neared, the exceptional hound let out a slight whimper at the sight of his beloved master.

"His back is broken," Arthur spoke softly without taking his eyes off the loyal dog.

Seth attempted to stand when Nathan kneeled next to him. Exhausted, the faithful hound collapsed into the dirt.

Tara crawled backward as Nathan tried to gently lift the hound in his arms, but Seth cried out in pain. He then eased his companion down and stood, never taking his eyes off Seth.

"Give me the rifle," Nathan said slowly, turning toward Jason.

"What?" Tara's eyes went wide, looking back and forth between the coon hunter and his fallen hound. "No! Mr. Ernst, we can get him home. Seth will be okay. I just know it!"

"Seth will die a painful death if we try to move him, children," Arthur explained gently. "This is the only way."

"No!" she cried, falling to her knees. "It can't end like this. Not again! *Not again!*" She fell forward, beating her fists into the ground as Painted Post stoically withstood the blows.

"Tara," Nathan's voice cracked slightly, and then added softly, "please don't make this any harder than it has to be." Turning again to Jason, he said, "Give me the gun, son."

With unashamed but silent tears streaming down his face, the young man handed the rifle over.

Standing, Tara buried her face into Jason's shoulder.

Holding the other rifle now, Bobby walked over to his friends "Will you be able to make it back to the farm, Mr. Ernst?"

"Don't worry about me. I'll be along soon enough," Nathan responded. Speaking to the youngsters, he motioned at Arthur's wounded arm. "I need you to do something for me. Make sure you

253

get Uncle Art home safe and sound now, you hear?" He looked away.

"Yes, sir, we will," Jason said, swallowing hard.

"I'd most certainly enjoy your company, young'uns." Arthur forced a smile and draped his good arm around Jason and Tara. Bobby stepped up quickly on the woodsman's wounded side as they began to leave.

After several steps, Jason took one last look back to see Nathan standing over Seth.

"Did I ever tell you the story about the time that I got into a fight with the Singleton Sisters up near Salamanca way?" Arthur began, slipping into his storytelling voice—a poorly veiled ruse.

"You got into a fight with two women?" Jason looked at the silver-maned woodsman and choked out a laugh despite his tears.

"I tell you what, young'uns! These weren't just any women!" Arthur explained, gently tugging on the boy's arm. "Some say they were half demon!"

Nathan watched as the teens and his animated uncle walked away, and the trees soon swallowed their figures.

Seth's breathing became labored, and he cried out in pain, trying to stand once more to regain his place by his master's side. The hound collapsed again.

"Easy, boy." Nathan gently placed his hand on his dog's head. "I thought today was my day to leave you—not the other way around." Peering into the sky, as if hoping to find Sharon there, he said, "Now, I understand." The coon hunter then beheld Seth. "I'll see you again, someday, my dear friend." Wetness rolled down his face. "No man ever deserved such an exceptional hound."

The King of Hounds, through pure will, raised himself as high as he could muster.

And for the final time . . . Seth roared!

The hills reverberated with the mighty sound.

A herd of deer jerked their heads up as one.

A raccoon woke and scrambled higher in the branches of its den tree.

And a severely wounded bear grunted in fear and hurried its pace to take it far away from the lands of the Painted Post.

Arthur and the children stopped, hearing Seth's wondrous voice. Tara gasped and tried to turn back, but Jason's strong arms gently held the young lady. Her body, her spirit, relented, and she allowed his strength to carry her. They continued their way home.

As Seth's echo faded, the magnificent hound sunk to the leaves and laid his head down.

Kneeling, Nathan used one hand to close Seth's eyes. He stood again, stepping back.

For a moment, the coon hunter shut his own eyes to see the image of a small ebony puppy standing before him. The little one released an incredibly loud bawl for a dog so tiny when Nathan and his father, Jacob, had sat on their front porch—so long ago.

Working the lever action to load a new shell, he lifted the rifle.

He remembered the proud day when Seth treed his first raccoon.

Nathan looked down the barrel. His aim had to be sure. Flawless.

Another memory flooded back—that of his brave hound, flying through the air to strike the chest of his father's murderer, and driving that villain to his deserved fate over the rails of a small bridge—saving Nathan's life.

It had to be fast, lest he lose his will.

There was Seth again, sitting proud as he always had in the front seat of his truck.

With every ounce of his strength, Nathan pulled the trigger smoothly.

And a lonely rifle shot cried out in the hollows of Ryland Creek.

Chapter 18
Closure

It had been nearly one week since the showdown with Scar Paw. On the sixth day, Nathan toiled at his barn's old workbench on a wooden masterpiece—a cross made of white oak. Rarely did he stop and ate but little. The only break from the task he took was to care for his hounds—that sacred obligation he was bound to uphold.

But always back to his uncompleted work did Nathan return. It had to be this way—to honor the true exception to all hounds. Determined, he would make it so.

This wooden cross stood much larger than the other crosses in the Ernsts' coonhound graveyard. All the cross's edges were gently beveled. The coon-hunter-turned-carpenter drilled and countersunk the holes for thick screws to hold the post and beam together. He hand-sanded everything. Finally, with painstaking precision, Nathan inscribed a name on the cross's beam. Each letter was perfectly drawn and then chiseled into the oak.

By the time Nathan had finished applying a golden stain to protect his monument from the elements, the sun had set several hours beforehand. Now, the third quarter moon rose late that summer night, and he stood back to admire his handiwork. The name inscribed there called to him, but Nathan collapsed, exhausted, to the floor against a bale of hay. He closed his eyes, pushing his ever-present gray fedora forward on his head, and promised himself that he needed just a short rest before retiring to his bed for the evening.

Soon, the coonhounds in their nearby kennels could hear the deep sounds of their master's slumber.

The din of his hounds' barking woke Nathan with a start. Squinting in the bright morning light, his mind tried to orient to the surroundings. Leaning against the hay bale, stretched out on the barn's wooden floor, his hand found the brim of his hat. He shifted the fedora forward to shade his eyes, still feeling the welcomed warmth of the dawning sun. The coon hunter moved slightly, with sharp pains of the wounds earned from the bear's attack, reminding him that he wasn't completely healed.

One day, his body would mend. His heart was another story.

However, there was an additional sound to the dogs' barking— the loud grumbling of a truck's engine coming up the driveway. Then a large frame filled the barn's open doorway.

"You sleep pretty sound, Nephew," Arthur said, smiling.

"Must have passed out," Nathan admitted, sitting up. "I was working on Seth's monument." He pointed to the golden cross held aloft by the clamps on the workbench.

"That's a beautiful dedication, young man." Arthur admired Nathan's craftsmanship. "I will take that cross and display it by my cabin near Salamanca. It'll stand as testament to such a great hound, and I'll tell Seth's story for as long as I draw breath."

Nathan could hear several people talking as the commotion grew outside, but he returned his attention to the woodsman. "Uncle Arthur, I made this cross for Seth's grave. I'll make another for your cabin, but I'd like this one to stay here."

"It must be this way, Nephew, I assure you. Besides, Gray Eyes will be quite upset to hear else ways, as he planned on helping me complete the monument."

"Are you sure the sachem would feel that way?" Nathan asked with a slight smile.

A slightly taller, noble man then stood beside Arthur. Wearing a bright, multi-colored ribbon shirt and brown leather boots, Gray Eyes smiled. The chief also wore the Iroquois traditional headdress, a *gahsdo:wa,* which had a single feather protruding straight up with other feathers pointed downward around the cap. "My son, The Ghost That Belongs to the Forest, has it on good authority I would be upset, young Nathan."

Still on the floor looking up, Nathan could only nod, his throat too tight for words. Further, the coon hunter caught the different address from the venerable sachem—he was no longer "Seth's Master."

"You should know," Arthur added, "that Seth's grave marker has already been attended to. I didn't want to tell you before today to not spoil the secret. If'n you wouldn't mind steppin' outside, we'd like to show it to you now." Arthur offered Nathan his hand, and the younger man took the firm grasp. Relying on the other man's strength, the coon hunter stood. If there had been any hint of remaining damage to Arthur's arm from his last encounter with Scar Paw, it wasn't apparent.

As Nathan removed his fedora for just a moment, he caught his reflection in a mirror on the barn wall. He could see a new, white shock of hair, about an inch wide, that had sprung overnight from his long, brown bangs. When Nathan looked at his uncle, he saw the woodsman studying the harbinger color on his head. Gray Eyes appeared to have also noticed the portent—only smiling sadly with the slightest of nods at Arthur—but remained reticent.

Quickly redonning his hat to cover the new white band of hair, Nathan took a few hobbled steps forward, his gait a reminder of his encounter with Scar Paw.

Grasping something just outside the doorway hidden from view, Arthur handed it to his nephew.

"What's this?" Nathan examined the smooth, yellow wooden staff that spanned over five feet.

"My Seneca friends bestowed it on me as a thank you a long time ago. It's solid oak, and you'd have to work very hard to ever break it. Now, I give it to you as a gift."

Reaching forward to take the heavy piece, Nathan hefted the perfectly balanced walking stick and nodded appreciatively. "Much obliged, Uncle Art. I shall carry it with me in the woods until the day I die."

"Let's hope that doesn't happen for many, many years to come." Arthur managed a smile.

Peering between Gray Eyes and his uncle, Nathan caught sight of Mead driving a forklift, carrying something draped with a large green canvas past the barn's entrance. Politely, Arthur waved for the younger man to pass through the doorway.

"Lead the way, gentlemen." Nathan motioned, and the three men exited the barn.

Stepping outside, using the new staff, Nathan couldn't contain his surprised look to see more than a dozen people waiting near Seth's grave. He watched as Mead lowered the lift truck's tines gently to place the still-covered object down at the head of the freshest-dug mound.

To one side of the grave stood Mead's wife, Sarah, cradling her sleeping toddler John in one arm while holding Lill's hand with her other. Beside them were Will and Beth Canton. There also stood Tara's father, Michael, and her little sister, Becky. Close by, J.P. Smith beamed when he caught sight of Nathan walking toward them. Father Simmons did likewise.

Bobby remained in the foreground near the foot of the grave with the pups, Buck and Tye, at his side. On the other, Jason stood slightly forward of the crowd with Tara immediately to his right, the young lady's shoulder pressed against his. While Arthur and Gray Eyes stopped just a few feet shy of the gravesite, Mead stepped away from the forklift to join his sibling.

All stared as Nathan approached. No one spoke. Even the nearby coonhounds hushed, honoring the solemn moment.

"Brother," Mead finally began, "we all know what a great hound Seth was. So, we meant to pitch in for something special to mark his grave."

"Meant to?" Nathan looked at the draped object.

"When I went to pay for it, the stone mason told me the tab was already paid in full. When I asked him who footed the bill, he handed me this and said to give it to you." Mead reached into the front pocket of his shirt and produced a folded piece of paper.

Nathan accepted the stationery. Reading the surrounding faces, it seemed clear only he remained oblivious to its contents. Unfolding the creased paper, which crinkled loudly in the air of Ryland Creek, he read the handwritten letter:

June 30, 1988

Dear Nathan,

It has come to my attention you have lost that spectacular hound named Seth to the same beast that killed my champion, Pride. I've also heard about your hound's heroics in his last moments on this earth, and I cannot write this with a dry eye to say how proud I am to call you a fellow coon hunter.

I could not allow such a great coonhound to ever be forgotten. To me, Seth will always be the greatest of world champions. Please accept this memorial and gift to honor such a truly exceptional hound.

Sincerely Yours,

Drake Wellington

"Mr. Wellington is a class act." Nathan refolded the letter and put it in his shirt pocket.

"If you would do the unveiling, Nate." Mead motioned for his brother to come closer.

Everyone kept their attention on the coon hunter, who only nodded. Words escaped him as he stepped closer to grasp the canvas with one hand. Nathan hesitated, but with a firm tug, the covering flew back to reveal a granite, slant monument nearly three feet tall. On the marker's angled face, it read a simple memory:

SETH

Jason came forward, with Tara and Bobby close behind. The teen seemed somehow taller, perhaps another growth spurt, and his voice a little deeper. "Seth will never be forgotten, Mr. Ernst."

"No, no he won't." Nathan agreed, looking from the stone to the young man.

Then Gray Eyes took a few steps nearer to the grave, focused intently on the freshly dug dirt. All remained reverent as the old chieftain sang in his native tongue for nearly a minute, raising his arms heavenward and back to the ground several times. Only Arthur truly understood the words, but through the sing-song nature of the chief's sacred inflection, all grasped the meaning.

The whipmaster nodded often during Gray Eyes' address. When the shaman had finished, Arthur's voice broke ever so slightly. "That was beautiful, my father."

The chief then stepped away from the grave.

From where he stood, Father Simmons spoke. "Please bow your heads." Everyone did. "Nearly two millennia ago, the Christ taught us there is no greater love than to lay one's life down for one's friends. Through the ages since, we have been given many saintly men and women who have followed that perfect example.

"This day, we are granted yet another lesson in this selfless hound and can only wonder in awe at our Father's wisdom in giving humanity such dear companions we have in dogs. In God's name do we pray. Amen."

The entire crowd repeated, "Amen."

Near Bobby, J.P. Smith spoke in his baritone voice. "The lands of our hometown are steeped in mystery—tales of ghostly hounds, swamps, and strange creatures, and even the Gandalark. But this day, a legend, one of many associated with the Ernst family, has been scribed in stone and forever in our hearts. A magnificent tale for the children of Painted Post to hear."

The crowd was silent but smiling now.

"What's a Gandalark again?" Bobby leaned over, whispering into J.P.'s ear.

The resident storyteller rendered a smirk and whispered back, "That would be a story for another time."

All present turned to Nathan. The coon hunter gripped his new staff and stood a little taller. "I am still young, but I have seen much of death in my lifetime. My father, Jacob, taught that those who have gone on ahead would want us to live our lives fully, to remember but not look back with regret or sorrow, and try our best to be good people along the way. He was right about that.

"As for myself . . ." Nathan paused to gather his thoughts. "I have seen the world of men and found it wanting. I prefer the company of hounds." He then scanned the woodlands surrounding his farm. "There is a peace in the forests, a sacred promise between hunters and their dogs that rarely exists elsewhere. Of this I am certain—it is in the deepest hollows where unbreakable bonds are forged."

There was a moment of silence, but then Arthur leaned close to Nathan and spoke in a not-so-quiet hush. "Didn't know you were such a poet."

"Neither did I." The coon hunter grinned for what seemed like the first time in a long while.

Then Buck and Tye placed their front paws on the wet earth of their sire's final resting place. Looking up to the sky, they let out a loud, mournful howl, and the other coonhounds in the kennels soon joined in.

When the young hounds finally stopped their crooning as suddenly as they began, Mead's voice held childlike awe. "That was a last open." When the crowd looked at him, he explained, "It's rare to hear one, but it's the hounds' way of saying goodbye to Seth."

"That *was* a last open." Nathan watched, equally amazed. "I haven't heard one sung since I was a boy. Well, I'll be da—"

"Nephew," Arthur interrupted with a twinkle in his eyes. "Remember—no cussin' around the young'uns."

Father Simmons gave Arthur an approving wink.

"Right." Nathan couldn't help but laugh. "Right you are, Uncle Art."

The group moved closer to Seth's monument, admiring the ornate letter carvings, with nearly everyone touching the gray stone. A tactile farewell to such a magnificent hound.

But one individual stood back. A small child—dressed in her pink dress, summer bonnet, and shiny black shoes—held a bouquet of bright-yellow dandelions. She remained there, motionless, staring at the grave from several feet away.

"Lill," Nathan asked, "would you like to come here, honey?"

"Yes, Uncle Nathan," the forest child replied. As she moved forward, everyone cleared a path for her.

Taking small steps, Lill carefully placed the golden wildflowers on Seth's grave. She proceeded to the headstone and stood before it. Reaching with her tiny hand, she stopped a fraction of an inch short of just touching the stone's surface. The child gazed at her parents. She watched her father motion for her to continue as tears flooded Sarah's eyes. Lill then spied Bobby with Buck and Tye, now grown so tall. She glanced at Jason and Tara, who said nothing but took a deep breath, watching the tender scene.

Seeking one final approval, Lill turned to her Uncle Nathan, whose kind smile urged her on. She then extended her fingers and closed her blue eyes as she felt the grave marker.

All held surprised looks, seeing an angelic peace come upon the little girl's face.

"Seth, my Seth," Lill whispered softly, reopening her eyes with her hand still on the memorial. Her blonde hair bobbed up and down beneath the bonnet as she then hopped about excitedly. "There's Seth!" she continued, pointing to the empty hayfield in the direction of the sun.

Watching their daughter, Mead and Sarah hugged one another with young John sandwiched between them. Gray Eyes and Arthur shared a knowing look at the child's special gift and sighed contentedly.

Nathan's lower lip trembled as he walked closer to his little niece and kneeled, using his new walking stick for balance, so their faces were almost touching. "Seth isn't hunting in the woods anymore, dearest," he slowly explained. "He's in heaven now."

"No, Uncle Nathan!" the little girl shouted with glee. "Seth is right there! And Grandpa Jacob, too!"

Looking about, Nathan first glanced over at Mead and Sarah, who only offered a bewildered shrug at their daughter's pronouncement. Despite himself, he then looked where Lill had pointed to see . . . nothing.

Only a gentle wind blew in a field devoid of man or animal.

Sarah walked over to take Lill's hand, and the child smiled happily as her mother led her away.

Reaching down to grasp a nearby green rucksack and a .30-30 rifle, Mead said, "Here's all the supplies you asked for, Uncle Art." He handed the gear to the woodsman.

"As we discussed," Arthur replied, accepting the pack first, "you can have my truck as payment for the gear." He slipped his arms through the pack's straps, made a few adjustments, and then accepted the large-caliber rifle.

"Something I should know?" Nathan raised an eyebrow.

"Time for me to take my leave, Nephew," Arthur explained.

"Guess I shouldn't be surprised you're leavin' as suddenly as you appeared." Nathan chuckled.

"It's been my way long before you were born," The Forest Ghost replied, grinning.

"You are always welcome here," Nathan limped close and clasped Arthur's hand, "and to stay for as long as you like, Uncle. But where will you go?"

"Out there." Arthur used the weapon to point west at the cascading, tree-covered hills. "I have a personal score to settle with a particularly ornery bear." The woodsman turned to Gray Eyes, who could not hide the pride on his face.

Bobby let out a low whistle. "You're going after Scar Paw alone?"

"Hah!" The Ghost That Belongs to the Forest cackled. "It's either it or me. I promise you that, young'un."

Jason stepped close to offer his hand. "How long will you hunt Scar Paw, Uncle Art?"

"As long as it takes, young man." The woodsman then spoke solemnly, grasped Jason's hand, and looked over at Bobby and Tara as well. "I'm proud of what you've learnt and certain you'll become great hunters someday." His familiar grin emerged. "But you still have a ways to go, young'uns."

"Forgetting something?" Tara smirked, producing Arthur's feathered black fedora and handing it to the silver-bearded man, who accepted the hat and proudly placed it on his head.

"Thank you, young lady." The older man smiled.

"Uncle Art." Tara's eyes watered slightly. "I'm going to miss you. Thank you."

"Thank me? Thank me for what?"

Tara searched for the words and then shrugged. "For just being . . . well . . . you."

Nodding with a smile, Arthur spoke directly to Jason. "You best treat Ms. Tara like a lady, young'un. Do we have a mutual understandin'?" Tara and Jason blushed slightly. The woodsman pointed a finger at the younger man. "And if'n I hear otherwise, once I'm finished with Scar Paw, I'll track you down. You know I will!"

"You have my word." Jason returned the grin. "Don't let your hair turn white, old man."

Arthur put his hand on the young adult's shoulder to give it a gentle squeeze and laughed after a furtive glance at Nathan and Mead. His eyes momentarily rested on the letters of the new grave marker, but then the whipmaster began to walk toward the forest.

Everyone in the small crowd watch in silence as the woodsman's figure grew smaller in the distance.

"Uncle Arthur!" Nathan called out, but his voice then broke slightly when his uncle stopped to look back. "Go get him!"

With a wave and holding the rifle above his head, The Forest Ghost turned to cross the field and disappeared effortlessly into the oaks of Ryland Creek.

Raising his hands toward the spot where Arthur had vanished, the Seneca chieftain closed his eyes and spoke for a while in his native language.

Hesitating for a moment after the sachem had finished, Nathan still ventured a query. "Chief, did you say a prayer for Uncle Art?"

The wise old man smiled at Nathan's use of his honorific title for the first time. Gray Eyes then squinted slightly. "Yes, I did. It was a two-part prayer that is hard to translate into English." He hesitated, searching for the right words. "I first asked The Creator of All Life to always watch over and protect my beloved son in his journeys."

When the sachem paused, Nathan prompted once more. "And the second part?"

"Knowing it is The Ghost That Belongs to the Forest who now hunts the Great Bear, I also thanked The Creator that I am not Scar Paw's sorry behind." The sage paused and then added, "Or something like that, anyway."

———— ◆ ————

It watched as the massive brute came closer. With its sharp olfactory sense, it could detect the slightest scent of the Enemy on the bruin.

How it longed to face the Enemy and exact vengeance!

At nearly 250 pounds, it was still less than half the size of the bear, although it would undoubtedly grow larger in the years to come. Even with its limited eyesight, the creature could discern the bruin gravely hurt and in no condition to attack.

The Great Bear looked at the alien refugee, a Russian boar, only a few yards away. Even if it had not been so severely wounded, Scar Paw would not have attacked the formidable beast. Instead, the bruin only grunted—not out of fear, but from a sense of shared destiny between the two terrible beasts.

The feral hog likewise grunted and slipped into the dense undergrowth, out of sight.

The marauder then caught the scent of its incessant pursuer on the wind. The Forest Ghost was not far behind, once again, and it must continue on quickly to survive.

Forever exhausted, Scar Paw hurried its path westward toward Salamanca.

Epilogue

Winter 1993

Sharon's voice broke, her face a mixture of sadness and anticipation.

"It is time, my love. Tonight is the night."

"I am ready." Nathan peered into the still pool on Ryland Creek, seeing the future it portended

"Now you understand the purpose of the children whom you've taught to hunt raccoon for all these years gone by?" She smiled sadly, regaining some composure.

"Yes, I know what it would've been like to have been a father," Nathan replied. "Will they be okay?"

"You have set them on the path to be good people." She took his hand in hers. "There is no greater legacy than that."

"And my hounds?"

"They shall be taken care of."

"And Lill?" In the dream and the mortal world, Nathan's breathing stopped momentarily.

"The forest child shall endure. She's an Ernst, after all." Sharon smirked softly, but a more somber look came over her pretty face. "And she will become legend."

Breathing again in both worlds. Nathan nodded.

"Be brave, as you always are, my beloved," she said, taking his hands to her cheeks to catch her tears. "I know you will."

Nathan looked up, uttering his eternal promise. "I won't run."

J ason's disappointment came over the phone line crystal clear. "Are you sure, Mr. Ernst?"

"Aren't you due back in college in two days' time to begin your next semester?" Nathan responded with a query of his own.

"Yes, sir," Jason replied. "But we can squeeze in one more coon hunt before I return to school."

"What is it you're studying again?"

"Industrial Engineering," the young man replied proudly. "It involves a lot of math, and I have a solid 4.0 grade point average!"

"Reckon you're happy Uncle Arthur and I insisted on you gettin' good grades." Nathan chuckled.

"My parents and I will be forever grateful you rode my keister about good grades through the years." Jason laughed as well, but then added somberly, "Do you hear much from Uncle Art?"

"Only stories from time to time of some wild man with a whip, wearin' a feathered black fedora and chasing an enormous bear through these hills."

"I miss him." Jason's voice underpinned a wistful nostalgia.

"Uncle Art?"

"Yeah, him too, of course, but I was talking about Seth," Jason said. "He surely was an amazing hound, huh?"

"Yes." Nathan paused for a moment. "Truly one of a kind."

The two men allowed the weight of memory to lift before continuing.

"Thank you, Mr. Ernst. Tara, Bobby, and I sure had a lot of fun over the years while we chased raccoon. I know they're grateful, too."

"My pleasure, and I'm sure Uncle Arthur would agree. How's Bobby doing in school now?"

"I saw him last week. He's studying automotive technology and loving it. I guess your old tractor breaking down all the time spurred his desire to become a mechanic."

"I suppose so." Nathan smiled. "How are you and Tara?"

"We're doing great. She's following her love of photography right here at the same college." The young man mustered his courage. "And you're the first I'm going to tell—I'm thinking of asking Tara to marry me. We're still in school, but I know she's the one." Jason hesitated and then added the sage advice that he had received a long time ago in a field on Ryland Creek. "I hear it in her laugh, and I see it in her eyes."

Although Jason couldn't witness the reaction, Nathan nodded his approval just the same. "I always suspected as much about the two of you. You know when she's the right one." He smiled, his thoughts drifting to another true love lost a lifetime ago. "I say ask her to be your wife, and I wish you both the brightest future."

"Thank you, Mr. Ernst, and you'll be invited to the wedding, of course, assuming she says yes."

"She'll say yes, I'm certain."

"You're absolutely sure you don't want me to go along for a hunt tonight, old man? Do you think the ringtails are moving?"

When Nathan glanced at the mirror on the adjacent wall, he saw the last remaining shock of his dark-brown hair, about an inch wide, turn completely white.

"Mr. Ernst? Is everything okay?" Jason spoke after the unusually long moment of silence.

"Oh, the coon should run tonight." Nathan then sighed deeply, repeating an echo across time. "But there are some hunts where we have to go it alone."

"I have a weeklong semester break early next month. Promise me that we'll go coon hunting then. Is that a deal, Mr. Ernst?"

"Sure," the coon hunter replied, making a commitment he couldn't keep. "And please, call me Nathan. You're a man now. There's no sense in treatin' you like a young'un anymore."

"Well, thank you, Nathan." Jason spoke the name like a ten-year-old trying out a new bicycle for the first time.

"Study hard in the meantime. Good grades are still required to go chasin' ringtails with me and my hounds."

"Yes, sir, Mister . . . uhm . . . Nathan—high marks it is!" More solemn, the college man added, "Thanks again for everything that you and Uncle Art taught us—about life as much as coon hunting. You were like a second father to me, and Uncle Arthur was like, well, like an uncle!" He laughed.

"You made the both of us and your parents proud," Nathan managed after a few moments.

"I'll talk with you soon."

"Bye, now." Nathan hung up the phone.

The sun had set over an hour ago, and Nathan looked out the front window to see the full moon rising. A white mist had formed in the barnyard.

Gathering his gear together, the hunter then loaded it into the truck. His gait remained slightly stiff, the result of the battle with Scar Paw all those years ago. Going back into the house, Nathan made a call to his brother, saying he'd stop over before going hunting this night.

"You're comin' by the house *before* you head to the woods?" Mead sounded perplexed. "One second, Nate."

In the background, Nathan could hear both Lill and John repeatedly shouting, "Uncle Nathan!" He swallowed hard, listening as Mead tried to calm his kids, promising their favorite uncle would be there to see them soon.

After his children had hushed, Mead said, "Kind o' difficult to tell Lill and John a story about a coon hunt before you actually go huntin', ain't it, big brother?"

"It's okay to break routine every now and again, little brother." Nathan then added quickly, barely able to keep his voice from breaking, "There's a beautiful moon out tonight. Bye now. See you in a bit." He hung up the phone and went outside.

Stepping onto the crusted snow, the hunter headed to the kennels.

In two kennels, a pair of black-and-tan hounds moved closer to him, just on the other side of their respective pens' wire mesh.

"Buck. Tye." He said their names softly. "It's time we go huntin' this wonderful night. Are you ready, boys?"

Buck whined happily and wagged his tail. Although they were littermates, Tye seemed older, much more stoic, like his exceptional father had once been.

"One more chase," he said, and then loaded the hounds into his truck's dog boxes.

When Nathan reached to open the vehicle's door, the coon hunter shook his head, chastising his forgetfulness. He walked to the front porch and grabbed his oak walking stick. As he'd told Arthur the day it was presented, he'd taken the now-weathered staff with him every time he journeyed into the woods.

Looking up at the silvery lunar surface, Nathan turned his attention to the hounds' graveyard. Something called him to visit that hallowed ground one more time. His footsteps make a soft crunching of the snow's veneer as he approached the unique monument. Reaching out, he touched the headstone. Instead of a cold reflection of winter, summer's warmth flowed into him.

As he glanced into the moonlit field, Nathan watched the mists of Ryland Creek take shape. There emerged a form—an ethereal body as dark as night, despite the moonlight's silver flood. The spectral canine looked to his master, bowing his head slightly and wagging his tail.

Beckoning.

"Easy, Seth." Nathan slowly patted the air between them. "I promise it won't be long now."

Next to the ghostly coonhound, a majestic figure stood, dressed in dazzling white with a sash, standing by the hound. The sash was a deeper scarlet than Nathan had imagined.

Upon seeing the apparition, the man who would not run—kneeled. Bowing his head, Nathan spoke the words that came like the welcomed relief after an arduous race. "I am ready now."

When Nathan looked up, both figures had vanished.

The last coon hunter stood, greeting the moonlit sky over Painted Post and sighed. "I'll be there in a bit, Seth. Just a while longer for some goodbyes to family, ol' boy, and then we'll be together once more."

Author's Note

Undoubtedly, the American black bear, *Ursus Americanus*, is a creature to be respected. A bear's sheer strength is awesome, and it's nothing short of foolhardy to not afford the deep respect due these beautiful creatures.

There are, albeit extremely rare, black bear attacks throughout the United States—often chance encounters where the human surprised the bruin or came between a sow bear and her cubs. Some bears are labeled "nuisance bears"—i.e., those that have shown tendencies to interact negatively (as defined by man) with humans or property

I've had several chance encounters with bears in the forests of Painted Post. These bears walked up on me—the wind wasn't in their favor (or mine, depending on your perspective)—when we came face to face. Each time, once the bear realized I wasn't a tree, the bruin stopped and wheeled in the opposite direction, disappearing into the forest in seconds. They wanted nothing to do with me, and for my part, I didn't take it personally.

All that said, Scar Paw in *An Exceptional Hound* should not be seen as a reason to demonize bear-kind—that view would simply be wrong. Instead, I wrote Scar Paw as a metaphor for the challenges each of us faces when we refuse to engage; reluctant (like Nathan Ernst) to even see there's a problem or recognize the need to become part of the solution. Whether those obstacles are personal or societal, eventually the individual must take it upon himself or herself to face these hurdles or risk losing—or perhaps worse, never achieving—something extraordinary. Perhaps something exceptional.

Will defeating your demons require Divine intervention? For my thinking, that answer is oftentimes yes, but it's you who must decide to take those first steps in the right direction.

And when you do determine it's time to face those daunting challenges in your life—don't run. —Joseph Gary Crance

About the Author

The author with Seth

Joseph Gary Crance was born in Upstate New York near his hometown of Painted Post. The author spent hundreds of nights with his father and their hounds, chasing raccoon through the hills bounding this historic and scenic land.

After a career in the U.S. Air Force (USAF), he returned with his family to Painted Post and the woodland hollows of his youth to again listen to the nighttime songs of hounds pursuing the wily ringtail.

Admittedly, Joe doesn't climb these unchanging hills as fast as he once did. But that's okay. His hounds and the oaks have a great deal of patience.

Mr. Crance is a member of the New York State Outdoor Writers Association and holds degrees in Survival and Rescue Operations from the Community College of the USAF and a bachelor's in Professional Writing from Mansfield University.

The Legends of Ryland Creek
Book III of the Ryland Creek Saga

Young Sharon "Lill" Ernst finds solace in the woodlands of her rural hometown of Painted Post. With her family, Lill has grown up following their coonhounds in the nighttime forests.

Andrew Renthro, orphan but heir apparent to a vast empire of drug dealers, has been ordered to prove his worthiness. Andrew leaves his native Chicago—a teen who eagerly seeks revenge for a father he never knew—and his success means destroying the unsuspecting Ernst family.

But the forests of Painted Post don't belong solely to the realm of man. Stories of guiding spirits, ghostly hounds, and hideous beasts abound in this mystical place of wooded hollows, streams, and pathways.

For many trails converge and diverge in these oak-strewn hills.

Some paths lead to redemption. . . while others may end in certain doom.

But all have the potential to become legend.

The Master of Hounds
Book IV of the Ryland Creek Saga

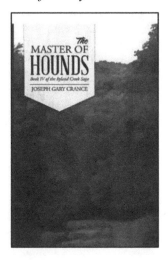

College student Jacob "Matthew" Ernst has a unique talent—he can see through the eyes of his hounds. Dogs obey him. For now, though, he needs a break from his studies. Time for Matthew and his faithful coonhound Monk to take a peaceful summer hike in the beautiful hills of their hometown.

Logan Willoughby wants to belong. She's fallen in with the Green Skulls—a gang with a long list of criminal exploits—and the price of admission may be too steep for her to pay. Logan accidentally learns too much and leaving the Skulls may no longer be an option.

A chance meeting puts Logan on a collision course with Matthew and Monk. Together, Matthew, Logan, and Monk will explore the wisdom only the magic of the forests of Painted Post can impart.

The Green Skulls see Logan as a loose end, and the gang's notorious leadership will do whatever it takes to protect their interests. The only thing standing between them and Logan is The Master of Hounds.

The Forest Ghost
A Ryland Creek Novel

In 1962, young Arthur McCutcheon hails from a well-to-do family who want ivied collegiate walls for him. Instead, Arthur is drawn to the tree-covered hills of Painted Post.

Just beginning to explore the forests, Arthur's life is turned upside down by villainous schemes, and his future quickly becomes murky.

Thrust into a new world with Renee, his loyal hound, Arthur learns about the woods and life from the venerable Seneca chief, John "Gray Eyes" Cornplanter.

It won't be easy as Gray Eyes, his daughter, Mist, and wife, Shell, try to teach the bumbling if eager teenager.

But one thing is certain.

There's something different about this youth from Painted Post with a foot in both worlds.

The exciting prequel to *The Last Coon Hunter!*